RIDE THE WHIRLWIND

By
Ernest L. Schusky

To: [redacted]

For all things done for
Collinsville

[redacted]

Bookman LLC
Publishing & Marketing
www.bookmanmarketing.com

ISBN: 1-59453-277-X

RIDE THE WHIRLWIND
ERNEST L. SCHUSKY

Ernie will
discuss the
background for
his novel at
Piece of Mind
Bookstore
1530 Troy Rd.
Edws,
Sunday, Nov 21
2-3 pm
See ya there!

RIDE THE WHIRLWIND

Domingo's love affair is shattered by the Pueblo Revolt of 1680. His knowledge of Spanish culture and language makes him an accomplice of Pope, brilliant Indian strategist, who leads the revolution. Through Domingo's eyes we experience the brutality of Spaniards--and Indians--in what was native Americans most successful war against white oppression.

A historic novel of epic proportions.

To order this book contact
Bookman
Publishing & Marketing
www.bookmanmarketing.com
1-800-342-6068

ISBN: 1-59453-277-X

TO THE CONTINUING STRUGGLE FOR INDIAN SOVEREIGNTY

SUMMER 1680

ONE

The whip pierced deep into Domingo's back. Pain stifled his scream. The tip of leather flicked his right eye. *Oh God, he's blinded me.* Fear blocked the agony in his back a moment. Then, torment set in. Blood trickled. He gagged. *I can't survive eleven more lashes.*

"It's all right to scream." Father Lucas waited, but Domingo made no sound.

The priest whirled the leather snake overhead, paused a moment, then hit full force.

"Jesu Cristo," Domingo howled.

"Thou shall not take the name of the Lord in vain." Lucas put every ounce of his shoulders into the next stroke. The whip coiled across Domingo's back and bit into his chest. The priest's crucifix swung around his neck. Domingo hoped it would cut his throat.

He lapsed into semiconsciousness, held to the whipping post by thongs that cut into his wrists. When he revived, he looked at the blood trickling along his forearms, feeling nothing in his wrists because of the agony in his back.

The priest leaned into Domingo's face. Through his stained black beard, his breath swirled onion stench in the white laden heat of *Nuevo Mexico*. "I'll use willow branches for the next nine if you'll confess your fornication." The Dominican's smirk might pass for grim determination to the San Juan pueblo onlookers, but Domingo sensed a stronger emotion. He choked back bile. He'd already admitted twice to lying with Cristina. After all, she had teased him to prove his sexual prowess ever since her first bleeding. He'd had a hard time believing her ardor since she claimed she'd known no other man before him.

"Where did you commit your sin?" Lucas' foul breath added insult to the torture.

"The willow grove along the Rio Grande." Domingo blinked his flooding eye.

"On the sand or a bed of grass?"

"On the sand." Domingo hesitated. *What does he want from me? I love Cristina—I guess.*

"How did you lure her there?

"She asked me to meet her, Father Lucas."

"How often?"

"She asked me several times."

"No! I mean how many times did you penetrate her?

"Once." Domingo had heard men in the pueblo brag of how often they could perform with women, but he didn't believe a man could have sex more than once a day.

"The first time you penetrated her, did she cry out?" Lucas licked his lips. A drop of salvia fell to his fat stomach.

"Why would she?"

"Wasn't it painful?"

"No. Not for either of us."

"Don't get smart with me." Lucas slapped him. Domingo turned away to protect his eye and glimpsed smoldering anger in the faces of his relatives, but none of them made a sound.

"She's thirteen. You're six years older. Don't pretend innocence with me."

What's he mean by innocence? It's as if he thinks I should be ashamed of sex.

Domingo tried to explain. "She wants a baby, Father."

"And you young devils are all too willing to make them! We've worked to educate you people for eighty years. If you—my most promising student—don't understand the sanctity of marriage yet, who will?" Lucas shook his head in despair, but his change in emotion lasted only moments. He leaned inches from Domingo's face to whisper. "The first time, did she bleed much?"

"I don't know." Domingo sensed the priest's disappointment with his answer.

"Didn't she cry out?" The priest breathed on Domingo's neck.

"No, Father."

"What about when you squeezed her breasts?"

Domingo wondered why he should squeeze her breasts. His dumbfounded look must have enraged Lucas. The priest screamed "confess." The people gathered around the edge of the plaza winced. Domingo's shame before his relatives cut as deeply as the lash.

He tried to appease Lucas. "Forgive me, Father" His throat choked with agony, his words muddled.

"Was it a tight fit?" Lucas hissed in Domingo's face. "Did she guide you in?"

Domingo failed to understand the priest's ravings but guessed he wanted him to promise marriage. "I want to marry her." *Is that what he wants to hear? Maybe I do love her. She's beautiful. I guess she'd make a good wife.*

Sweat dripped from every gaping pore on Lucas' balding forehead. "What about the pain when you first penetrated her?" Domingo shook his head, growing confused at the man's insistence for detail. He thought he'd understood the confessions required of Catholicism. If the religious believed Domingo to be his favorite student, as he so often said, how could he relish such punishment.

"Did she wrap her legs around you?" The priest's tongue flicked over his puffy lips. "Pull you into her?"

"Yes. No." Domingo struggled for the answer Lucas wanted.

"The details! You must confess the details if you want forgiveness." The priest screamed the word, forgiveness. Before Domingo could speak, the man grabbed the willow rods and lashed twice. The people nearest the whipping post gasped. The priest's wild eyes reminded Domingo of a stallion mating with a mare. "Did she get on top? Plunge down on you?" Despite the dry heat saliva dripped from his mouth.

"Father, forgive me!"

Lucas stood back and paused each time between the next seven lashes. His face grew pallid. The ashen white creeping to his hairline made his thick eyebrows grow even blacker. After the count of twelve, he circled Domingo to stare into his face.

The last thing Domingo remembered was a dark stain spreading below the belt of Lucas' cassock.

When Domingo gained consciousness, he drew comfort from the familiarity of his one-room home. The cool stone walls contrasted with the mid-day heat. The darkness radiated protection like a womb. Domingo was prone, face down in his father's lap. The head man of San Juan, the *cacique*, stood behind them. His stern features failed to hide his concern. A medicine man knelt over Domingo, dipped a cloth into a bowl and applied the poultice to his back.

"How are you, my son?" His father tried to smile.

"My eye. The right one. He whipped it."

His father examined the eye. "It's bloodshot but not bleeding. It may leave a scar. Otherwise, it looks alright."

Domingo blinked, looked around. "I guess it is."

His father brushed the hair from Domingo's forehead. "Who will ever understand the Spanish rules? Cristina is not a relative. She's the daughter of my father's sister's daughter's daughter. She'd make a good wife for you."

Domingo rolled his tongue over dry, cracking lips. "Before Lucas whipped me, he claimed we committed incest."

The cacique snorted. "By their rules we'd never be able to find a wife." He grinned. "Or anyone else for a good lay."

The medicine man snickered. "What do you know about a good lay? How long's it been?"

"Not as long as it has for you. I can tell by the way your wife looks at me." The cacique's eyes sparkled.

"She's just sorry for you. And for your wives. There's no way you can make both of them happy." The medicine man fingered the few drops of medicine in the bowl and touched a scratch on his ankle.

"You're jealous because I have twice the fun you do."

"Twice my fun would put you in the grave, you old fart." The medicine man covered his jar of remaining medicine and turned to Domingo. "I'll be back tomorrow. One more treatment will do it."

The three nodded to him as he left. Domingo sat up. The humor had been for his benefit, but its relief was only momentary. He looked at his father. "Why do the gods allow us to be humiliated?"

Before his father could answer, the cacique said, "Be patient. The gods haven't deserted us. They are just unhappy with the priest around." He sighed. "You have danced with the kachinas. You know their power."

"They are only men of the pueblo in masks." Domingo's uncles had given him a cursory explanation about how gods entered men's souls in the kiva. His faith had been shaken, and he had reservations about the theological concept of men being transformed into gods. It struck him almost as incredulous as wine being turned into blood at the behest of a priest.

"You know we become more than human." The cacique smiled wryly. "After you've danced more, you'll understand how we become the gods' persona. You'll feel their presence inside, guiding you. You'll know you've become them."

"But why don't they help us?" Domingo's pain made him doubt everything he had learned in the kiva. Perhaps the kiva was only an underground chamber, no closer to the gods than a church was.

"One day the kachinas will drive out the Spanish. When that fetish of a dead man on a cross is destroyed, the gods will return with rain. Even the Apache will be able to grow enough corn so they'll stop raiding us."

Domingo's father sneered. "The cacique before you took over claimed we'd drive the Spanish out when the devils cut off my foot. I'm still waiting." He pulled his leg to his knee to massage the purplish stump at its end.

Domingo bit at his lip. His father was one of the most morose men in San Juan. A childhood memory of a loving father full of jokes contrasted with the present. He knew the man had attracted any number of women after his mother died in her second childbirth. Yet, his father never showed any interest in even the most beautiful women who left food at their door. Any mention of his mother brought a scowl to his father's face, interrupting his customary frown.

Domingo turned to the cacique. "When the time comes, I'll tie Lucas to the whipping post. Or, better yet I'll kill him!" Domingo winced as he raised himself to his hands and knees. "All this pain simply because I made love to a woman."

"Lucas would like the girl for himself," the cacique said. "He's jealous." He chuckled. "But with that belly of his, he probably couldn't get it in."

"He should be going hungry like the rest of us." Domingo attempted a joke about the priest's belly, but the bitterness in his tone hid the humor in his words.

"Celibacy did something odd to Lucas." Domingo's father said. "If he enjoyed girls the way other priests do, he might stop being the sadistic devil he is."

"Why don't we kill him and the other brown robes?" Domingo said. "There are thousands of Indians, only hundreds of the Spanish."

The cacique's brow wrinkled. "It's always been each pueblo for itself, but a day of reckoning is coming."

"What do we do then?" Hope flickered inside Domingo.

The cacique frowned. "Are you ready to ride the whirlwind?"

Domingo felt certain he was but wondered what to expect when he mounted the whirlwind.

TWO

Domingo's father was examining the scabs from the whipping when a messenger from Fray Lucas summoned Domingo.

"He must be crazy," Domingo growled. "I never want to see him again. I may go to Taos to live with grandpa."

"Maybe you should see what he wants. It's important that we know what the priests are thinking," his father said.

"They're always thinking of how to plunder us for our labor. Nothing more. It was a mistake for me to learn their ways."

"No, my son. We need people who know their ways. Now more than ever."

"Are you thinking of an uprising? Our pueblo could never defeat all the Spanish soldiers." Domingo stared at his feet.

Domingo's father put a hand on his shoulder. "There will be a time when the pueblos unite."

"Are you thinking it'll be soon?" Domingo's enthusiasm waned as he recalled what a dreamer his father was.

"Nobody can know when, but right now it's important the Spanish think nothing is out of the ordinary." A glint animated his eyes. He removed his hand from Domingo's shoulder. "Cooperate with Lucas. We must know what's on his mind."

Domingo nodded and left for the convent. The children playing in the plaza stopped their game and ran to him. He reached for a pebble, shifted it between his hands, and nodded at a boy to guess where it was hidden. The boy laughed, pointed, and gasped in surprise at the empty palm. Domingo reached behind a girl's ear to retrieve it. After a few jokes he hurried on, but not before teasing women about lumps in their corn meal. Their manos danced a little lighter in their metates as their eyes followed him across the plaza.

A hint of scorched corn filtered through the smoke from scores of cooking fires. His stomach rumbled even at the smell of burnt food. The two tortillas for breakfast had disappeared in the far corners of his gut. The last time he had filled his belly was when a Catholic feast day coincided with a pueblo ceremony, sometime during winter. *That was the last time I tasted squash. And beans seasoned with chili!* His mouth watered, and his stomach churned at the memory.

At the entrance to the convent, anger replaced hunger. He couldn't imagine cooperating with Lucas. Domingo wanted only revenge on the fat, balding priest whose beard provided sanctuary for lice. He almost turned on his heel but remembered his father's admonition. He made himself knock.

Lucas opened the door. "Thank you for coming, Domingo. I'm glad to see you." He put both hands on Domingo's shoulders and looked him in the eye. At sight of the scar near his eyebrow, the priest blinked. Domingo stared a moment before looking down. "Let me see your back." Lucas turned him with his hands.

Domingo raised his tunic, imagining deeper, bleeding gashes on Lucas' back. The priest traced the scab with tender care but couldn't resist a probe at the end. Domingo swung around to catch a strange gleam in the priest's eye.

"I regret I had to punish you, my son. But it was for the sake of your soul. No one is above the rules of the Church."

Domingo nodded as if agreeing. *And one day I'll help your soul on its journey!*

"The penance is behind us. Let's forget it."

Domingo swallowed his retort.

"As I've told you many times, you are my most promising student. I've found no one else so capable of writing, I guess because you speak Spanish so well." Lucas shook his head to confirm his praise. "Yet, you remain modest. And so willing to help other students. You're an exemplary Christian."

Such praise was the last thing Domingo expected although he had heard it before. "A thousand thanks," he mumbled.

"In return, God has given you an artistic talent that comes close to matching that of a Spaniard. Your text illuminations prove God has singled you out." Lucas reached for a page that Domingo had illustrated and leaned toward him with it. The swarmy onion smell of his breath reminded Domingo of his flogging. A shiver of pain ran down his back.

"I've studied this page a dozen times to find a way to improve it, but the work is flawless."

"It's nothing that others in the pueblo couldn't do if given the chance." Domingo recalled the caliber and beauty of pueblo sand paintings that exceeded anything he did on paper.

"Don't be so modest. You have a duty to God to perfect your talents. Doubtless, you can sculpt as well as draw if given the opportunity."

Domingo thought Lucas meant to trap him. He probably wanted to know if men still carved the beautiful masks of the pueblos. Representatives of the gods that were abominations to the priest.

Domingo would love to carve a kachina, but he had not met anyone willing to teach him. He wondered if Lucas knew what a sacrilege it would be if Domingo attempted to carve a mask without ritual guidance.

"I know nothing about sculpting." Domingo's words were ernest. "There's no one in the pueblo to teach me." As he twisted the truth, he resented the guilt he felt by lying, even to a Spaniard.

"Unfortunately, I don't have the training to teach you." Lucas shrugged. "But Fray Nicolas in Taos is a master sculptor. He will help you fulfill yourself."

"Is Fray Nicolas coming to San Juan, then?"

"No, he is needed in Taos. I'm sending you there. He can perfect your talent for the printed page as well as instruct you in wood working." Lucas went to a cabinet and rummaged in a shelf near the floor.

"My father needs me here to tend the fields." Domingo began to sweat. Kinsmen would help his father, but he didn't want to leave Cristina. On the other hand, Domingo had just said he wanted to see his grandparents in Taos.

"The cacique can arrange for someone else to help your father. Since you'll be doing God's work, God will provide." Lucas took tools out of a cabinet and laid them on a frayed sheep skin. "Study these chisels. They're going to be an extension of your soul while you apprentice with Brother Nicolas." Lucas handed the points of steel to Domingo, obviously expecting him to exclaim in delight.

"They seem sharp, father. I can see how helpful they'd be in carving. But don't you need them?"

"I haven't used them since my eyesight began to fail."

"Couldn't you teach me to use them?"

"You mustn't pass up the opportunity to study with a master carver." Lucas' tone showed irritation. "You'll be eternally grateful, once you've finished."

"How long will it take?"

"A few months at most." Lucas bit at his lip. "Not that long. If you dedicate yourself to the task, you'll be back before harvest." He reached to another shelf for two letters. He rolled them and the chisels into the worn sheepskin, then tied the scroll with leather thongs. "I'm sending instructions for your training with you. Give Brother Nicolas these letters along with the tools."

Domingo didn't feel like continuing work for Christians after the beating Lucas had given him, but his father and the San Juan cacique needed information about the Taos priest. True, he'd miss Cristina, but Taos was only a long day's run up the Rio Grande.

"I assume you can stay at the convent in Taos until you or Brother Nicolas find a family to accommodate you. Do you have relatives there?"

"I'd be imposing. Food must be scarce there, too." In fact, Domingo looked forward to a welcome from his beloved grandparents.

"Trust me, my son. God will provide."

Domingo had more faith in his grandparents. His grandfather, so unlike his father, was a famed story teller. When he was not embellishing on the most recent practical joke he had originated, he was holding listeners in suspense with a tale of supernatural drama. Best of all, his grandmother used the sweetest masa in the whole Rio Grande valley to make her tamales. Domingo's stomach begged him to go.

Domingo was thinking about missed opportunities with Cristina when he returned home. His scowl must have matched one of his father's.

"What's that stinking devil done to you?" his father asked.

"He wants me to go to Taos to learn how to carve wooden santos. At least, that's what he said. But I suppose he means to separate me from Cristina." Domingo held up the packet of sheepskin. "He gave me tools and a couple of letters for Fray Nicolas in Taos. He's a master sculptor, and Lucas would apprentice me to him."

"He didn't pry into what's going on in the pueblo?"

"I thought he might be tricking me when he talked about carving. Trying to find out what I know about kachina masks." Domingo rubbed at his scarred eye. "But he only spoke about my artistic talents and how I should put them to God's use."

"Let's see what's in the sheepskin," his father said.

Domingo untied the cord and rolled out the skin. His father picked up the chisels and ran a finger over them. "Most stone tools are sharper than these."

Domingo shrugged as he flattened the letters.

"Read them to me," his father said.

Domingo skimmed over the first one. "He exaggerates the way I write Spanish and how well I know it. Do you remember how I told you I painted what they call illuminations? Lucas has different colored paints for it. Even different sized brushes. I've learned to use them all."

Domingo hesitated; his eyes pleaded for forgiveness. "I didn't mean to say that I'm better than anyone else."

His father smiled. "It's alright. We all know that some men are better wood carvers than others. We just don't brag about such skills when we're lucky to have them. That's not the San Juan way."

Domingo breathed easier at his father's reassuring answer.

"What's in the other letter?"

Domingo picked up the second sheet, smoothed it, and studied it. "It's in a language they call Latin."

"Is it like a code?"

"It is as far as I'm concerned. I gave up trying to learn it when Lucas told me about declensions and all sorts of things I'd never heard of. It was easier just to memorize the parts of the mass that are in Latin. The hymns were the easiest."

"Maybe you should tear it up. It must be something Lucas doesn't want you to know."

"Don't you think he'll expect a reply to it?"

"I suppose you're right," his father said. 'You have to deliver it, but first show it to your grandpa. Maybe he can guess what it is."

"Can he read Latin?" Domingo looked perplexed.

"No. Nothing like that." His father chuckled. "But he has powers that tell him a lot."

"He's a medicine man?"

"He never told me, but something like that. I saw a few things. If he doesn't control any mysterious power, he sure is a shrewd old man. He was always one step ahead of everybody else."

Domingo was musing over what he might expect in Taos when someone coughed at the door. His father opened it and nodded a welcome to the cacique.

The man entered and inquired about Domingo's back. Domingo assured him it was alright and told him about Lucas ordering him to Taos.

The cacique fingered his chin. "It may be an opportunity for us. You can find out where the Taos priest's loyalty lies. And our young men should get to know the men of other pueblos better."

"But I hate how the priests burn our kivas and beat us with the whips they use for cattle."

"Our kivas are well hidden now," the cacique said. "It's we who must get inside the minds of our enemy. And you have a head start with your knowledge of their ways. But can we trust you?"

Domingo's stomach flip flopped. He wasn't old enough to be trusted by the elders. Yet, he did know far more about the Spanish than most Indians. *It can be a way to take my revenge.*

His father nodded his agreement with the cacique. "You can also help your grandfather with his fields."

Since he'd no longer be helping Lucas but undermining him, Domingo's choice was clear. "I will go."

The cacique gripped Domingo's shoulders. "Remember everything about the Spanish you can. We don't know what will be useful. Gain their confidence anyway you can." He squeezed Domingo's shoulders, then nodded his farewell.

"I'll be glad to see grandpa." Domingo retied the letters and wrapped them in the sheepskin with the tools. "I'll leave tomorrow."

"I'd feel better if someone were going with you. You never know when those Apache savages will show up."

"All my friends are busy in the fields."

"We'd best get our hoes, too," his father said.

At the end of the last row of corn, Domingo's father grew quiet as if lost in thought. He said to Domingo, "Your grandfather gave me a fetish that has protected me for years. My partner will protect you while you're on the trail and in Taos." He took a leather pouch from around his neck and handed it to Domingo.

The sack had mystified Domingo for years. He looked for permission to open it as he fingered the lacing. His father nodded. Domingo stretched the bag open to reach inside. His fingers encountered the smoothest stone he had ever felt. He pulled it out. A red deer, the size of his finger tip, stared at him from alert turquoise eyes.

THREE

Domingo and his father stirred as the first light crept under their rawhide door. Neither spoke while they stretched and rolled their bedding, tucking it in an alcove. Domingo's father went outside to put twigs on the banked fire, then added splintered wood. The still warm grill absorbed the heat while Domingo patted cornmeal into flat cakes. The lumps he felt reminded him of how he had teased women at their metates.

He laid out eight patties on the stone. Two each for breakfast and two for mid-day. With luck they might add roots or cactus buds to their menu, or a kinswoman might take pity on his father late in the day and share a bite of her food.

The ripples in the browning patties teased his tongue as much as the smell of roasting corn. If his mouth watered like this all day, he wouldn't need to drink. His stomach rumbled as saliva set off its juices.

His father stooped over the grill stone. "What are these hills doing in my tortillas?"

"Those lumps stay in your stomach longer so you don't get hungry." It was a familiar joke between them, but they still enjoyed it. His father poked a mound.

"I hope you get lucky on the trail." His father winked. "With game, not a girl." He turned serious. "If you keep up a good pace, you'll have time to roast a rabbit." He jabbed a finger at one of Domingo's prominent ribs. "You could use it."

The thought of fresh meat made Domingo drool. He wiped his mouth with the back of his hand. "You think grandma's storage bins will be as empty as ours?"

"That's hard to imagine. When I was young, Grandma fed everyone."

"You never experienced drought when you were a kid?" Domingo tried to picture reliable rains.

"Oh, sure. But the Spanish took less of our food." He looked at the cloudless sky. "We had more rain. Nothing like the drought of the last five years." His face grew solemn. "Since the Spanish whipped those medicine men in Santa Fe, the gods punish us for doing nothing but squatting on our heels."

His father's conviction that the Spaniards had caused the drought by rounding up forty-seven of the medicine men condemned by the priests was a widely held pueblo belief. The unusual alliance of civil authorities with the clerics had convinced many Indians their cause was hopeless. Despair reigned when four of the men were hanged and the other forty-three publicly whipped. The brutality caused bitter resentment.

"How can we go on?" His father hung his head. "I'm sorry to be so glum. Now I've depressed you." He looked again at the sky. "It snowed hard in the mountains this winter. At least, the river will soon be full. We can irrigate the corn and beans though the melt is late for the squash."

Domingo forced a smile. "The first squash won't be long." He and his father peeled their tortillas from the grill, tossed them from hand to hand until they cooled, then squatted, and ate.

His father offered his superficial smile. "Guess your body can make it on four tortillas. You need some flesh on your bones."

"I haven't been running the way I should. Lucas demands so much time. At least sitting all day to write doesn't make me as hungry."

"Maybe your mother was mistaken when she insisted you learn their ways." His father slowly chewed each bite of his tortilla. "I think we'd be better off without them. What would we miss if we returned to the old ways?" He'd asked the rhetorical question before.

"Do you think I shouldn't go to Taos?" Domingo raised an eyebrow.

"The cacique wants you to go. Learn what the devils are plotting while you sculpt. You can also learn from your grandfather. The old men in Taos are known for their wisdom."

"Do you think that way because you grew up in Taos?" Domingo teased.

His father shrugged. "It's time you left. You up to a day's run?"

"Sure. Especially with help from the deer," Domingo said.

"Deer are vigilant as well as swift. You need to be on guard as well as fast." His father stared hard at the sack around his son's neck. "If you get in trouble, listen to what you hear in your heart as well as in your ears."

Domingo fashioned the roll of sheepskin to fit across one shoulder. He slung his quiver and bow across the other and started. Except for the sweat caused by the sheepskin, the morning run was like any other. He stuck to the high trail above the Rio Grande. The arduous path gave frequent vantage points to see travelers along the river. Twice, trickles of water from the mountain side refreshed him. When the sun reached overhead, he stopped to eat. He chewed slowly, as much to rest as to relish the corn's nourishment. His scarce rations reminded him of the drought. He searched the sky for a cloud. *Have the kachinas deserted us? Maybe there's no room for them and Jesus. I'd give my life to rid the country of the Spanish!*

When he looked down at the valley, two men on horseback rounded a bend. He caught no glint of sun off metal, but the Spanish sometimes rode without armor. He waited.

The two rode without saddles. Black hair reached half way down their buckskin tunics. One man looked to be as thin as the stick figures of petroglyphs. The other was strangely fat, the lower part of his stomach distended. An Apache scouting party.

Domingo hid behind a rock, glad that he hadn't killed a rabbit to roast. The two would have spotted his smoke. Just below him, they turned down a draw to the river where they dismounted. The emaciated one dropped to his stomach to drink while the other held the horses and scoured the terrain. When the one who was drinking rose, he squirted the other with water from his mouth. The fat one uttered a string of incomprehensible words. The first laughed so loud that a rabbit broke from a nearby bush. Domingo felt a moment of companionship with the Apaches. He had never imagined savages having a sense of humor.

He crept to a larger rock, never taking his eyes off the two Apaches. After the other man drank and the horses were watered, they mounted and continued downstream. *I must warn the pueblo, but how can I get ahead of the horses? Maybe they're headed for Santa Clara pueblo or an encomienda so it's not my problem.*

The trail toward Taos tempted him, but his conscience made him turn. When the Apaches were almost out of sight, he trotted back down the trail after them. He could keep up with horses, but avoiding loose rocks and anything else that made a sound was a challenge. The smallest rock slide would convert him into the hunted.

The Apaches vanished behind boulders for a while. When he caught up, he saw their tethered horses. The two men were circling a clump of willows on foot, bows in hand. Domingo guessed they'd seen a covey of birds. They loosed arrows at the same time. Yips of laughter followed. They rushed into the brush and returned with rabbits skewered on arrows. The animals kicked and squealed. The Apaches broke their necks. The skinny one used flint and steel to start a fire while the fat one gathered wood and prepared a roasting stick.

The smell of smoke caught Domingo's nose. The scent of roasting rabbit caused his saliva glands to erupt. He would have been glad to eat the meat raw. The Apaches' pause for a meal made him want to get ahead of the savages so he could warn his pueblo, but only barren mountainside lay before him. He had no choice but to stay put, forced to lay on his stomach and watch the Apaches eat and joke. After they had torn the last bit of flesh from the rabbits' bones, they lay on their backs pointing at a lonely cloud and jabbering incessantly.

From the slow pace they set after their meal, Domingo knew they would camp that night well before reaching any pueblo. A plan formed in his mind. Instead of racing ahead, he'd wait until night and steal their horses. On foot, they'd have to return home. Adrenalin swept through him. He had joined war parties twice to face Apaches, but the threat never materialized in either case.

But what if he did manage to steal the horses? He hadn't ridden a horse since adolescence when he and friends slipped onto an *encomienda* and stole rides before daybreak. He was just beginning to feel comfortable on a horse when the encomienda overseer caught him and his companions and reported them to Lucas. He had to write Thou Shall Not Steal one hundred times. Yet, if he could take the two mounts, the Apaches would have to return to their mountains, and San Juan could feast on horse flesh.

At dusk, he realized his plan was nothing but a dream. He'd never outmaneuver an Apache guard. He decided to run back to San Juan after dark to warn his people.

When the two Apaches stopped at dusk, Domingo sat to watch. After they hobbled their mounts, the skinny one searched the river bank while the other built a fire. It wasn't long until the hunter returned with a snake squirming on his arrow. His banter brought a laugh from the other man. Soon the roasting snake spoke to Domingo's nose. He held his stomach, fearful that its rumbles might be heard.

When the Apaches finished eating, the fat one reached under his buckskin shirt and pulled out a flask. He was no longer fat. The man tipped his head back for a long drink. The lean one shouted harsh words. The other said something that made the first man laugh, and he reached for the extended flask. After a few exchanges between them, the two laughed loud and long.

It seemed forever that the Apaches kept bantering. Domingo thought it best for one of them to be asleep before he tried slipping past them. He sang a dozen childhood songs under his breath. Finally, a sliver of moon showed both Apaches prone. The snores of one rumbled over the rocks of the river bed. The second man never stirred. Domingo couldn't believe his luck.

The horses grazed downstream from the sleeping men. Domingo felt ahead with one foot, making sure the ground below was firm before he lifted the second foot. Twice, the horses lifted their heads to study his approach, but his stealth seemed to reassure them. Domingo gave thanks that they wore crude halters. They continued to graze, moving away from their sleeping owners. Domingo crept along. The wind carried the last of the campfire smoke to him. He stifled a sneeze.

Beyond the campfire, the grass grew thick and the horses slowed. A narrow cloud strayed across the moon when Domingo drew within an arm's length of the first horse. It snorted at him. He raised his hand to its muzzle. It explored his hand, thankful for the sweaty salt it licked away. Domingo seized its halter, patted its cheeks and neck.

The other horse's curiosity grew. It inched toward Domingo. He held out his other hand. The horse threw its head back but couldn't resist. It took its taste of salt. When Domingo reached for its halter, it tossed its head. Domingo held tight to the rope. The snoring at the campfire stopped. Domingo hid between the horses. One of the prone figures sat up. He looked toward the horses, then lay back down. Domingo held tight to the halter ropes while he petted both animals.

When the snores resumed, Domingo headed slowly down the river toward San Juan, keeping the horses in the grass to let them graze. At one point the second horse halted for an eternity, burying its muzzle in the forage. Domingo jerked the halter, the horse jerked back. It freed itself. Domingo's insides flared. The horse returned to its grazing. Domingo reached for the rope, but let the horse feed. His pulse pounded. His mouth went dry. His knees felt numb.

After grazing farther, Domingo could barely see the Apaches. If one of them awoke to check how far the horses had grazed, he might pursue them. Domingo thought of the chisels in his sheepskin. One of them could cut the hobbles, but he didn't dare remove the sheepskin, let alone unwrap it. Instead, he fingered his arrows to find the knife-like one.

Domingo stooped beneath the first horse, raised the rope hobble, and sawed at it with his arrow head. Its rider had stolen Spanish rope. It did not cut easily. He pressed hard until he cut through. A finger bled from the effort. The other horse was hobbled with twisted grasses that gave way with little trouble.

Domingo gripped both halter ropes to lead the horses a few paces farther. The second one whinnied at being denied its grassy feast. Domingo looked toward the Apaches. One was sitting up, shaking the other. He leaped onto the back of the first horse, held tight to both halters and dug his heels into the horse's ribs. His heart would have leaped through his mouth, but his throat was too constricted.

FOUR

An arrow ricocheted off a rock behind Domingo. He turned on his horse to look back. The other horse raced past him and almost jerked its halter rope free. Moments later the Apaches were lost from sight as Domingo rounded a bend. He slowed his horse to a trot. In his mind he pictured the savages returning home, their friends ridiculing them for losing their horses.

His daydream shifted to imagining his entrance to San Juan. He'd hide the horses until dusk, tie them at the edge of his pueblo, and steal in after dark. Once he could be sure Lucas had retired, he and his father would awaken their relatives and friends to butcher the horses. The fresh meat would be a feast; the dried flesh might last into winter.

His horse balked in the stream bed. Domingo shook his head to rid his mind of daydreams. Ahead lay boulders from a land slide that foretold a waterfall. The right bank rose in a sheer cliff side. Rough boulders blocked the left bank. Domingo had to retreat upstream. He remembered a draw that led to the path above the river. If the Apaches were in pursuit, he had time, but he cursed himself for failing to be vigilant. How could he have forgotten this hurdle? His carelessness made him think of the deer at his neck. "Brother deer," he pleaded. "Warn me next time." He shivered, sensing movement at his neck.

At the draw, his horse hesitated. The path rose over loose rock, not difficult on foot but hard for a horse. He'd climbed half way up when the second horse's hind legs gave way. It jerked its head to recover, pulled the rope from Domingo's hand and slid to the river bottom. It turned and trotted upstream. Domingo dismounted and unslung his bow, made sure of his footing and shot. The horse howled from the arrow embedded in its flank. It ran up stream limping.

The horse he had ridden bolted at its companion's screeching and jerked free. Domingo had no idea where it would go, but he couldn't risk it ending up in Apache hands. He drew another arrow and shot. It struck the horse in its side. The animal went down screaming but rose and trotted away. Domingo's second arrow struck near the heart. His dreams of feasting San Juan pueblo vanished, but at least he might satisfy his own stomach. He raced to the downed animal and drank the spurting blood. The gushing red nourishment splattered his face and chest. He swallowed so rapidly that he choked. He cupped two handsful more. When the blood slowed to a trickle, he sucked at the wound. The red liquid meant strength—the strength to reach Taos.

The quarter moon did little good after Domingo left the river path and struggled back up hill toward the high route to Taos. Rocks cut through his moccasins, and his hands bled from the prickly stems he grabbed to pull himself upward. He was exhausted when he reached the high ground path. He fell to his knees to catch his breath before he looked down at the river. From such a distance he had little chance to see anyone.

But the death screech of a horse echoed along the canyon walls. The Apaches must be butchering it. No doubt they were gorging on the animal's heart and liver. They'd take time, too, to carve themselves the best cuts of flesh that they could carry. He envied them. His mind knew the blood he drank would sustain him, but his stomach craved something solid.

The images of the Apaches butchering their horses comforted Domingo as he tread up the trail, every step putting distance between him and the enemy. In a few familiar places, he jogged. But the pace caused pain. Even small rocks cut his feet through the gashes in his moccasins. A nasty cut on his right foot made him limp.

By dawn Domingo was half way to Taos, but his limp slowed his pace. It would be late afternoon before he saw his grandparents. If he saw them. *How desperate are those Apaches? If they want revenge on me as much as I want it on Lucas, they'll likely catch me. They surely have picked up my tracks by now if they didn't head home.*

By noon, Domingo believed the Apaches had given up. He stopped at a mountain side trickle of water to drink. His confidence grew. He took time to line his moccasins with two handsful of grass. Resuming a trot, the soft padding made the pain bearable. He again pictured the Apaches heading north to their homeland, regretting their foray into Pueblo country.

A war cry from above shattered his fantasy. His innards pushed upward, seeming intent on stopping his heart. He stopped to clutch the sack at his throat. A large rock crashed in front of him, setting off an avalanche of smaller rocks. *I must be out of arrow range, or I'd be dead. If I can reach the river maybe I can outrun them. The path there is nearly level.*

He started down the trickle's draw. Its sides offered a few handholds. When he stopped to look for the river path, he saw an Apache below him dive behind a rock. He'd almost plunged into an ambush. He scrambled back to within arrow range of the Apaches. The first one shouted to alert his comrade of what Domingo had done. Their screams to each other made Domingo forget the cuts on his feet.

His mind raced. The Apache below him no longer constituted a threat, but the Apache above could be within arrow range. The thought spurred Domingo's legs to take over his body.

He glanced up but saw nothing of his enemy. *Perhaps I have outrun him.* His foot began to hurt. He glanced down. Blood oozed from his moccasin. *I can never make it to Taos.* He imagined Lucas conducting a funeral service for him. *I can't let that furry chin outlive me.* His body picked up momentum. His feet felt nothing.

When he came to a large boulder, he remembered a crevice above it where he once played as a child. Slim as he was now, he might be able to slip in and hide. He leaped for a handhold careful not to leave a bloody footprint, hauled himself to the top, and found the crack in the rocks. He slid into it sideways after taking off the sheepskin and bow. Half squatting, his knees against one side of the crevice, his back against the other, he tried to calm his breathing and listen. If the Apache was running fast, he'd bypass Domingo. Then Domingo would somehow find a way to elude his two pursuers.

A cry from behind told Domingo the Apache on high ground still tracked him. No doubt, he signaled his companion below that he was closing for the kill. In moments, Domingo heard muffled footsteps, even a gruff pant. *He hasn't slowed. He's passed me by.* Domingo suddenly realized how hard he was rubbing the deer at his neck.

Moments later, he back tracked on the trail to find a place where he could descend to the river. His heart raced because of the need for ant-like progress. Any moment, the two Apaches would be returning to pick up his tracks, assuming that the one along the river had joined his companion after their ambush failed.

Finally, Domingo reached the river trail to Taos. The multitude of tracks on it made it unnecessary for him to cover his own. He ran, grimaced at the pain, ran harder as he imagined what the Apaches might do if they captured him. They had ways of making their victims plead for death.

When Domingo reached the stream that led to Taos, his hope for safety grew. He passed a farm where squash ripened and corn tasseled. Although an overpowering thirst struck him when he saw the field's irrigation ditch, he kept running to be safe.

At the next field, men of Taos dropped their hoes, picked up bows, and ran toward him. Domingo felt like stopping for their welcome, but his legs refused. He took four more steps before they did freeze. The pouch had tingled at his neck. An Apache arrow whizzed by him to pierce the earth where he would have been had he continued.

FIVE

Domingo struggled to free himself from the ant hill where the Apaches had buried him. He freed one arm before realizing he was trapped in a blanket. His grandmother's blanket. He sat up with a sigh of relief. His grandmother came in, a wide smile on her face, carrying a bowl of steaming mush. She handed it to him, then examined the cut on his foot. A wider smile said it would heal.

He ate slowly, relishing the thought of last night's tortillas and corn soup while his grandmother massaged his foot. When he finished eating, she winked. "You're fast as a deer to outrun twenty Apaches."

Domingo cocked his head. "There were only two, Grandma."

"I know, but the rumor says twenty. When Fray Nicolas tells the *encomendero*, all those Apaches will be to blame for stealing his sheep."

Domingo licked his lips and laughed. "I can't remember the last time I had mutton stew."

"You rest your feet. Tonight the pueblo enjoys meat."

Domingo's grandfather entered, blinking in the darkness. "So how's the hero? Out-running half the Apache nation."

"You stick to our story there were twenty." His grandmother looked stern. "Fray Nicolas is gullible but not a fool."

"So it was only twenty." He looked quizzically at Domingo. "You were lucky to stop when you did. My heart leaped when I saw that Apache arrow coming at you."

Domingo grasped his pouch. "My fetish warned me."

"May I see it?"

"My father gave it to me just before I left." Domingo handed the sack to his grandfather. The elder removed the deer gingerly. A smile crossed his face.

"That looks like your deer," Domingo's grandmother said.

"I gave this to our son-in-law." His grandfather handed it back, and Domingo retied the pouch around his neck.

His grandfather motioned to the door. "You feel like sitting outside? We can watch what's going on in the plaza and gossip like old women." He pursed his lips at his wife.

"You think we don't know what goes on in the kiva when you claim to be praying?" she said. Her husband chuckled.

He and Domingo went outside to the plaza. His grandfather found a piece of firewood for his grandson to sit on. He squatted beside him. "So, you are here."

"I am here." Domingo wasn't sure where to begin. He recalled his father's words about his grandfather being able to see what others couldn't. "But, I'm not sure why I'm here,"

The elder cocked his head, a bemused smile on his lips.

"My father told me to ask your advice, but I must get something first." He went to the room where he had left the two letters and brought the one in Latin to his grandfather.

"I can't read this. It must be a message to Father Nicolas, perhaps explaining why Father Lucas sent me here." Domingo handed the letter to his grandfather.

The old man ran a finger under the lines. Doubtless, he had seen Spaniards do this. Then he held the paper to his ear and listened to it, then inhaled the letter's essence.

"What trouble did you have with the San Juan priest?" he asked.

"There was a girl I laid with. He claimed we committed incest. He gave me a beating and sent me here."

The old man gazed at the letter a long time before he asked, "What did he say was his reason for sending you here?"

"To learn how to carve."

"Perhaps there is some truth to that. Perhaps also he wanted to separate you from this girl."

"Should I go back and confront him?" Domingo exclaimed.

"No need to go right away. Your grandmother has missed you. Besides, you could learn what goes on in Nicolas' head better than any of us. He's more secretive than the last priest we had."

"What good would that do?" Curiosity filled Domingo. The concern was the same his San Juan cacique expressed.

"If we know how the Spanish think maybe we can convince them to leave." Domingo heard an ominous note in the word, convince.

"Are Taos people thinking of a revolt, grandfather? My father thinks the time may be near."

"The kachinas taught us to be peaceful, but the Spanish lords are starving us. We may have to chose between our deaths or theirs." He grinned lopsidedly. "Not a difficult choice, is it?"

"What drives the Spanish to steal our land, then work us like slaves to grow food for them?" Domingo sighed. "What are we to do?"

"We wait. But not much longer."

Domingo saw no sense in waiting. Indians far outnumbered the Spaniards. *We can kill each and every one of the stinking priests. Why don't we strike now?*

His grandfather must have sensed Domingo's anger. "You know how Indians are," he said. "When everything else fails, our humor keeps us going." With a sly smile he began a story of what Keres speakers of the in-between pueblos thought when they first saw horses. "They were shocked when the horses ate grass because they believed the animals were giant dogs." If his stories were true, the Keres speakers were all retarded. The humor matched his grandmother's cooking for the comfort it gave Domingo. He held his sides.

The old man took a different tack. "So tell me about that worthless son-in-law of mine."

"Aren't you ever going to forgive my father for taking your daughter to San Juan?"

"Well, it could have been farther. I know he loved my daughter as much as she loved him." A tear came to his eye.

"But you don't seem to like him."

"Well, when he's not frowning, he wears a scowl."

"You can't expect everyone to have your sense of humor."

"I know. But he was so good humored when they married. Until those hairy animals cut off his foot."

Domingo hated to be reminded of the incident. "Just because they caught him riding a horse." Domingo gritted his teeth, tears in both eyes.

"There's more to it. He didn't tell you everything." The old man paused. "Your father was the fastest runner around. That's why I gave the deer to him." He dug at wax in his ear. "When he was young, he was so fast the old timers challenged runners in San Ildefonso." He stared over the plaza as if picturing the event. "You know Indians. Everyone from throughout the valley came to the race. The odds all favored your father. Even at three to one, it was hard to find takers."

"You were there?"

"Wouldn't have missed it. Funny, the rivalry among pueblos didn't cause hard feelings. Your father flew so fast he was everyone's hero. Could have had any woman there, but he loved your mother too much to ever look around.

"Well, the Spanish feared your father might unite the pueblos. So, when they caught him riding a horse, they used that as an excuse to end his fame."

"I can see why he became depressed." Domingo's shoulders sagged. Hatred whipped up his stomach.

"He would have survived that, I think. But the next year your mother died in childbirth. He gave up. If he hadn't had you, he'd have killed himself."

"He had you and grandma."

"Yes. We got along fine, and it was good to have you here during the times he came to visit. But your father never tried to fit in at Taos. He had a terrible accent. I'm proud of how you learned it. You speak like you were born here."

"Well, it's not all that different from Tewa." Domingo blushed at the praise. "Spanish is the truly weird language."

"Well, if you can't find a wife at San Juan, you can come here. Or if you get desperate, you can go all the way down river to Sandia. They speak Tiwa there almost as good as we do."

"I heard there are pueblos in between us where the language is about as different from us as Spanish."

"That's the Keres speakers. Funny how the southern and northern Tiwa got split so far apart." He scratched his chin. "Guess some pueblo drove their in-laws out and let strangers settle in between." He chuckled at his joke.

"I suppose you think we don't speak *properly* at San Juan."

It was his grandfather's turn to blush. "Well, you Tewa speakers come close to proper." He found his own log from the wood pile to sit on while Domingo greeted passersby.

Later, Domingo's grandmother called. Domingo smelled mush boiling, tinged with a scent he couldn't identify. "Grandpa?"

His grandfather blinked sleep from his eyes. "Is that the old woman calling?" He rose, straightened stiffened limbs, and headed to their room. "Hope you don't starve. We have a good enough breakfast, but only a light meal the rest of the day."

"That's more than I'm used to." Domingo's stomach offered a mild protest at the reminder of his starvation diet.

"Between the Spanish wolves and the Apache vultures, we're lucky to eat at all." His grandfather glanced upward at a cloudless sky. "Not to mention the kachinas forgetting us."

His grandmother ladled him a full bowl of soup. Her's and his grandfather's bowls were only half full. When Domingo protested, she said, "We've lost our appetites."

Domingo felt shame, recalling the tortillas he had wolfed the night before, not realizing his grandmother's storage pits might be empty. When she went inside for salt, he poured some of his soup into her bowl. His grandfather chuckled. "Won't you take some of mine?" Domingo said to him.

"Eat up. She's flavored it with squash blossoms. Shouldn't be plucking them since we'll need every squash we can get, but it's her favorite recipe. For her favorite grandson."

The two sipped in silence until she returned. "It's so good you're here." She looked him over. "Eat up. There's more."

"This is plenty. Been a long time since I had blossoms."

"There's a little garlic, too." She looked around nervously. "We've been saving it for a special occasion."

"An occasion when Fray Nicolas isn't in sight," his grandfather said. "That dirty brown robe made everyone hand over their garlic for a Christmas offering." He spat his contempt. "We didn't have time to hide much."

"We're almost out of water," Domingo's grandmother said to her husband. "If you would—my joints are acting up."

His grandfather rose with a nod to find a pot. "Don't let her put you up to anything," he said. "She claims the men won't do anything without a push from the women."

Domingo's grandmother watched her husband until he was out of sight. Her eyes sparkled her love for him. Then, she studied Domingo's features. "My eyes are getting old. This morning I didn't see the scar near your eye." She looked from various angles. "It makes you even more handsome." She paused. "I bet there's a story behind it."

"The San Juan priest whipped me. He almost got my eye."

"The village priests are worse since the governor whipped all those medicine men, and the Indians did nothing to resist. Now they believe they can get away with anything." A lump caught in her throat. "Why did the brown robe whip you?"

"Because I laid with a girl."

"Was she good?"

"Very good."

"Is she a hard worker?"

"Yes. She's young, but everyone says she helps around the house and in the fields." Domingo wondered why he hesitated to declare his love for her.

"Well, it is about time you married."

Domingo nodded. *She is beautiful. And the sex is great.* The thought of lying with Cristina the last time made his groin tingle. Maybe if he returned to San Juan at night, he could avoid any Apaches. "I haven't thought much about other women since I met Cristina."

"That's a sign of love. Do you dream of her?"

"A lot of day dreaming." Domingo felt his face flush. But not all the dreams were of sex. She sometimes worked beside him in the corn fields. He imagined jokes he told her. *That must be what love is about.*

"Wouldn't you like to be a father?"

The question startled Domingo. He had expected to be a father. Yet, the idea of holding a baby in his arms made him sweat. What would he do when it wailed? An image of Cristina with a baby at her breast gave him pause. His grandmother waited. He muttered, "Sure, I guess."

"What about her, grandson? Would you risk another whipping to be with her?"

Agony infused Domingo's back at the mention of a whipping. He craved for Lucas to feel the pain of the lash, or better to feel Domingo's hands wrapped around his throat.

SIX

Fray Lucas hovered over him with a whip, yelling an inarticulate speech. He breathed onion into Domingo's face. The stench made Domingo sit bolt upright, sweating in his grandparents' cool room. The distant cry of a Taos priest greeting the sun awakened him from his nightmare.

His grandfather came in, placing a hand on his back. "Let's greet the sun."

The two went to the wood pile and found the logs they had used the day before. On a third story roof a man stood with arms raised, his prayer-chant mesmerizing. Domingo understood few of the words. The powerful prayers spoke to his spirit, not his mind. He drifted into nothingness. When the chant stopped, he felt an inner peace, his dream forgotten.

"I missed his call yesterday," Domingo said.

His grandfather nodded. "No greeting yesterday. The stupid priest labeled the morning prayers pagan. The elders told him they weren't religious, just preaching morality to the children."

Domingo laughed. "Did they convince him?"

"A few of our priests are born con artists. They continue their turns. Others wouldn't lie to the fool priest so they quit." His grandfather grimaced. "No wonder we're plagued with draught."

"I must visit your priest this morning."

"Let's first see what your grandmother has for breakfast. You don't want to see turd tongue on an empty stomach."

Domingo choked on a laugh. "Why do you call him that?"

"The girls who work for him grind up dog turds in his corn meal." He dug into an ear with his little finger, frowned his disdain at the wax. Domingo recalled the gesture was a prelude to his stories.

"The old fart's belly makes you think of a pregnant bear about to hibernate." He wiped wax on his moccasin top. "Every time I see him, he's gnawing a tortilla. He keeps one hidden in his robe at mass. At Lent, the only thing he gives up eating are the lice eggs in his beard."

"No doubt, he teaches that gluttony is a sin?"

His grandfather shrugged. "The man's worse than an Apache raiding party. At least, they grind their own corn. The girls that he drafts musta worn out a dozen metates."

"Is the girls' labor all he wants from them?" Domingo had heard of more than one priest who forgot their vow of celibacy.

"None have complained if he's taken a fancy to them." His grandfather pried into his other ear. "His belly bulges so much he couldn't get close enough to a woman's sweet spot to make her happy." He guffawed. "The girls add a lot of salt to his tortillas so he won't taste the shit." He paused but the twinkle in his eyes raced. "The old fart must love salt. He eats with gusto." His laugh convulsed him. "And farts like a dog." He paused for emphasis. "An improvement over Spanish farts."

Domingo was still smiling when he arrived at Fray Nicolas's convent.

He cleared his throat, waited, then remembered Spanish custom. He knocked. A voice asked who it was. Domingo explained and the door opened. Nicolas's belly greeted him, followed by piercing green eyes. "Have you recovered from your wounds so soon?"

Domingo had no idea how to answer.

"I heard a large war party of Apache almost killed you. You didn't get away unscathed, did you?"

"God was with me, father. Some cuts on my feet, but He looked over me otherwise."

"I'm glad you came to see me, son. Such a loyal servant of the Lord."

"Like you, father." Domingo bit his tongue. He'd found a little flattery went a long way with the Spanish. "Fray Lucas sent me to apprentice with you. So I can learn to carve santos."

Nicolas knit his eyebrows. "Have you practiced much?"

"No, father. Perhaps these letters will explain." Domingo handed him the two envelopes.

Nicolas beckoned Domingo into a room with a desk. He lit a candle and sat to read the letter in Spanish while Domingo stood. "He praises your illuminations. How are you as a scribe?"

"Passable, father."

"Modesty is a virtue, my son!"

Nicolas opened the second envelope, stroked his chin at the Latin. He reached for a dictionary, underlined words with a finger as he labored over the contents. He looked up with a smirk. "My mornings are busy. Report to me Monday through Saturday when the sun is overhead. We'll begin after a meal. Bring something for the two of us. A little garlic wouldn't hurt. I trust you have relatives here?"

Domingo acknowledged his grandparents.

"Bring them to Mass each Sunday. I'll reserve a place in the service for you."

Nicolas reached for another book. "The santos I carved, I gave to a chapel in Santa Fe. Take this work outside to study the drawings. Leave the book on the desk when you finish. Tomorrow we'll start lessons—after lunch. Now I have work."

Domingo went into the courtyard. In two corners, young girls were grinding corn. They pretended not to look at him just as he feigned to ignore them. He leafed through the book. The drawings caught his breath. The crude carvings at San Juan hadn't prepared him for the beauty so often caught in santos.

When he returned the book, the office was vacant. He went out the back door into the church. He called softly. A snore answered him. The priest lay curled up on a mat behind the altar. Domingo retreated to his grandparents.

"Harelip has invited us to his house," his grandfather told him.

"Should I know him?"

"He's one of the winter people so he lives on the other side of the river." His grandfather pointed with pursed lips. "He's a couple of years older than you. When you were a boy, we came across him fishing. He'd caught four. Skinny ones, but he bragged about them."

Domingo bit at his lip seeking to recall the incident.

"The fish were in a net he held up like a war trophy." His grandfather stretched an arm high. "After a while he fished upstream. You replaced the fish with four ears of corn. Remember?"

"You told me to." Domingo laughed. "He believed the fish turned into corn."

"The man's still dumb as crow shit. When he told his grandfather, the old man said it was a joke, but Harelip wouldn't listen. He went to the priest. Claimed he'd witnessed a miracle." He laughed a low rumble. "When the priest wouldn't acknowledge it to be a miracle, Harelip asked him if wine could be turned to blood, then why couldn't fish be turned into corn."

"I didn't know that."

His grandfather guffawed. "The priest cuffed him good."

His grandfather motioned him toward the bridge. "A few years ago Harelip campaigned to become cacique. You wouldn't believe how onerous he made the job sound and how thankful he was he didn't have to do it."

Domingo raised an eyebrow. "Isn't that how campaigning is done?"

"But one needs to be subtle." His grandfather said. "His ambition stuck out like a butt's carbuncle. Besides, he was too young."

"What do you think Harelip wants with us?" Domingo asked.

"He kissed Spanish ass. The governor appointed him *gobernadoreillo*. Do you have 'little governors' at San Juan?" His grandfather didn't give him a chance to answer. "He had no problem being chosen since no one else would do it."

"What's he get out of it?"

"The Spanish play to his vanity. They gave him a cane as a sign of authority. Went right to his head. He doesn't notice how the people avoid him. We've even kept the presence of a new kiva secret from him."

"If you all ignore him, how can he ever find out what's going on."

"We pass on gossip to him so that the governor's bureaucrats believe he's on top of things."

Domingo nodded. Life was much the same for the little governor at San Juan.

After the two crossed the bridge, they walked to the end of the pueblo. A room featured a frame encasing a wooden door.

His grandfather knocked. "Harelip would like a casita, but the authorities insist he live in the pueblo."

A man wearing his hair cut short in the Spanish style answered. His lips curved up on one side in a permanent half smile. His eyes darted from grandfather to grandson to beyond the river as if scouting danger.

"Welcome," he gestured to Domingo's grandfather. "And you, boy. I heard you outran two dozen Apaches."

Domingo started to protest, then caught himself. "I wasn't able to count them."

"Too numerous to count," Harelip whistled in admiration. "Good thing we have Spanish arms to protect us."

"Did soldiers pursue the savages?" Domingo's grandfather asked, his sarcasm ill concealed.

"They haven't reported to me yet." Harelip turned to Domingo. "I'm surprised they weren't mounted, Did you see horses?"

Domingo thought fast. "When they first saw me, I was on a rugged part of the high trail. They might not have wanted to risk their horses." His mouth dried. He had never lied except to Spaniards. "I never saw much of them. Too busy running."

"Well, have some corn mush. Touch of meat in it." He called to the next room. "Wife. We have guests."

A woman just reaching maidenhood came in carrying bowls. She handed one to Harelip, and then served the guests. The smell of meat ordered his stomach to rumble in anticipation.

The three men squatted and slurped the soup. The wife sat in a corner, her legs bent to the side. When they finished, Harelip went outside. The girl dashed to Domingo, took his bowl, and returned with another helping. She teased him with her lips as she handed it to him.

Harelip came back, glancing over his shoulder, then staring at Domingo. "Why are you here, son?"

His rudeness startled Domingo. His mouth gaped, but he answered. "I've been sent by Fray Lucas to learn carving."

Harelip inquired about Domingo's other activities in the church.

He knew nothing of illuminations and little of wood carving but obviously was impressed by the extent of Domingo's involvement in Catholicism.

"All your study must leave little time for training in the kiva." Harelip glanced at Domingo's grandfather for his reaction.

The hair on Domingo's neck bristled. "It's a regret, I suppose."

"Your mother and father must be disappointed."

"My mother is dead. My father is not active in any kiva. I don't know when people meet—if they do meet." His mouth dried.

His grandfather rose. "Got to stretch my legs." He went outside.

"You can bet the old kiva members here meet, even if they no longer have a kiva. Your grandfather would make sure the old ceremonies continue."

Domingo flushed. He tried to be non-committal. "My grandparents haven't said anything about kivas."

"I have no concern about kiva meetings. The Spanish fail to understand our ways." He waited for a reply but got none. "We need the old customs to get rain. Go when your grandfather invites you to a kiva meeting. You needn't tell Fray Nicolas nor me. I'd worry less if I knew the old ways are kept up." He shrugged. "Since I became governor, the people hide things from me. Jealousy, you know."

"I can't think of anything my grandfather would have to hide." Domingo spoke with force, glancing at the young girl to see her reaction. She looked down to hide a smile.

Harelip scowled. "I've glimpsed strangers in the pueblo. Obviously hiding from the priest."

Domingo searched for a reply. "You know how Indians value their independence."

"Yes, but the Spanish have changed things. We are all one family now."

Domingo almost choked on the thought of including Lucas as kin. The young wife covered a reddish face with a cough.

"The soup was very good." Domingo rose as his grandfather beckoned from the door.

At home, his grandmother greeted them with tortillas. Domingo's mouth watered from the touch of their warmth. His taste buds had a fiesta with their scent.

"You had much better at Harelip's?" she goaded the two.

"That young wife is so good looking, I can't remember what her food tastes like." Domingo's grandfather fingered his chin as if recalling her looks.

"She'd have you crawling back here to recover for days, after one night with her," his grandmother said.

His grandfather grimaced. "I'll borrow some salt for these tortillas. Can't tell what you put in mine."

His grandmother's eyes danced as she watched her husband leave. "I suppose Harelip wanted to know why you're here."

Domingo told her of his inquisition, especially of Harelip's curiosity about strangers. "Does everyone know he's an informer?"

"His older wife knew. They say she wouldn't live with a traitor. Convenient for him. The Spanish didn't want a bigamist for a little governor. Anyway, everyone says the young wife is more than he can manage in bed."

"No wonder grandpa envies him," Domingo teased.

"That old man has more imagination than endurance. She wouldn't give him a second look anyway." She chuckled, then said seriously. "You watch out, though. Don't let her catch you alone!"

SEVEN

On his way to the convent, a girl's smile reminded Domingo of Cristina. He hadn't thought of her since his discussion with his grandmother. For a moment he wondered what that meant about his love for Cristina. *She is beautiful. And good humored. But when I'm old, will she look at me the way grandma looks at grandpa?* He still toyed with the question when he arrived at the convent.

Domingo carried half a dozen tortillas in a crude basket his grandmother had given him for lunch. The way she had said, "I salted 'em the way he likes 'em" caused him to wonder if she had used anything besides corn in preparing the meal. At the convent door he knocked. When he got no answer, he called.

Nicolas grumbled a reply and opened the door. He was wiping his mouth with the back of his hand. "Good. You've brought lunch. It'll nourish you for a long afternoon of work." Before Domingo could answer, the priest took the basket, nodded for him to enter. Nicolas sat in his chair while Domingo squatted. He took four of the tortillas, tossed two to Domingo, muttered a grace and devoured one while Domingo chewed his first bite. The religious finished the next three, licked his lips, and stared at his apprentice half way through his second tortilla. He was about to speak when Domingo told him that his grandmother had used the last of her garlic months earlier. The priest screwed up his nose.

"I've looked at the tools you brought from Fray Lucas. Most useful for an apprentice. You won't be carving up yourself. Cut your fingers, and you won't be of any use." Beads of sweat appeared on Nicolas' forehead, and he flapped his robe around his knees. "Let's go into the courtyard to see if there's a breeze. Bring your tools."

Nicolas carried his chair, expecting Domingo to squat while he worked.

Domingo selected a chisel and examined its edge, placed it on the board and ran a small groove. He looked at Nicolas.

"Let me show you." Nicolas peeled away a sliver, then molded Domingo's fingers around the chisel. "Too much pressure and you lose control. Too little and you'll end up frustrated."

Domingo tried again. The chisel went the way he wanted until he hit a knot. He shoved hard and the board splintered.

"You see what happens with too much pressure." The words showed impatience. "I'll get another board."

Domingo spent the rest of the afternoon trying to shape the wood into something resembling a santo, but nothing like a human face appeared. Nicolas offered occasional advice, but more often he snorted himself awake after his head drooped. Once he almost fell from the chair.

It was Domingo's turn to sweat. He did his share, frustrated at his lack of progress. Neither of Fray Lucas' chisels cut into the wood in a satisfactory way. The few times he made headway, he ran into hardened grain or knots at critical places.

"Perhaps, I don't have the talent for carving," Domingo shrugged. "Maybe I was meant to work with paper."

"Too early to tell, my son."

"I'll be here weeks." Domingo spoke with exasperation.

"Patience. The basics require months." Nicolas grinned slyly. "You clearly have the potential, and the time you spend as a servant of the Lord is never a waste."

Domingo swore under his breath that he wouldn't serve the religious or their Lord one moment longer than it took to undermine them.

Later in the afternoon, a breeze brought cool air from the mountains. Domingo stopped sweating, and Nicolas stopped napping. The priest told his apprentice to rest. Domingo sat while Nicolas faced into the breeze and sucked in the fresh air. After he picked up the last crumbs in his lap, he flapped his cassock.

"It's almost like my home in Spain. I grew up in mountains north of Madrid." The priest straightened in his chair. "Have you learned the geography of Spain?"

"A few cities and rivers."

"The central plateau is high with wonderful weather. Something like here except we had rain." His eyes half closed. "My father grew grapes and sheep. We never lacked for wine nor cheese. Nor bread." He opened his eyes wide. "Have you ever tasted bread?" Before Domingo could ask what bread was, Nicolas rubbed his stomach. "The *encomendero* on the way to Picuris grows a little wheat. But he seldom shares with me." He sighed.

"Is wheat like corn?" Domingo asked, massaging his aching fingers.

"You can make bread and beer with wheat." Nicolas' tone was sharp. "What can you do with corn? Mush and tortillas. Tortillas and mush. Grain to rot the teeth. Lord knows what it does to the guts. I've never felt full since I've been here. Stomach's always upset. A little garlic helps, but I've had none for months."

"Isn't there any way to return home?" Domingo tried to hide his hope.

"I have two older brothers. No chance for me to inherit. I could only live on their charity."

Domingo hid his confusion behind a mask of ignorance. *Is he saying that brothers do not share the family wealth? Surely he can't mean that.*

The priest continued in his revery. "My father was right to send me to seminary. My wealth consists of the souls I save—and helping saved souls like you to become better Christians."

"God recognizes your dedication." Domingo decided vanity must be another weakness of the priest. "Not only do you suffer the pagan ways of my people, but also the Apaches threaten your life daily."

"Every minute. We're lucky that the war party who chased you didn't invade us."

Domingo smiled inwardly to find the priest believed the exaggeration. "Instead of attacking us, they're probably raiding for sheep and cattle."

Nicolas sucked in his breath. "I hadn't thought of that." He shivered a moment. "The Apaches are worse than the Jews were in stealing our wealth."

Raiding Jews didn't conform to the picture Domingo had of them from the Bible. "Did they raid you?"

Nicolas chortled. "They're too cowardly to raid. They stole our wealth through usuary."

"I'm sorry." Domingo had never understood the concept despite Lucas' explanations. He couldn't imagine a society where everyone didn't share what they had. Only witches accumulated wealth.

"No need for regrets. King Ferdinand and Queen Isabel expelled the Jews from Spain in 1492, along with the Moors. That was their greatest accomplishment." Nicolas laughed. "Too bad the Crown can't do the same to the Apaches." He burped, slumped in his chair and his head fell.

Domingo resumed his carving. He exerted a bit more control, but the slivers remained too large or too small. Nor could he picture any shape emerging from the block. He considered asking Nicolas how to draw on the wood, but he hesitated. The snores that accompanied a flow of drool from the priest's mouth were too deep.

Domingo went into the convent to look for the book of drawings. On a top shelf he discovered four different sized chisels and other tools he couldn't name. He picked up a chisel, ran his finger over the cutting edge, and sucked in his breath. He'd sliced his finger without realizing it, the cut so light it stopped bleeding when he blew on it.

He found the book, took it and the new tool to the courtyard, and set two logs from the wood pile upright. He sat on one and used the other as a work bench. The curls of wood he peeled off were of uniform size. For the first time, he felt control. He propped the book open to the drawings, selected a simple example, and projected it onto the wood with his mind. When he turned to carve, the book slid off the log. The noise startled Nicolas.

"What are you doing?" the man roared. When he saw the book face down on the ground, he lectured Domingo on how irreplaceable books were on the frontier and threatened him with a whipping.

"I'm sorry." The thought of another whipping inflamed Domingo's gut. He'd kill Nicolas before he'd submit to such humiliation again, but he assumed the threat was an idle one.

Nicolas came over to retrieve the book. When he saw his tool in Domingo's hand, he screeched at him. "You thief." Livid with anger, the priest slapped Domingo's cheek, grabbed his ear and stomped into his room dragging Domingo. "You disobey me again, and I'll never teach you anything. You understand?"

"Yes, father. Forgive me. I'd never steal, I swear."

"Well, you do show potential." The priest released Domingo's ear. "But you need to practice with the apprentice's tools first. You must always be grateful to Father Lucas, you understand?"

"Yes, father." Domingo paused as Nicolas slumped into his chair. "I wondered, father. How do I bring a shape out of the wood? Should I draw it on the wood?"

"You may. Master carvers see shapes in the wood and have no need to draw what they intend to sculpt. They simply peel away the wood from what they see hidden in the wood." He clasped his hands behind his head. "So I've been told, but I never managed that. Don't you expect to." He waved Domingo away. "Go practice your whittling until I dismiss you."

Domingo returned to the courtyard. He found a piece of pine and ran his finger over its grain. The sweet scent made him smile. The wood smiled back. Cristina peered from the wood.

EIGHT

Domingo cursed himself for failing to carve Cristina's face when he first saw it. Weeks had passed yet his lover had not again appeared in the wood. One dawn he rose early to beseech Mother Kachina's help. His prayer ended as the morning crier's began. When the trilling call stopped, Domingo sat on a log outside his grandfather's home searching for an excuse to skip his session with Nicolas. His grandfather came out to squat beside him. "You look like you need help."

Domingo had told him little about his apprenticeship. As he explained how his talent for illuminations had failed to extend to wood carving, his grandfather raised an eyebrow. "Most of us sculpt kachinas. The Spanish have no monopoly on wood carving."

Domingo shrugged. "Nicholas tries to help me. He teaches a few things most days. When the chisel—a kind of knife—slips, he grins. Tells me to keep trying."

"You need a change. You've helped me with my weeding. Let's go to the kiva instead of the fields this morning."

Domingo's grandmother must have overheard them as she brought their morning tortillas. "You'll get the boy in trouble. What if Fray Nicolas sees him go in the kiva?"

"Fatso is too busy swilling mush. The boy needs time away from the farming. Between the hoe and the knife, he has nothing but blisters."

"Well, don't go on an empty stomach." She waved the tortillas under Domingo's nose. "There's a little mush when you finish these." She handed both of them four tortillas.

Domingo's grandfather took a bite. "No salt. Guess you didn't flavor them with anything special?"

The woman covered her laugh with a hand as she returned to her rooms. The two men followed after they finished. Inside, Domingo finished a half filled bowl of mush.

"Time for kiva business," his grandfather said.

"All you do is gossip," Domingo's grandmother said. "How's our grandson going to fit in?"

"You don't know what goes on in the kiva, woman. The kachinas will frown on your impudence." His grandfather spoke sternly but didn't do well at hiding his smile.

"So you paint and scratch wood while you talk about everyone who doesn't show up." She matched his gruffness.

"You think you know so much about the kiva? I guess you want to be initiated? You think women could stand up to that?" His wife shrugged off the threat as if she'd heard it before.

Domingo and his grandfather left for a remote edge of the pueblo. His grandfather nodded to a slab of rock covering a hole. "We use a notched log instead of a ladder in order to hide the entrance." He glanced around. "If Nicolas knows the kiva's here, he doesn't want to confront us. Same with Harelip. Still, we make a point of knowing they're not around before we use it."

"It's certainly well hidden."

"Besides those two meddlers, it's good to be away from women's chatter." His grandfather chortled. "We have serious work this morning. There'll be a dance tonight, and everything must be in order for when the gods return." Suddenly, he drew a deep breath. At the edge of the plaza a tall, dark figure commanded attention. Even from a distance, Domingo felt the man's eyes. When he flipped his head, Domingo felt compelled to approach. He and his grandfather hastened to the man's side.

"You're a stranger here?" The man's eyes bored into Domingo.

"I spent time here as a youth. With my grandfather," Domingo nodded toward him. "My home is San Juan."

The stranger's smile flickered. "My home is San Juan, too. But that was long ago."

Domingo looked puzzled. The stranger said, "Even when I was there, you weren't likely to see me."

Domingo couldn't imagine how that could be, but he didn't question it. The man's features weren't unusual except for the penetrating eyes. That and a backbone straight as an arrow.

"Let us talk." The man gestured to a small door that looked like an entrance to a storage room. Inside, the room was lined with benches. It smelled of close, constant human occupation.

"How has the priest at San Juan treated you?"

Domingo sensed that the stranger had an idea of his relation to Lucas. Nevertheless, he went into detail about being a student and why Lucas had sent him to Taos. He paused, but the man's eyes continued to question him. "He gave me a public whipping. For nothing more than fornicating."

"So why do you help this devil by learning to carve santos?"

"My mother thought Spanish ways were necessary to know. My father loved her dearly." Domingo paused, wondering if he should include the cacique's admonition. The man's eyes forced him to continue. "My cacique urged me to spy on the Spanish."

"How do you feel about the Spanish?"

"I hate them. I wouldn't be here if it weren't for the cacique asking me to come. I pray to serve the revolution."

"No one speaks of revolt." The command in the man's voice made Domingo shudder. "But, you follow your cacique's orders."

Domingo nodded he understood.

"Have you learned to read and write?"

"Yes. By enhancing the text with art work—what are called illuminations—the priest believes I can learn to carve."

"This writing that you do, can all Spanish read it?"

"Not all, but many."

"Can they tell who wrote it?"

"Each man has his own style of handwriting, yes."

"So everyone would know if the governor wrote a letter?"

"Well," Domingo paused. "I suppose a scribe or secretary writes the governor's correspondence. The governor only signs his name. That is, makes his signature."

"So it's his signature that is important?"

"As far as I know." Domingo began to stammer under the penetrating eyes. He felt he was being tested. "The Bishop's signature is all important in church documents."

"So can you write the governor's signature?"

"No." Domingo stammered.

"But you make…what did you call them, illuminations?"

"I would have to have a copy of the governor's signature. I have no idea where to get one."

"That can be arranged." The stranger put a hand on Domingo's shoulder. The touch burned. "You can help send the Spaniards back to Mexico if you learn to make that signature."

As they left the room, his grandfather whispered that he should tell no one about meeting Po-pe. Domingo gasped. Po-pe was one of the medicine men the Spanish had whipped in the plaza at Santa Fe. Since then, the man's influence had become legendary.

"Was I wrong? Isn't Po-pe talking of revolt?" Domingo whispered to his grandfather.

"We'll see," he replied. "I'm not sure he's the right man to lead us. He seems to want power too much."

The two edged to the kiva entrance, glanced around, saw no one, and descended a notched log amidst laughter. The joking halted long enough for Domingo to pass among the men, greeting each one. Then they returned to their masks and costumes, touching up paint, gluing feathers, sewing loosened seams.

An elder approached making oblique inquiry into Domingo's background. No one would be brought into the kiva who was not initiated, yet custom obligated the elder to seek credentials from strangers. Domingo described his initiation. The elder seized the opportunity to bore Domingo with a long description of Taos practices until his grandfather came to his rescue.

He led his grandson to a niche in the wall where he retrieved a mask. Domingo smiled at its well worn features, realizing it had seen almost as many years as his grandfather. The two sat on a stone bench along one wall, the mask staring at them, waiting to be called to life. His grandfather muttered a prayer, hummed, and tried on the mask. It quivered with life.

Others in the kiva donned their masks and danced in place to ensure their headgear was secure. His grandfather borrowed a paint brush from a neighbor and dabbed at red dots, repainted a line where a fleck had blistered off, and hummed a tune. Domingo took the cloth that his grandfather used to store his mask and asked for the paint brush.

He made small images of the masks he saw around him, concentrating on details that identified the kachinas. He was so intent on painting that he didn't notice Po-pe until the man stood over him. "Let me see," his eyes demanded more than his words. "You've captured every detail. I know I can count on you." He handed Domingo a dusty scroll tied with a blue ribbon.

Domingo's grandfather had heard little of the conversation, he was so absorbed with his mask. He took back the paint brush, failing to notice Domingo's drawings. "We're ready for tonight." He spoke to the mask, not to Domingo.

Domingo slipped the ribbon off the scroll and spread it open. The note thanked a friend for two Apache slave children sent to the governor as a birthday gift.

Domingo's fingers ached from a miserable afternoon that matched Nicolas' mood. He'd exhibited none of his usual patience, and Nicolas' sarcasm cut sharper than the tools that failed to find a proper groove. Domingo returned to his grandparents' with aching body and heart.

His grandmother greeted him at the door. "Did the glutton share my lunch in his usual way? Twice as much for him as you?"

"And he complained it wasn't enough. Besides that, I couldn't carve anything right."

"Well, tonight's dinner will cheer you up. The pueblo is sharing one of those sheep the Apaches stole. We'll have mutton soup. No corn for once."

When the time came to eat, Domingo asked where his grandfather was. His grandmother smiled and told him he had been volunteered to make sure Nicolas stayed at the convent so his nose wouldn't detect the smell of mutton.

The women had dished out the last of their stews before Domingo's grandfather returned. When his wife told him that they had finished the mutton without him, his mouth dropped and his face reddened. But he caught himself before he spoke, realizing that she joked.

As darkness set in, Domingo's grandfather nodded, and the two headed for the kiva. They descended into a rumble of singing, stomping, and joking. The elder who had questioned Domingo handed him a mask and skirt. As he and his grandfather changed into kachina costume, Domingo noticed that Po-pe was donning a mask and stepping to the drum beat.

The drumming stopped. The elder began a song that everyone echoed. The men danced in place a moment, then without direction fell into a line, circling the kiva. Domingo was just succumbing to the hypnosis of the dance, when the elder climbed the notched log. Panic swept Domingo's chest. *How can we dance in public? What if Nicolas sees? Or Harelip?* His panic subsided as he realized that someone must be keeping the little governor and the priest busy just as his grandfather had done earlier.

Above ground, the drum seized him in its rhythm. The majesty of the dancing men, each locked in step with the other, felt an awesome weight, an awesome weightlessness. The masks overpowered him. The sacred symbols spoke to him with their solemn meanings. The figures were no longer men but personifications of the gods. *The kachinas have returned. I am one of them. We will bring rain. The old ways are not lost.*

NINE

The men who had danced and prayed most of the night slept late in the kiva, undisturbed by the wise man calling the sun. Domingo awoke when his grandfather shook him to help pack his costume. When his grandfather reached for the cloth to wrap the mask, he noticed Domingo's painting. He drew back in awe, studied the art, then asked his grandson if he had drawn the representations. Domingo nodded modestly. His grandfather praised the work but warned that the gods did not want their images lying around. He'd have to burn the cloth. Domingo understood.

Outside the kiva, his grandfather looked upward. "The kachinas have sent a few clouds." He rubbed his arms. "Cool for summer. The mountain snow remains. It keeps the river high."

Domingo yawned. "Be good to go back to bed."

"The deer and rabbits will be raiding the fields. We must check."

His grandfather uttered a short prayer under his breath when they found no damage to the crops. "We've got a while before you see Nicholas. It's time you learned to carve."

"You're serious?" Domingo raised an eyebrow. "I'll get my things." He went for the chisels that Lucas had loaned him. His grandfather had walked upstream and sequestered himself under a cottonwood. Its quaking leaves whispered a shady welcome. Domingo sat next to his grandfather on a slab of rock that served as a workbench.

"Let's see your tools." He examined the two chisels. "You couldn't cut baby shit with these. It's like someone wanted to drag out your lessons. Did Nicolas give you these?"

"No. Lucas sent them. Said he cherished them."

Domingo's grandfather shook his head. "I doubt they'd hold an edge, but it's hard to tell about Spanish steel. You try this." He handed Domingo a stone blade, fitted into a wooden handle. It felt like a chisel. Another stone tool handled like a knife. His grandfather demonstrated how to use each one on a block of cottonwood.

Domingo sucked in a breath. As a child he had watched carvers but never appreciated their skill. Now his gaze followed every move. In no time, the rough form of a kachina emerged from the cottonwood. "You finish the details. Put them into the wood the way you painted them on the cloth."

Domingo took the wood, studied its grain, and edged the stone chisel along with care. He felt a cooperation between fingers and tools that he had never before experienced. His tool peeled off chips no thicker than a fingernail. He couldn't decide if his grandfather had started Mother Kachina or if he saw her in the wood. She took on her identity as details about her materialized. Once or twice, his grandfather showed him how to gouge the smallest of chips or peel an almost invisible groove. He smiled his pleasure as Domingo made a head of hair that looked as if it had just been combed.

"It's time you worked on the real thing," his grandfather said. He reached for a piece of wood at his feet. "Here's cottonwood root."

The consistency of the wood was ideal for carving. Its soft light texture responded as if begging to be carved. His grandfather chuckled at Domingo's delight. "One more thing." He reached under his tunic to retrieve a Spanish knife of steel. It's handle of carved horn was roughened so it would never slip from one's grip. "Try this. It was a Spanish killing tool until I reshaped it for carving." He half grinned. "Still might be useful to kill with." He winked. "When my eyes were young, I put it to good use. Now it's for your eyes. Keep it."

Domingo ran his finger over the edge. "I've never felt such steel. Nor seen such a handle."

"It's bison horn. A Comanche trader gave it to me."

Domingo wondered how he could ever repay his grandfather.

The man spoke as if reading his mind. "Use it for the people."

Domingo grooved a line with his new knife. He felt a presence in the wood that responded to him the way Cristina did to his caresses. He carved a second Mother Kachina that resembled his first attempt, but he added intricate three dimensional details that he could never include with a paint brush.

"I've never seen anyone learn so quickly," his grandfather said. "I guess that painting you do prepared you."

"Don't forget the practice I've had. I couldn't carve well with those dull chisels, but they gave me a feel for the job." Domingo turned over the doll to complete the beads of a necklace. "Do you know a child who would like this?"

"Once you have it painted." His grandfather pointed at the doll's hands. "Work on her fingers. Make them more like a woman's. I like the way you've sculpted her knuckles, but the fingernails could use more attention."

"It's tempting to make her come to life. Show her dancing, for example. Give her an individual identity."

"She's a god, not a person. Concentrate on the symbols of Mother Kachina, not her actions." His grandfather studied Domingo closely. "Your santos are live people. They are born and they die. Make them lifelike, but the gods are immortal. We can't know them as people because they aren't people. They're gods." Domingo inhaled deeply. He wasn't sure he understood, but he felt compelled to portray an individual.

Three women came to the river to wash clothes. Domingo recognized Harelip's wife and nodded to her. She returned the nod, smiling warmly. He picked up another cottonwood root, worked it into a form to frame a human face and edged off bits of wood. In no time, Domingo had sculpted a face. Its coy smile invited touching.

His grandfather recognized Harelip's wife. "You've caught on quickly. You'd better rest now to be ready for whatever make-work Nicolas has in store." Domingo bit his lip. He'd forgotten about his appointment with the priest. He hid the forbidden tools and handed his grandfather the kachina dolls. In his rush, he forgot about the sculpture of Harelip's wife. His grandfather dropped it at the foot of the stone slab.

"Best not surprise Nicolas with what you can do. Looks to me like he wants to keep you busy for a while. Let him think he's a master teacher, though, and you can hasten your progress." He barely suppressed a grin. "I suppose you want to get back to that San Juan girl?"

That afternoon while Nicolas dozed, Domingo carved a fair human likeness, employing the dull chisels, but touching off the work with his grandfather's knife. Nicolas' mouth dropped when he woke.

Domingo responded promptly. "I remembered all you taught me."

"You learn well," the priest muttered in confusion.

"Teaching must be a divine gift that God gave you." Domingo hesitated to say more. His sarcasm might show if he continued.

A week later, Domingo carved a santo that rivaled ones Lucas displayed at San Juan. Nicolas was unable to contain his enthusiasm. "You must try a different wood. Harder but beautiful. And use other tools."

Nicolas went into his room and returned with two slabs of mesquite, several chisels, two knifes, and the book of drawings. He demonstrated use of the tools, then opened the book to an image of St. Nicolas. "You may have the honor of carving this saint."

Domingo studied the picture. Nothing of particular interest caught his attention. *I wonder if the artist failed to capture what made the saint distinct. No interesting symbols here.*

Domingo rotated the wood. It's texture did not inspire him though its grain held a beauty cottonwood lacked. He tried one of the new chisels. It hardly bit the wood. He felt the edge, recognized it as sharp as his grandfather's stone tools and tried again. The wood seemed as hard as stone. As he chiseled away, he recognized the tool's potential. After much sweat, he had a resemblance to the picture, but the carving fell short of inspirational art.

He coughed hard to awaken Nicolas. When the priest came to the courtyard, he studied the image, grunted inaudibly, and handed Domingo the second piece of wood. "Be careful. I don't have much more." He flapped his cassock before he sat. "Study the grain, get a feeling for what speaks to you from the board. Peel away the wood from the image that you see within." He laughed. "Maybe it won't be St. Nicolas." He yawned and headed back to the church.

Domingo held the mesquite in both hands, turned the piece over and over. One side was of uniform color. On the other side, dark grain contrasted with a reddish brown. He held the wood to his ear but heard nothing. He closed his eyes, opened them half way and gazed at the wood. The dark side rippled. At first, he thought he saw water, then he recognized the rippling of long hair being flung back. *It's Cristina tossing her hair.*

The chisel went exactly where Domingo needed to part wood from hair. As the mane took shape, he was reminded of how she'd undo the knot to let it flow free. Sweat stung his eyes. He thought his innards churned from lust, then realized it was a desire to free her hair from the wood. Each strand. He knew instinctively which tool would bring the hair to life. When he finished, he was panting, thirsting for water.

But he passed up a drink to study the wood. The hair outlined Cristina's profile. A dark knot in the red was the small mole on her neck that he teased her about. He forgot his thirst. He forgot everything except the face that lay waiting to be freed from the wood.

It was past the hour when Nicolas came to dismiss him, but Domingo had no idea of time. Nor did he recognize the cramps in his fingers. Knife and chisel did their work. Cristina emerged from the wood, her face beautiful in its reddish brown complexion, her hair lustrous and as seductive as ever. He had captured her teasing eyes and the way she wrinkled her nose. He sighed and ached for her. *How could I have left her? I love her more than life! I'll marry her as soon as I return.*

His rapture made him oblivious to Nicolas' presence. "It's a beautiful image," the priest said. "But I don't recognize which saint it is." When he held the slab closer to his eyes, he realized the image was of an Indian. He gasped, turned to Domingo and cuffed him to the ground. "How dare you suggest an Indian be a saint. And a woman at that." As Domingo got to his knees, Nicolas struck him with the carving. "Such blasphemy! And this good piece of wood wasted."

Domingo needed to be alone. He headed up river to the cottonwood where his grandfather had instructed him. His despair ate at him. The thought of his beautiful Cristina being cast on a wood pile brought tears to his eyes. *How could I have been so careless to let Nicolas see the image of my angel?*

His body trembled. He thought to flee to San Juan. Suddenly he felt hands over his eyes. He expected an Apache knife in his side. He swung round to the sound of a giggle. Harelip's wife plopped herself into his lap, wrapped her arms around his neck, and pulled him tight. He struggled in her grasp. She ran her hand to his belt and tugged at its knot.

"It's not right. You're married," Domingo gasped.

She paid no attention to his protests, loosened his belt, and reached under his breechcloth to massage him. When that did not arouse him, she lifted her blouse and put one of his hands on her breast. The soft flesh tempted him to caress it. When his finger strayed and touched a nipple, she whimpered, slipped off his lap, and pulled him down to the ground rolling under him.

"I can't do this," Domingo murmured. "I love another."

The woman was panting so hard, she probably didn't hear. She thrust her hips into his groin, grabbed his buttocks and pulled him to her. "I want your baby."

Domingo rolled off her, protesting that he could not love her, that he had a true love at home.

"Do I not appeal to you?" She reached under his tunic and ran a hand up his chest.

"You are a beautiful woman. If I did not love another, I couldn't resist you." Domingo got to his feet. "And you are married!"

"That old turncoat will never give me a child. He thinks more about pleasing the Spanish than he does about pleasing me."

"I'm sorry." Domingo took a step back. "There must be many men here who would gladly father your child."

"But I don't want those men. I want you." She ran at Domingo.

He sidestepped and held her at arms' length. "I love Cristina. It can't be."

She walked over to the rock and pulled the carving of her face from below it. "It can be. If you don't come to me, then I'll show this to my husband and tell him it's love medicine. How you seduced me with it!"

TEN

When Domingo told his grandparents about his encounter with Harelip's wife, they teased him for not taking advantage of the attempted seduction. But, they listened with sympathy as he told them of his dedication to Cristina. Later, his grandmother warned him his good looks could get him into trouble but not with Harelip. Serving as a Spanish lackey made him a pariah in the pueblo. No one paid attention to him.

Still, Domingo felt it time to leave Taos. For once, he looked forward to seeing Fray Nicolas, convinced he had learned all he could. The anticipation of seeing Cristina in person instead of in wood raised goosebumps and made his insides quiver.

At the convent, Nicolas searched the bottom of the food basket that Domingo brought, fingering the last few crumbs. He shrugged as he handed Domingo his share. When the religious finished eating, he led the way to the courtyard. "I trust you've learned your lesson." He licked his lips and stared at the tortilla Domingo was eating. Domingo handed the rest of it to him. "You'll carve saints now and not fantasies?"

"I will indeed, father. No more Indians." Domingo intended to keep on the good side of Nicolas. "If you'll let me see your book, perhaps I can sculpt St. Nicolas?" Domingo kneeled at the saint's name for effect.

"That's more like it." Nicolas patted Domingo's head and lifted him by his chin. "You must know what to carve as well as how."

"You've taught me well, father. I owe it all to you. I am eager to show Fray Lucas the miracle you worked on me."

Nicolas beamed. "We have indeed done well." For a moment, he seemed uncertain. "There are a few more techniques to demonstrate. You must stay longer," he said without conviction.

"Please decide after you see my work today." Domingo bowed.

"If you work in oak. It's a useful wood for santos." He retreated into the convent and returned with a long slab. "Take your time. You'll need a few days. I'll be inside praying if you need me."

"Please include me in your prayers." Domingo uttered a short prayer of his own to an unidentified god asking that the priest sleep well. He didn't want to be seen using his grandfather's tools.

Domingo held the wood to the light, wondering for a moment if he should ask for a blessing. He decided study of the grain would prove more useful. He examined both sides of the slab, ran his finger over the wood, and listened to it. It made no sound. He decided on a side and inspected the grain again. He saw nothing of a human face or figure. He studied the book of saints for inspiration. St. Nicolas inspired him not at all.

Domingo turned the wood over again, squinting at it. An arm took shape under his scrutiny. He stared and saw a side profile dressed in a cossack. He explored for a neck or head, found a nose and a lock of hair. He turned his chisel to the body that he watched rise to the surface.

The sharp tools worked well. He knew by intuition when to use stone and when to use steel. The first fold of the cossack emerged. Domingo felt the cloth, glowed with pride as it twisted into folds, saw a sandal near the bottom of the wood. Tracing the cloth upward, he drew a sharp breath at a knotted cord around a narrow waist. Sweat worked its way into his eyes. He wiped it away with the back of his hand.

He'd concentrated so hard that he leaped when he felt someone breathing on his neck. Harelip hissed, "More of your love magic, I see."

Domingo had no idea what Harelip meant.

The man snarled. "My wife told me what pains you took to seduce her. I'll have the priest punish you for your sins." His lips curled into a vicious grin. "Unless you leave Taos immediately!"

"I did not use love medicine on your wife."

"Anyone can see her face in the wood you carved. Are you going to deny it?"

"I carved her image but only for practice. I chose her by chance."

"Are you saying she isn't beautiful?"

"Yes, she is beautiful."

"So you did try to seduce her!"

"No." Domingo screamed his denial, disgusted at such interrogation.

His shout brought Fray Nicolas to the courtyard. "What is this all about?" The priest frowned. He yawned when he saw Harelip.

"Your apprentice here is trying to seduce my wife." Harelip waved a black cane trimmed with a silver tassel under the priest's nose. "Haven't you preached to us about adultery? Doesn't the church believe it's a sin?"

"It's a terrible sin, we all know." The priest stared at Domingo. "Have you forgotten why Fray Lucas punished you? Don't you know that adultery is worse than fornication?"

"Yes, I know, father. And after the whipping I received, I'd never commit adultery." Despite the seriousness of the accusation, Domingo worried about how Harelip's jealousy was going to delay his departure.

"Has your wife told you that she was seduced?" Nicolas stared at Harelip.

"She wasn't seduced," he stammered. "But she told me this stranger used love medicine on her."

"Love medicine?" Fray Nicolas' surprise showed in his face. "What are you talking about?"

"He carved her image in wood so she'd be attracted to him."

"That's more like witchcraft. Do you think Domingo is a witch?" Nicolas's voice filled with concern.

"No!" Harelip was visibly shaken. "Just whip him and make him leave."

"So you don't think he's a witch?"

Harelip trembled. "No. No evidence for that. Everything would be better if he just left."

"You haven't yet reported any cases of witchcraft to me. Are you sure you haven't heard anything?"

"Yes. I mean no, I haven't heard of any. The people have given up witching since you told us how evil it is."

"They didn't give it up at other pueblos. It could be you're failing in your duties as little governor."

"If this intruder would leave, that would solve everything." Harelip clearly didn't want to discuss witchcraft.

Domingo volunteered, "My apprenticeship is nearly finished. I could leave tomorrow."

Harelip shrugged and backed away. As he left, he called over his shoulder, "It can't be soon enough."

"I've never heard of love medicine," Nicolas said. "There are enough pagan ways of witching without that." He looked at Domingo. "You ever hear of it?"

"No, never." Domingo laughed inwardly at the priest's ignorance. "But it would be best if I left. I can perfect my carving back at San Juan. I know I need practice, but I'm ready to work on my own."

"Fray Lucas could help you, I suppose. You have learned most of what I can teach you."

Domingo hid his joy behind words of feigned respect he showered on the priest.

His elation was short lived. Harelip had also taken his accusation to the elders, and they asked Domingo's grandfather to bring him to the kiva that night. A shiver ran down his spine at the sight of the elders sitting along one bench, the youth at the sides. Every initiated male of Taos must have been present.

"Bring your grandson forward." An elder nodded to Domingo's grandfather. Domingo shivered again as two elders took his arms to lead him before the Summer Chief.

The Summer Chief rose. The room went quiet. "You have been accused of using love medicine on a wife of Taos pueblo. What do you have to say for yourself?"

Domingo mustered all the dignity he could. "I intended no love medicine. I love another woman, and she loves me. I have no need for love medicine. I was practicing my sculpting when I made an image of Harelip's wife."

A murmur rose from the assembly. He hadn't intended to use Harelip's name. He glanced around, failed to find him, and couldn't fathom what custom he had violated. If Harelip weren't there, he wondered why the name aroused such a response.

"When you carved her image, didn't you intend to capture her spirit?" The Winter Chief spoke so sharply that Domingo guessed the man to be a close relative of Harelip's wife. He gulped at the thought of how many of her relatives must be present.

"I was only practicing. Fray Nicolas is teaching me to carve santos." Domingo searched the elders for a friendly face. He saw nothing but scowls.

The Summer Chief spoke. "Perhaps, San Juan customs differ from ours. Perhaps they don't condemn love medicine." He paused, hope rose in Domingo's chest. "But we are not in San Juan."

Domingo's chances of claiming innocence vanished. The use of love medicine was considered a serious matter at San Juan although not one to be condemned by the whole community.

Domingo took a deep breath before beginning. "We at San Juan consider love medicine as dangerous. Disputes about it are settled by the families involved. I regret that my ignorance of your custom has caused a problem." He evaded the implication of adultery by skipping it while scrambling for a solution. "The problem could be solved if I left immediately. My work with Nicolas is finished. I could be gone in a day or two."

"But what about the woman who now finds you irresistible?" the Summer Chief said. "What if she follows you to San Juan because you are irresistible to her?" Something about the way he repeated irresistible sounded strange to Domingo.

Before he could figure what it was, the Winter Chief stood. "What's to keep you from using your magic on our wives?

Domingo gulped. He had never heard such a serious accusation about love medicine. Taos pueblo must have exaggerated its importance out of all proportion. He searched their ranks for Po-pe who might better explain the San Juan custom, but he was nowhere to be found.

The Winter Chief continued. "What happens when you carve their sweet spot? Does that get you a really good lay?"

The question was too much for Domingo's grandfather. He burst out laughing. The other men joined him. Domingo flushed. He'd been the butt of a joke, so taken in that he had to force his own laugh. His stomach continued to quiver with anxiety.

The two leaders left the bench to tell Domingo he was a good sport and would always be welcome at Taos. They nodded for him to take his place with the young men.

The Summer Chief spoke. "Now it's time we decide what to tell Harelip."

An elderly man answered. "We say one of the medicine men knows the antidote for love medicine, and this lad paid for him to use it." Murmurs of assent filled the chamber. The old man continued. "The antidote consists of several parts. First, his wife has to go through three of her periods before she can have sex again." Laughter erupted.

Another man spoke out. "As a second part, he should cool her sweet spot. Every time she menstruates, he has to fan her vagina." The young men guffawed. A low grumbling made its way among the elders.

One said, "That goes too far. Besides, it punishes his wife." Murmurs of agreement followed. The men started talking to each other, searching for more ideas.

Domingo's grandfather stood. "Harelip is dumb enough to believe anything we tell him. Why don't we say the antidote requires that he help grind corn, carry water, all the things women do. He must prove he's fearless about his manhood by showing that he's not afraid to do what females do."

The laughter and the cries of assent made it obvious the council had reached a consensus. As people left, they passed by Domingo to tell him they hoped he'd return to Taos. Although they made him feel at home, thoughts of Cristina filled his head. He'd soon be on his way to San Juan.

ELEVEN

Inspired by Cristina's image, Domingo needed only two days to finish carving Nicolas' santo. He'd failed to capture any lifelike glint in the eyes, and he'd taken a short cut by covering the saint's hair with a hood. Still, the image surpassed the drawing in its lifelikeness.

He took the santo to the convent the next morning. The priest's eyes lit up, and he invited Domingo inside. He offered Domingo a stool while he sat behind his desk, studying the santo's features. He fingered the robe and whistled at its knotted cord.

"You've learned well, my son. Use your talents for the church. Don't be tempted by the black arts of your people."

"I never could have achieved anything without your guidance, father." *You stupid Spanish fool!* Domingo knelt and kissed the priest's hand. He rose and looked the man square in the eyes. "I'll be leaving tomorrow."

"There's one more thing," Nicolas said. "Since I spent so much time tutoring you, you can take a while to tutor me."

Domingo's heart raced, anticipating more delay. "I can't imagine what I could offer a man of your learning. I'm just an ignorant savage."

"I understand that your native Tewa is like the Tiwa spoken here. Teach me the language's rudiments. I'll find someone here who knows the language and perfect my skills with him." Nicolas' smile would have been ingratiating if Domingo didn't know him so well. "One never knows when I might be needed at a Tewa speaking pueblo."

Domingo's spirits plunged. He could conceive of no excuse to evade the request. Nicolas had mastered Tiwa grammar and acquired an impressive vocabulary. Although his accent marked him as a foreign speaker, he was at ease using the language. Domingo tried one last evasion. "But I'm not a teacher."

"I've had training in languages," Nicolas said. "I know what to ask. I won't impose on you long."

"How do we go about it, then?" Domingo asked.

"We'll start now. I'll write down basic words I need to know." He reached for pen and ink on a shelf beside him. "What are your words for man and woman?" He smiled when Domingo told him. "Quite similar to Tiwa." He proceeded recording another fifty words, licking his lips at the words for soup and corn. He slobbered over the word for garlic.

Domingo wondered for a moment if Nicolas used Spanish magic. The words he chose were quite similar in Tewa and Tiwa.

Nicolas blew on the ink, then held the sheet close to his eyes. "Let's practice these." He recited the Tewa words, asking Domingo to correct his accent. Domingo pronounced each word distinctly. The priest made no headway with his pronunciation, and Domingo gave up correcting him, praising his accent instead.

Nicolas handed the sheet to Domingo. "It's time to test me." Domingo asked the words in Spanish, and the priest responded correctly to every item. His face beamed with pride. "I'll soon have this mastered."

Domingo asked about expanding his beginning dictionary. Nicolas yawned. "I have other work to do. If you returned at lunch time—perhaps your grandmother would make us tortillas—I could learn another fifty words."

Domingo returned to his grandparents heartbroken, wondering if he'd ever return to San Juan. His grandmother asked what was wrong, and he explained.

His grandfather smiled. "Teach him well so we can get rid of him. Some Tewa pueblo must need a priest."

His grandmother shook her head. "We'd probably do worse with his replacement, but you best teach him as fast as you can."

"He learns quickly. Somehow he picked out words in Tiwa and Tewa that are much alike." Domingo gave examples.

His grandfather's eyes sparkled. "The devil is cunning. He's figured out that the everyday words have much in common."

Domingo frowned. "So when we get to less used words, he's not going to do so well. He could keep me here another month."

"Here's what we'll do." His grandfather's eyes sparkled. "Let's think of words that aren't so common yet ones useful to a priest. Then we'll give them our own meanings."

"I'm not sure what you mean?" Domingo said.

"Well, has he asked you the Tewa word for water?"

"Yes."

"So he'll want to know the words for holy water, next." Domingo's grandfather grinned, then explained how he could be taught holy urine, given the accent that Domingo had mocked.

Once Domingo stopped laughing, he and his grandfather composed fifty more phrases that would make a fool of Nicolas. Domingo's favorite was changing the meaning of fine-ground corn meal to dog turd corn meal.

"Won't he find out what I've done when he talks to a Tewa speaker?"

"The few traders who speak Tewa fluently are away on business. I'll let them in on the joke when they return."

"I'm sure he'll look for someone soon to practice on."

His grandfather nodded. "One of Po-pe's lieutenants is from San Ildefonso. He's a great practical joker."

"I don't know if that will satisfy Nicolas," Domingo said.

"You can tell him I speak Tewa. I'll teach him good."

They both howled.

That afternoon Domingo instructed Nicolas in his grandfather's list of words. He had a hard time keeping a straight face at the priest's practiced diligence, especially when he repeated urine water with such piety.

Nicolas was so pleased with himself that he agreed to Domingo's departure, provided he would write out his word-list. Nicolas excused himself while Domingo wrote. He returned, licking his lips, just as Domingo finished his task.

Nicolas stared at the writing. "The work of a remarkable scribe. You can do one more thing for me. Come by in the morning. I have one more favor to ask."

TWELVE

Domingo chewed at a ragged fingernail as he approached the convent. He hoped to leave Taos but suspected that Nicolas had contrived another delay. The priest might not be a sadist like Lucas, but he must be conspiring with him. Domingo fantasized what life would be like when the Spanish were driven back to Mexico—or killed. His hand went to the knife at his belt. He visualized Nicolas being stoned to death, but he saw himself slitting Lucas' throat.

Domingo's nail split, and he concentrated on the image of Cristina that he had carved. It would be so good to see her in person. To hold her. To ask her to marry him. He sighed with longing and forgot his fingernail.

Beside his desire to reunite with his true love, he suspected Harelip would create problems for him if he stayed longer. Relatives of the young wife had told his grandmother how unhappy Harelip was with his punishment. Although his wife was amused by her husband grinding corn, she had grown angry when she suspected a prank. If she told Harelip of her suspicion, he'd want revenge and cause more trouble for her family.

At the convent door, Domingo concocted a story as to how excited he was to carve santos for his San Juan church. He was rehearsing his story when Nicolas opened the door. The priest hid a yawn and stared at Domingo with a raised eyebrow. "Aren't you early for your lesson? Didn't you bring any tortillas?"

"You asked to see me before I left," Domingo said.

"Oh, yes," Nicolas touched his forehead with a finger. "I want you to illuminate a letter to Señor Martinez. Nothing fancy but enough to impress a crude *encomendero*." Nicolas ushered Domingo into his room, pointed to the stool, and sat at his desk. He readied pen and ink. "You can write the letter, also. Leave space for an illumination. I'll get paints for you while I dictate."

Domingo suspected another delay. He'd write a page and then the priest would find fault with the illumination. The first thing he'd mastered of the art was to illuminate before writing.

The priest offered pen and paper, then dictated a salutation to a Señor Martinez and proceeded to the letter's contents. "The bearer of this letter is a faithful Christian and loyal supporter of the Crown." Domingo's spirits dropped. It might take days to deliver the letter. "He is devoted to the Lord's work, has mastered the art of a scribe, and has finished an apprenticeship with me in sculpting santos." Nicolas allowed Domingo time to finish. "That should ensure you of a good meal." He laughed while Domingo bit his lip. *All this time I've been cooped up here when I could have been loving Cristina, and I've found out nothing that will help my cacique. Now this nonsense of delivering a letter.*

Nicolas continued. "I know you will show him Spanish hospitality. Times here at Taos have been unbearable, and I've had little food to share with him. I am near starvation and have to rely on Indian gratitude for my services. If you can find it in your heart to share your bounty with me, I'll be forever in your service.

"I have forgotten the taste of garlic and worse, I've existed for months on nothing but corn. I dream of bread made of wheat. Two nights ago I awoke from a wonderful dream when I was spreading a slice of bread with honey. Have your bees been productive this year? Lord only knows what a diet of nothing but corn does to the digestive tract." The priest paused to ask Domingo, "Do you need help spelling any of those words?"

Domingo thought he knew the spelling of digestive but asked to make sure. He suspected Nicolas would be happy to make him rewrite the letter, but the priest continued.

"Could you send a soldier with supplies? My apprentice was attacked by twenty Apaches on his way here. I pray daily that those savages have not attacked your ranch, that your wife and children are safe, and that your fields prosper. I sent word about the Apaches to the authorities in Santa Fe, but they did not grace me with a reply." The priest snorted.

"I know you must be low on imported supplies, but if you could spare a cooking pot, I'd forever be in your debt. My silly servant girl lost mine. Why the Viceroy can send supplies only once in three years I'll never understand. Lord knows what will happen if the Apaches raid the convoy. But surely God watches over our *Nuevo Mexico* mission.

"The high snows in the Sangre de Cristo mountain range are melting and have raised the river level. I pray the flooding will not delay the wagon train. The colony must be low on powder and arms. For protection we must rely on the prayers of the religious for the safety of Spanish men, women, and children." Nicolas turned to rummage through a shelf. When he turned back, Domingo caught a stench of cheese that made him gag.

Nicolas raked his tongue over his teeth before dictating more. "Fortunately, we need protection only against the savage Apaches. If the other pueblos are as content as Taos we have nothing to fear from them. This pueblo has destroyed its kiva and ceased its devilish dancing. Neither I nor the little governor has seen anything but devotion." He paused while Domingo finished.

"Am I right, Domingo?" Domingo sat bolt upright. The use of his name startled him. He assumed Nicolas had forgotten it, if he had ever bothered to learn it.

"Sorry. What did you say?"

"Has your grandfather given up the old ways? Has the kiva been destroyed?"

"That's right, father. The people filled it in. If any dances were held, you'd surely hear the drums and songs."

"It's good to know I've made a dent in the heathenish ways." Nicolas sighed and wiped his brow. "Now, if I could only induce more faithful attendance at mass." He studied Domingo. "You've helped, my son, with your grandparents, but the others make constant excuses. At least, those who will talk to me."

Domingo felt exhilarated. He'd be able to report to his cacique the priest's ignorance of kiva activity and his lack of suspicion of revolt. He blew on the letter to dry the ink. "If you have the paints for the illumination, I can begin."

"Your hand must be cramped from my rambling. Go home and rest. You can finish this afternoon." He scrutinized the letter. "Fine work!" He nodded a dismissal. As Domingo rose, the priest added,

"Don't forget your grandmothers's tortillas. She does wonders with corn meal."

Domingo's grandfather told him that the Martinez ranch laid between Taos and Picuris. The journey would require two or three days, depending on how long the rancher kept him. His grandfather instructed him on the shortest route while his grandmother prepared corn mush. While Domingo ate, his grandfather explained what information would help Po-pe. Domingo's jaw dropped at the thought of returning to Taos. His grandfather laughed telling him to report to a Po-pe lieutenant in San Juan. He added that he might inquire into the rancher's attitudes toward the clergy and civil authorities. It would be useful to know where the rancher's loyalty lay. Domingo's heart pounded at the thought of helping Po-pe.

At the convent he felt another elation. He'd be reunited with his true love soon. He'd ask her to marry him. The thought of a baby in his arms no longer frightened him.

Nicolas had laid out the necessary brushes and paint, and Domingo set to work. However, Nicolas insisted they eat first. For once, Domingo finished his tortillas before the priest did.

The illumination consisted of the letter T, one of Domingo's favorites. The ends of the horizontal line could circle in flamboyant style while balancing each other in a subtle manner. A vine curled up the vertical line, a plant he'd adorn with flowers. An afternoon hardly sufficed to do justice to the letter, but since Nicolas had only red and green paint, Domingo kept the design simple.

As Domingo traced an outline of his T, he saw intuitively how the embellished letter fit into an intricate background. He went into the courtyard to picture in his mind the total piece. The vine started growing, red buds forming, then bursting into full bloom. A bee darted from one flower. He closed his eyes to the letter's beauty, but before he could open them, the flowers trembled. The letter bent, then was uprooted by a violent tempest. Domingo broke out in a sweat.

He returned to the convent in a daze. He finished the letter as it might be drawn in a practice book, but it still drew Nicolas' admiration.

THIRTEEN

"You must not stay away so long next time." His grandfather's voice cracked.

Domingo nodded a promise to return soon.

"This is for that rusty piece of steel my man gave you." His grandmother handed him a doeskin sheath. The brown and white spots of the soft leather blended with the knife's handle. Domingo beamed at its beauty, tying the sheath to the belt. He tucked his tunic behind the knife handle to display the sheath.

He shrugged a goodbye, wiped away a tear, and wondered when he would see them again. He backed away, eyes on his grandparents until he turned for the convent, fearful that Nicolas might have further delaying tactics.

The priest ushered him into his office, folded and sealed the letter, and found a leather pouch for it. "You'll keep it dry? We wouldn't want our illumination ruined, would we?" He stared at the pouch Domingo wore around his neck.

Domingo guessed Nicolas was aware of his people's use of personal fetishes but avoided making an issue of them. Once in a while the Dominicans showed a little sense. When Nicolas handed him the pouch, Domingo tied it to his belt.

Nicolas probed at a dusty collection of artifacts on a top shelf. "I have something else for you, a gift in remembrance of our friendship." He held up a small wooden cross as he might offer the chalice at Sunday mass. "When I had good eyesight, I carved this. It's all of one piece." Domingo fingered the soft aspen. The amateurish carving resembled his own first trials. He was at a loss for a response.

The priest picked up a small bag much like the one that held Domingo's deer. "The cross fits in here. It makes a companion for what you are wearing, and, God willing, one day you'll realize it's all you need to wear.

"A thousand thanks, Father. I'll treasure it." *And watch it float down the river as soon as I get home. If I don't need it for firewood before then.*

Nicolas repeated his instructions for finding the Martinez *encomienda* and sent his blessings to each family member. Domingo asked if he wanted to send greetings to other Spaniards there, and the priest told him of four men. Domingo smiled inwardly. He had gleaned useful information even before reaching the ranch. Mulling over other possibilities for helping Po-pe sustained his run there.

The next day he arrived well before dark. Two Indians herded sheep on the outskirts. Domingo spoke to them in Tiwa, then Tewa, but they replied with blank stares. He resorted to Spanish, and both grinned, ready for gossip about Taos or wherever he had been. When he discovered they were Mexican Indians, he asked about their relatives before inquiring about Indians working on the ranch. From their gossip, he supposed they'd remain loyal to the Spaniards in an uprising.

While the two herded their animals toward a corral, Domingo jogged to the large adobe building beyond. Four majestic shade trees held it in their arms. An older Indian sitting on the porch steps, greeted him in Spanish and asked what he wanted. Domingo informed him of the letter he carried for Martinez. The man ushered him into a front room and pointed to a chair. He left, then returned with a Spaniard, taller than most, bearded, and wearing black pants and white shirt. A black beard and mustache hid the lower half of a weathered face. A black eye patch added mystery to the upper face.

Domingo stood and bowed his head. "Fray Nicolas sends you a letter."

Martinez nodded for Domingo to sit, dismissed his servant, sat at his desk, and read. His stern look changed to one of warmth. He pointed toward the dining room. "Will you join me for dinner? My wife is ill." He led Domingo to a dining room where a large table was covered with dinner ware. The settings of forks and knives made Domingo bite a lip. He searched his mind for the little Spanish table etiquette that Lucas had taught him, then decided to follow his host's example.

"Is Taos truly on the verge of famine?" Martinez asked.

Domingo hadn't been instructed to give false information. He decided he'd best go along with what Fray Nicolas had written.

"Everyone is short on food. The beans and squash are half what they should be. The corn languishes from lack of water."

"But I've heard the Rio Grande is higher than usual."

"The river at Taos got little runoff, and the drought has lasted so long."

"I see." Martinez rang a bell and a young Indian woman brought them soup.

Domingo whispered to her in Tiwa, and her smile told him she understood. Perhaps she, too, could garner information.

"I was lucky earlier in the year hunting deer," Martinez said. "We haven't butchered any sheep until lately."

"Are you still hunting?"

"I stopped because our powder supply is running low. I've even melted the lead from used balls to make more."

"Can't you make them from iron?" Domingo said, trying to sound naive.

"I suppose you don't know much about guns. We have to rely on Mexico for powder and shot."

"I've never seen a gun up close," Domingo said.

The *encomendero's* face lit up. "I'll show you my collection after dinner. Three fine pieces and eight old harquebuses. At least, I can arm all my men against the Apaches."

"I'd love to fire a gun. The one time I saw one go off I couldn't believe how much fire it belched."

Martinez laughed at length. "Your metaphor of belching fire is both entertaining and accurate. I can see why you've become a favorite with the Dominicans."

The two continued chatting during a meal of venison stew. Domingo hadn't tasted venison for months and overate. When he tried to suppress his burps, Martinez asked when he was going to belch fire.

Domingo used the joke to remind Martinez he intended to show him his weapon collection. The hunter took him to his study. A engraved wooden cabinet, with a locked door, served to store the firearms. Martinez took out the three modern pieces and showed Domingo how they worked. He expressed regrets that he could not allow Domingo to make one belch.

"If the Apaches were foolish enough to attack you, would you defend yourself from here?" Domingo asked.

"Not if we can help it. They'd burn our home. My men built a stockade of rocks on a nearby hill. A spring trickles through, and there is a rock roofed room for the women and children. We could last several weeks—longer than any Apaches have ever attempted a siege."

But if Po-pe's men got to your fort first, you'd be vulnerable. Domingo imagined the shock to Martinez when he fled to his fort and found his foe waiting for him. With a straight face he said, "I can see you're well prepared. You should have nothing to fear." He guessed that a locked cabinet next to the gun cases held powder and shot. "What happens to gun powder in a fire?"

Martinez laughed. "If one is lucky it burns up, but it can also explode. Right now I have so little, I needn't worry."

"You can arm all your men, can't you?"

For the first time, the rancher's eyes glinted suspicion. "They'll be well armed, and they are crack shots."

Domingo knew to change the subject. He talked of his experiences at Taos, mentioning Fray Nicolas' craving for garlic.

Martinez chuckled, "Maybe he'll attract more people to his mass without such bad breath."

"I wonder if he ran out of incense or garlic first," Domingo said.

Martinez bellowed. "I keep some incense handy in case he visits." He pointed down the hall. "Would you like to see my chapel?"

They entered a small room through a door of the study. It could hold half a dozen people. An altar below a window was adorned with white cloth, two candles, and a bronze cross. A hint of incense lingered in the air. Martinez pointed to an incense holder. "My anti-garlic defense."

Domingo laughed, then studied the room. "I admire your taste, señor. Simple but pleasing to the eye."

"Too simple, I'm afraid. Life on the frontier is dreary." Martinez' eyes lit up. "Perhaps you could add to the decor?"

Domingo raised an eyebrow. "I, señor? I know nothing of architecture."

"Perhaps you could carve a santo for me?"

Domingo's heart raced. A santo would require an additional three or four days, providing he could find the right wood. Yet, he could not very well turn his back on Martinez' behest. He held his chin in his hand as if contemplating a carving but in fact searched his mind for a way to evade the request.

"You do me an honor, Señor Martinez. Allow me to show you a sample of my work." Domingo took Nicolas' cross from the sack around his neck and handed it to Martinez. The man tried to hide his disappointment. The words that he mumbled revealed he was ready to excuse Domingo from the carving.

"I do not have any tools with me. Perhaps you have some?" Domingo had Lucas' dull chisels and the knife his grandfather had given him, but he had provided Martinez with reason enough to dismiss him. The rancher suggested that he carve a santo in San Juan and bring it on his next visit. Then he showed Domingo to a bunk house and invited him for a morning meal.

Before breakfast, Domingo sought out the serving girl he had met the night before. He asked her to tell his grandfather when supplies reached the ranch and if she could find out where the rancher kept his gun powder. She promised to relay any news to Taos. After eating, Martinez escorted Domingo to the trail toward San Juan, warning him of Apaches and urging him to return. Domingo was about to leave when two vaqueros rode up. Domingo exclaimed what fine animals they were and asked the size of the herd. Martinez answered without thinking. Domingo took his leave, storing the size of the horse herd for Po-pe's lieutenant.

On the run to San Juan, Domingo mulled over the intelligence he had gathered. A chill spiraled down his spine despite his sweat as he realized he had spied. *But what good is information about a single ranch?* Suddenly he realized he was likely just one of many spies that Po-pe had recruited.

After a noon rest, Domingo's thoughts turned to Cristina. Desire swept through him. He wondered why he had not thought more about her when he had ended the San Juan finishing rite that made him eligible for marriage. The memory troubled him. Cristina had talked about her own finishing ceremony although she did not know a date for it.

Nevertheless, he planned to ask his father to find a go-between as soon as he reached San Juan. If his father's older brother was away on a trading expedition, the cacique could take his place. With him as go-between, Cristina's parents would surely hasten her finishing ceremony.

His head was so full of wedding plans, that he plunged into the Rio Grande crossing without thought. When he missed a footing, the high water caught his legs and tumbled him against a boulder. He rolled down stream cursing himself for his carelessness. He regained his footing at a sand bar, then swam down stream using the current to take him across.

He trotted to Cristina's home, waited at the entrance, but no one came to the door. He bent over two small children playing nearby, showed them a trick with his fingers, and asked about Cristina. Neither had seen her.

He headed for his father's home but found no one there. Anxiety crept into his innards even though he knew most men would be working in the fields. He went to the cacique's, waited at the door longer than customary. As he stood in frustration, Fray Lucas approached. He called a greeting, and Domingo was obliged to discuss his apprenticeship with Nicolas, promising to show his skills in the next day or two. He was reluctant to ask the priest about Cristina, but he couldn't help himself.

The priest's nod couldn't be interpreted, but he said, "She may be the wife for you, once you are prepared for marriage."

Domingo couldn't contain his joy. "She was planning her finishing ceremony when I left, Father. We could both be ready soon." Domingo bit his lip. The San Juan finishing ceremony meant nothing to the Catholics.

Lucas rubbed his chin. "I was thinking of something more important." He put a hand on Domingo's shoulder. "She wants to be by your side in the Spanish world. She wants to learn our language, so

I arranged for her to live with a family on an *encomienda*. She works as a servant while she learns."

"Where is this family?" Domingo suspected the priest of another trick to keep him from his love. He leaned forward for the answer. A stale onion odor mixed with the priest's reply.

"Her parents knew of a family. An *encomienda* where one of them once worked, near San Ildefonso. I can't be more helpful."

Domingo suspected Lucas lied, but he stood helpless to confront him. One day he would.

FOURTEEN

Domingo went home to rest. He was dozing when his father returned to joke about Cristina running off with someone else. When Domingo scowled, his father claimed that late night discussions in the kiva had left little time for gossip. He did know that she had danced in the finishing ceremony. Domingo sighed in relief.

"I thought you'd have forgotten her by now," his father said, attempting a final jest.

"Being away made me want her all the more," Domingo replied with fervor.

"You're sure she's the one?"

"I'm ready to marry." Domingo had never felt so certain about anything in his life. "Will you find a go-between for me?"

"We could wait for my brother. If he's been lucky trading, he should be back in thirty or forty days." His father stretched out on his sleeping mat and yawned. "But if he's had no luck, it might take longer."

"Could you look for someone else?" Since his father wasn't close to his older brother, a substitute shouldn't be a problem.

"I have a friend who's served as a go-between. He'll do a good job." Before Domingo could ask who it was, his father's snores stopped him. A coyote barked for its mate to join in a hunt, and Domingo fell asleep lulled by their familiar jabber.

At dawn, a San Juan wise man wailed a greeting to the sun. As it climbed past the horizon, the greeter admonished the youth to respect their elders, then urged everyone to the fields. The day threatened to be another white hot eternity.

His father sat up, felt his back, and laid back down. When he rolled over, he saw his son, and rose. "You must be starving. I didn't save any food for you last night."

Domingo told how he'd banqueted at the Martinez ranch, and the cook had given him so many tortillas that he had enough for their breakfast. He undid the corn husk wrappings and handed his father three of the four. While they ate, his father described how a recent rain had urged the weeds to overrun their fields. Between late night talks and travel to other pueblos, the men of San Juan had fallen behind in their work. Domingo noted that his father avoided reporting the discussions. He wondered if they involved politics or religion. But if his father wouldn't tell him, Domingo knew not to ask. His father did volunteer that they might find the cacique after weeding, and he might know something about Cristina.

Soaked in sweat from weeding, Domingo sighed with relief when his father suggested they find shade while sharpening their stone hoes. Cousins were eating under the trees, and they shared their noon meal of corn and beans. Domingo restrained himself from asking for a second helping.

Bent over his hoe, rasping its edge, a cousin asked how the Spanish sharpened their metal hoes. His father explained grinding wheels and steel files, adding that when their tools broke, they had no way to repair them. He wiped sweat from his brow as he chipped away. "I used their metal once. The hoe was no better than mine, but the Spaniards would never think to use stone."

"They depend on new hoes from Mexico City, don't they?" the cousin asked.

"That's right. The supply wagons scheduled for this summer should have new hoes—if the wagons get through."

Domingo's eyes widened. "You think there's some reason they won't?"

His father muttered. "Who knows? The wagons have been delayed before." The men headed back to their fields.

At day's end, when father and son ended their weeding, they met the cacique, his tunic stained with sweat. The man congratulated Domingo for outrunning half the Apache nation on his way to Taos. Domingo knew from his exaggeration that the cacique had received reliable reports on the encounter and must have appreciated the rumors that followed.

His father switched the talk to Cristina. The cacique pointed to a fallen cottonwood where they could sit in solitude. "Lucas asked Cristina's kin for her services after you left," he nodded at Domingo. "They did not object but I worried. When I talked to her, she had no complaints until a few days later when she asked me if she could leave. I told her I'd talk to her kin. The day I saw them, Cristina came home in tears." Domingo's insides churned. "I feared Lucas might have sexually assaulted her, but she said no. When he pinched her cheeks or ears hard enough to bring tears, she had endured. But this time he had accused her of flaunting herself to an altar boy, and he held a candle to her arm. She showed us a burn festering white pus."

"I'll kill him." Domingo gripped the handle of his knife. His heart raced. *Why did I ever go to Taos? I should have been here to protect her.*

"We sent her to San Ildefonso, her mother's pueblo. I told Lucas her family needed help. He offered to place her with an *encomienda* nearby. Claimed she'd learn Christian virtues so she'd be a fit companion for someone like you," the cacique said to Domingo.

"Christian virtues like brutalizing the innocent," Domingo's father said.

The cacique grimaced. "We had to take the chance. The girl can send food to her family, the way other servants do. She's more valuable there than at home grinding corn."

"But what will the *encomendero* want beside her labor?" Domingo said. *I'll castrate him if he rapes her and make him eat his balls.* Domingo tasted bile.

"The man has a wife and kids." The cacique spoke softly. "His reputation is better than that of most Spaniards."

"What if we married?" Domingo said. "She should come here after marriage, shouldn't she? I could protect her from Lucas. Or we'd move to San Ildefonso. Live with her mother."

"That's up to her," the cacique said. "Or the two of you."

"I want to marry as soon as possible."

The cacique shook his head. "It's not just the food she sends." The cacique chose his next words carefully. "The ranch occupies a strategic position between the pueblos and Santa Fe. It's essential to know where the *encomendero's* loyalties lie. The governor and ranchers get along because all they're interested in is making money from Indian labor. However, the governors don't last long in office the way the priests do. So the religious often develop more influence."

"You mean priests such as Lucas?" Domingo glowered.

"Not Lucas. The priests at Santa Clara and San Ildefonso are the ones who interest us." The cacique sucked in a breath.

"Who cares what the rancher feels toward them? Or those devils in Santa Fe?" Domingo didn't hide his irritation.

"Let's just suppose," the cacique looked around, "that Indians attacked the *encomienda.* The rancher would flee to Santa Fe with his family. But would he go out of his way to rescue any priests? If he did, it would be easy to lay a trap for him."

Domingo felt a chill. An uprising must be closer than he imagined. And his beloved Cristina would be in its midst.

He hit his head with a fist. When he had thought about other Indians spying on the Spanish, he never dreamed his beloved might be one of the spies.

"You're asking more of Cristina than my grandfather asked me of me."

The cacique half grinned. "And what do you have to report to me?"

Domingo's jaw dropped. "You're the lieutenant of Po-pe?"

"One of many. I'll see he learns whatever you found out."

Domingo recounted the numbers of men and horses and the shortage of ammunition at the Martinez ranch. "There was one other thing. Martinez has built a fort on the hill south of his ranch, equipped for a siege. It would be difficult to take unless Indians occupied it before the rancher had any warning." He pictured the befuddled rancher when he fled to his fortress to find it occupied.

"They don't need to know if Martinez would help any priests," the cacique chuckled. "He won't be going anywhere."

"But what about Cristina?" Domingo's whisper was harsh. "She's too young to learn what the *encomendero* plans."

"She is. But San Ildefonso servants work for him who have been at the ranch for years. They'll tell a fourteen year old girl whatever gossip she shows an interest in."

Domingo smiled with pride, certain that his beloved could stir such gossip. Still, the thought did not relieve his anxiety. "How long does she have to stay?"

"Not long." The cacique looked past Domingo to the fields. "Your father needs help with his corn. Every ear, every bean will matter. Help us catch up before you think of leaving. That will give Cristina time to learn more from the Spanish."

For the next few days, Domingo's hoe flew faster than the eye could follow. He was collapsed with fatigue on a Saturday evening when Lucas came to ask his help with the morning mass. Domingo clenched his fists, ready to refuse, then realized he might glean more information.

After mass, the priest invited Domingo to his quarters where they talked about his apprenticeship. Lucas emphasized the debt Domingo owed for all his education, then asked him to carve a santo for San Juan.

"It must be after the harvest." *And after I see you to your grave.* Aloud Domingo settled for a sarcastic barb. "I find I work much better with sharp tools."

If Lucas comprehended the remark, he ignored it. "I believe I know who might help you."

Domingo suspected a ruse but maintained a facade of innocence. "Our stone knives aren't of much use, and no one seems to remember how to carve anyway."

Lucas laughed. "I know where you can get the best Spanish steel." He waited, toying with Domingo's curiosity.

"Where would that be?" After all of Lucas' deceptions, Domingo wasn't about to count on his promise.

"Señor Baca has excellent wood working tools. Also you can learn more about sculpting. One of his ranch hands is a cabinet maker. Once in a while he turns out a santo. He'd guide you."

"The family must be wealthy to have a cabinet maker."

"Señor Baca employs five Spaniards and a dozen Mexican mestizos. His herd of sheep is the largest north of Santa Fe."

If Lucas would supply more information, Domingo could report to the cacique. "I suppose he employs pueblo people, too?"

"Yes, indeed, like your Cristina! If you'll dedicate yourself to carving the patron saint of San Juan, I'll use my influence with the *encomiendero*. In a few months you two could marry and work together on his ranch. It would do my heart good to see you well placed in a Christian family."

For a moment, Domingo imagined Lucas helping him live in bliss. Until a twinge of pain cut a path down the scars on his back. He nodded to imply he'd do the carving, but in his mind he pictured his knife at Lucas' throat.

FIFTEEN

Domingo attacked the last weeds and helped his father irrigate a final time. The two feasted on five fresh squash before slicing others into lengths for the drying racks. He guessed the scant harvest would only last until the winter solstice. Father and son hid their anxiety but could not disguise their dependence on summer rains no matter how much devotion they poured into the irrigation ditches. Domingo longed for the lush, abundant green the corn wore the last time the kachinas descended from their mountains to bring proper nourishment.

"We can harvest the corn in sixteen or so days," his father said. "I'll clean the storage pits."

"I'll be back to help," Domingo swore. "I may join Cristina's family in their fields, but I won't miss our harvest. I want to taste my sweat in our corn."

"Feed your deer while the corn pollen is abundant."

Domingo's hand went to his throat. In the hard work, he had forgotten his fetish. He considered giving it back to his father. The Apaches would be lurking near by at harvest time. "Would you wear it now? The Apache vultures will be here."

"They're as likely to scout San Ildefonso as here. You keep it." His father clasped his son's shoulder. "I see you've acquired a knife."

"A gift from grandfather. It's wonderful to carve with."

Domingo unsheathed the knife and handed it to his father.

"Useful against Apaches, too. It and the deer will protect you from them. And other danger."

"Is the revolution near?" Domingo knew he shouldn't ask such a direct question, but he worried about protecting Cristina if war broke out. "Is it time?"

His father grimaced. "If I knew, I couldn't tell you." He released his grip on his son's shoulder. "Just be extra alert. Everyone is in more danger than usual."

"At least, I'll have Cristina by my side. Send the go-between to her parents." Domingo sucked in his lip. "Her parents can't say no, can they?" He waited in vain for reassurance. "May I leave tomorrow?"

"The fields are finished. It's time you're going." His father smiled. "Make a good impression so my go-between will have an easy time of settling arrangements."

The next morning Domingo left after breakfast. The journey to San Ildefonso was an easy day's jog, but he rushed along. He'd spend the rest of the day visiting Cristina's father and mother and do everything he could to gain their approval. He tried to recall his cousin's likes and dislikes. The two had been constant companions in their youth even though she was ten years older. When Domingo's mother had died in childbirth, the cousin became like a second mother to him. He felt lost when she married a San Ildefonso man and moved to his pueblo.

The run was uneventful. He'd scrutinized the path for Apache tracks but found none. The times he rested, he talked with his deer and day-dreamed of Cristina. He imagined a dozen ways to convince her parents he'd make a good son-in-law. He decided to emphasize how hard-working he was, rubbing at the callouses on his hand. He'd mention his illumination and carving but worried how Cristina's father might react to his knowledge of Spanish ways.

He decided to emphasize, if not exaggerate, the part he took in the Taos kiva. He imagined recounting everything that had transpired between himself and Po-pe before recalling his vows of secrecy. After his last rest, he finished his run in a quandary, still unsure how to present himself to his prospective in-laws.

At the edge of the pueblo, he surveyed the buildings. The kiva ladder no longer protruded from its customary spot. He guessed the men had filled it in and dug a secret one. He studied the doors trying to recall which one belonged to his cousin. He had visited her only once after her marriage.

He would have asked someone in the plaza, but it was empty except for a young woman surrounded by a swarm of children. She had each one's full attention, leading them in a stick game. Judging from their laughter, she must be joking and telling stories as much as playing. Domingo decided not to interrupt her but to rely on his intuition to find his cousin.

His feelings served him well. He stood before a door only moments before it opened. "Good to see you, Mingo." His cousin beamed a smile of welcome. "How many years has it been?"

"Too many." Domingo warmed at hearing the nickname that only she used. He had resented it as a child and chased her around the plaza whenever she dared call him Mingo. Later he realized the warmth she invested in the endearment.

"I suppose you've come to help with our harvest?" She kept a straight face, but her tone was teasing. "You're early."

"Cousins should help each other—even when one of them deserted her pueblo," he said.

"I suppose your hands and back are in no condition to farm since you spend so much time drawing pictures for the Spanish."

Domingo listened to her tone more than to her words. He couldn't yet judge what she thought of his work for the Spanish. He wasn't even sure Cristina had relayed news of the whipping Lucas had given him.

"My mother urged me to learn Spanish ways." He hesitated yet got no response. "But you must know that?" Again she said nothing. "If she hadn't died so young, she might have changed her mind. My father didn't interfere with her wishes since he loved her so much."

His cousin said, "Would he have loved her if one of the Spanish devils had whipped him because of it?" She burst out laughing.

"You'll never stop teasing me, will you?" Domingo said. "You know very well why I've come."

"I expected you long before."

"Did Cristina tell you everything about us?"

"Everyone but Cristina told me. You didn't expect Indians to keep something like that a secret, did you?"

"I didn't know how many people knew about our love for each other," Domingo said.

His cousin's mouth dropped, but she recovered quickly. "They told me how the priest whipped you for sleeping with your cousin. Some gossips thought she really was a cousin." She turned up her nose. "One thought you had lain with me." She laughed hard at the thought. "I heard all kinds of rumors but nothing about you being in love with Cristina."

"My father will send a go-between." Domingo spoke with determination. "We want to marry."

His cousin's eyebrows arched. "I'm not sure she's ready to marry. She's so childish at times."

"She often told me she wants a baby."

"As often as she wants to lay with you, no doubt. You don't think you've been the only one, do you?" She tapped his shoulder with a finger. "But you're the first to talk of marriage."

"We have discussed it." Domingo stammered. He couldn't remember exactly when they had talked of marriage nor what they had said, but he felt like they should marry. He couldn't be more positive of anything since he had sculpted her face. "Certainly I want to marry her. My father's sending a go-between."

"How well do you two know each other?"

"I've seen her since she was a child." Domingo felt a chill. The answer was unsatisfactory.

"Can you put up with her vanity?"

"I haven't found her vain," Domingo protested. "She's rightly proud of her beautiful hair. Her beautiful face." He lingered over the word, face.

"How will you feel after a day of weeding, and you come home to find her combing her hair instead of cooking a meal?"

"I'm sure she'll cook for me!"

"Can you imagine her cooking and taking care of a baby?" His cousin asked the question so sincerely that Domingo had to think hard.

"She'd make a wonderful mother. She wants a baby, I know."

"You can only be sure she wants *to make* a baby." A teasing tone returned. She paused, then asked in a serious voice, "How does she feel about your work for the brown robes?"

The question caught Domingo unawares. Her use of the phrase, brown robes, suggested his cousin's family had little contact with the Dominicans. "She's listened attentively when I've described how I illuminate manuscripts for Fray Lucas. She has attended mass—on occasion."

"Like at Christmas?" His cousin snickered.

"I'm sure we'll be happy." Domingo spoke more forcefully than he had intended. "We dearly love each other!"

His cousin shrugged. "It's up to you two. Her father will want to give the go-between a hard time, but he's always let Cristina do what she wants." She chuckled. "Maybe he'll be glad to have one less mouth to feed."

"I'll take good care of her, I swear."

"We'll see." His cousin sighed, then teased. "You'd be better off marrying her sister, but she's probably too old for you. Almost your age. And with a mind of her own."

"Cristina's never mentioned a sister."

"Francesca's the black sheep of the family." She offered no explanation.

"I'd like to meet her."

"Tomorrow she'll guide you to the Baca *encomienda* where Cristina works. Or you can meet her now if you wish."

"I'd like to," Domingo said.

"Did you see her in the plaza? She's likely surrounded by children."

Before Domingo could return to the plaza, his cousin insisted he eat something. The stew was warm enough that it gave off the scent of venison. Its sight and scent sent Domingo's mouth into rapture.

He spoke with his mouth full. "Your husband must be a good hunter."

"Francesca had to track the buck for three days. Killed it with her first arrow."

Domingo was dumbfounded. He'd never heard of a woman hunting large game. He finished the bowl in silence puzzling over whom he was about to meet.

When he reached the children in the plaza, they were spell-bound from a story. He expected Francesca to dismiss them and talk with him. Instead, she reached for four sticks on the ground. "One last game. Who wants to take me on?"

An older boy scrambled to his knees before her. She handed him the sticks, one scraped clean, another with its bark. The other two had different parts of their length peeled away. Domingo recognized the game as one he had played as a child.

The boy threw the sticks. Francesca pointed at one of the smallest girls. "Your turn to count." The girl counted hesitantly. Domingo realized that Francesca was making a game of learning.

After a few more turns, the woman dismissed the children promising a story later. She rose to greet Domingo as if she expected him. He was surprised at her height. Taller than he. Her long legs had the thigh and calf muscles of a runner. When she drew close, he saw her eyes slanted in toward the nose more than customary for a pueblo Indian. In contrast, her eyebrows flared up at the sides, pointing to the top of her ears. The brown irises were close to being black. Politeness called for less than a glance, but Domingo felt, as much as saw, flecks of gold in the deep brown.

Francesca stared at his eyebrows, almost into his eyes. The gaze unnerved him. There was nothing demure about the look, so unlike Cristina, yet the eyes were balanced by an intriguing smile highlighted by broad lips. It was hard to believe she was Cristina's sister.

"Your mother said I'd find you here," Domingo stammered, not expecting such a tall woman nor such a bold gaze.

"She told me you'd be coming to see Cristina." Francesca shifted her gaze to Domingo's forehead but stared far longer than custom allowed. "You're from San Juan?"

Her directness unsettled Domingo more than her height or eyes. He was about to answer when she said, "I hear the people from San Juan run like turtles. You any faster, Mingo?"

Domingo's jaw dropped. *How dare she call me that.* He fought to find a sarcastic reply, but the best he could do was, "If we are turtles, San Ildefonso people must be snails."

"Well," she snickered, "tomorrow we'll see how well you can stay on the track of a snail."

"What do you mean?"

"I'll be showing you the way to the Baca *encomienda.* Aren't you in a hurry to see my sister."

"Of course, I am." Would this woman never stop her teasing? Domingo thought.

"Then you'd better be sure your runty little legs are well rested tonight."

SIXTEEN

That night Domingo slept on his cousin's roof. He dreamt of Cristina, but a curious glitter in her eyes disturbed his sleep. Half awake, he reveled in the dream waiting for the wise man to greet the sun. When the morning call finished, he rolled onto his back imagining Cristina in his arms.

"You can't lie around all day if you want to see my sister." Francesca's head popped from the top of the ladder.

Domingo rolled to his side. Slanting sun rays sparkled off the flecks in Francesca's eyes as if the gold were real. His rapid heart beat made him wonder if she might be a witch.

"You waiting for me to carry you down the ladder?" she teased.

"I thought you'd bring tortillas to me." Domingo got to his knees, rolled up the sheepskin his cousin had furnished, and turned to Francesca. "Guess I'll have to come down."

"You've been around the Spanish lords too long. Expecting a servant to wait on you. Will you train Cristina to wait on you?" This time, her voice carried more taunt than tease.

Before Domingo reached the ladder, Francesca had slipped into the room below. Her behavior irritated him. *She doesn't know her place. Like her mother. Maybe she'll grow out of it. Her mother seems to have.*

Francesca's mother was adding wood to a small cook fire below a stone grill. On one side, a pot of mush steamed. The dry wood crackled. Its perfume mixed with the fragrance of fresh tortillas. His cousin turned the flat cakes.

The bursting bubbles on their surfaces did to his eyes what the smell did to his nose.

"Shall we go?" Francesca came up behind him without a sound.

Domingo jumped. "Go where?"

"To see where Cristina lives. Surely, you don't put tortillas before seeing your bride to be?"

Domingo's mouth dropped. It had been so long since he had seen Cristina, their meeting could wait for a bowl of mush—and especially for fresh tortillas. Yet, he felt committed to the run and bent down to tie his moccasins.

His cousin laughed. "She's teasing you, Mingo. I swear, you're as gullible as ever."

Domingo flushed. He turned up his nose at Francesca.

She rolled her tongue over her lips. "Maybe you'll want to nap after breakfast, Mingo. I could run down a rabbit while you sleep. After that I might be tired enough so you could keep up."

Domingo's cousin handed him a tortilla and a bowl of mush. He rolled the tortilla to scoop the mush, burning his mouth with the first bite. "It's very good," he sputtered, his mouth open to suck in air.

His cousin hid a grin with the back of her hand. "She gathers a wild seed on the mountain meadows," nodding at Francesca. "It makes them taste better, and they fill you up." She winked. "We keep the plant a secret."

Her husband came to the grill. Juan's little finger on his left hand was missing. He massaged the other three fingers as if counting his blessings. He had said little to Domingo since his arrival, but the few words were warm. Domingo felt his prospective father-in-law would have no qualms about offering him his daughter.

Juan was short, barely reaching Francesca's shoulders. His hair was pulled back and tied with a piece of rawhide. "Has Francesca spiced the tortillas?" He took one from the grill as his wife handed him a bowl of mush. He dipped the tortilla in, waved it in the air to cool it, then wolfed it down. He grinned his pleasure at Francesca. "You'll make some man a wonderful wife. If you can find one to stand up to you."

Francesca's cheeks flushed. She looked almost demure. "I'm at home here. Why should I look for another?"

"You need to start another family," her mother said. She looked at Juan. "She's not a bully. She just stands up for herself."

From the way his cousin spoke, Domingo guessed the topic had been discussed before.

"I'm off to kiva business," Juan said. "I'll go to the fields afterwards."

"Don't gossip too long. The Apaches could take half the crop while you men blather in the kiva."

"It's our blather that protects the crops. We've got to schedule guards, assign work loads and beseech the gods. Be grateful you're a woman." He turned to Domingo. "We'll expect you tonight for a welcoming dance."

His wife made no reply as Juan walked away. She spoke to Francesca instead. "I hope they get guards out. The savages always raid us this time of year. You'd think we planted our corn for them." She sniffed the air. "I can smell the scum."

"Mingo and I will watch for them, if he can get his mind off Cristina." She stooped to retie her moccasins. "Or if he ever finishes breakfast."

"I made extra tortillas for you. Mingo looks gaunt." His cousin lifted eight of the patties from the grill. "Take the pouch with the venison jerky. You can use it for the tortillas."

"I'll get the flask. A couple of the water holes between here and there were dry the last time." Francesca returned with flask and pouch. Her mother put the tortillas in the pouch while Francesca filled the flask from an olla at the doorstep. She looked Domingo up and down. "You are gaunt. You up to an all day run?"

"I'll be treading on your heels each step of the way."

The path from San Ildefonso crossed a dry stream bed, then led upward in a series of switchbacks. The rocky way reminded Domingo of the path to Taos. Rocks and thorny plants laid in waiting. Domingo fought to catch his second breath as he avoided the sharpest stones and cactus spines.

He'd kept up in the stream bed, but after that he never came close to treading on Francesca's heels. Twice she disappeared from his sight. When he did catch up, he suspected she had slowed to wait for him. At least, she did not taunt him.

The way led into pine country, and the stony path gave way to a carpet of pine needles. When the path leveled off, Domingo guessed his lungs might survive.

Francesca disappeared in a draw. At its edge Domingo stopped. He had a clear view of the path she must have taken. He searched for a sign as he treaded forward.

"You're dead!" Francesca leaped from behind a ponderosa pine near the path, jabbing a finger into his ribs.

"What?" Domingo shrieked.

"I could have been an Apache," she said. "What if that had been a knife instead of my finger?"

"The Apaches would have killed you first. That's why I've let you keep the lead."

"What if they thought you were my husband? They'd let me go by so they could kill you. And carry me off." She flung her arms in a dramatic gesture.

"What would they want with you?" Domingo panted his sarcasm.

For a moment Francesca grimaced, but she recovered her humor. "He could sell me to the Mexicans. Don't you think I'd make a good slave?"

"You're too uppity. Unless they beat it out of you." Domingo still breathed hard while she didn't seem the least bit winded. "What about a sip of water?"

"You can have two. I don't need one yet." She handed him the canteen, keeping the cork.

He would have liked to refuse the water, but his thirst was too much for him. He took two quick swallows, wiped his mouth with the back of his hand, and gulped a third.

She corked the flask, slinging it over her shoulder, "This is one Spanish innovation that's worthwhile. I can go two days with a canteen of water. Almost always broke a pot or cracked a gourd when I carried them."

"I suppose you've been all over these mountains," Domingo said.

"I love running up here alone. It's so good for my spirit. Farther on, the hunting is the best there is."

"You're the one who will be captured by Apaches some day." Domingo wanted to be sarcastic, but he heard a note of concern in his words.

Francesca looked down and sighed. "Don't think I don't worry about it. Maybe the danger is what makes it exhilarating."

"Do you know anyone captured by Apaches?"

Francesca cocked an eyebrow. "You don't know?"

"What?" Domingo suspected a jest.

"My mother," she said.

"What about your mother?"

"You didn't know Apaches captured my mother?"

"No." Domingo's jaw dropped. "When?"

"Shortly after she married. I know relatives wanted to keep it secret, but I thought gossips would spread the word."

"What happened?"

"They tell me she stayed in the fields too long. Weeding a final row. Two of the savages carried her off."

"How did she get away?"

"She didn't. They kept her three moons. Two other men joined them. They all slept with her. Once they finished scouting, they let her go."

Domingo swallowed anger, couldn't think of a suitable response. "At least they didn't take her to Mexico to sell." The thought sent a chill down Domingo's spine.

"Maybe they thought she'd hold them back. She started throwing up in the mornings."

The news made Domingo's knees go weak. "You mean she got pregnant?"

"She gave birth to me." Francesca's laugh was bitter.

Domingo had no idea how to reply. He didn't need to. Francesca turned and ran but not before she shed a tear.

Most of the afternoon the path followed the mountain ridge. Francesca settled into a pace that Domingo could maintain. He enjoyed the cool air and scent of pine. Twice they stopped at points where the view to both sides showed rocks in contrasting layers of burning red and misty white. Domingo thought the gods must construct mountains the way his people built their homes. Francesca turned her face to the sky and sucked in air. The chamisa fragrance was pungent. She jerked her head upward to call attention to a hawk circling overhead.

As the trail began its switchback descent, Francesca pointed to a meadow on the opposite side. Domingo glimpsed smoke. Later on he spied a herd of sheep, wondering if they were running wild. He forgot about them when they stopped by the trickle of a spring. Francesca dropped to her knees and drank. Domingo knelt beside her. He'd never tasted anything so satisfying. After drinking his fill, he sat and listened to nothing until the chatter of a blue jay scolding a squirrel broke the silence.

Francesca said nothing, her brow wrinkled in a frown.

"Still thinking of Apaches and your mother?"

"Sort of."

"Can you ever stop hating them?"

"It wasn't just them." Francesca blinked away the furrows. "I had a hard time growing up in the pueblo. The kids made fun of me because of my long legs."

"Your eyes are special, too." Domingo spoke on impulse.

"No one teased me about them. I don't think it was the long legs either. I guess it was because their parents told them I was half Apache." She swallowed hard. "I grew up hating my own people."

Domingo shivered at the thought. "But the children love you now. I saw the way they flock to you."

"I guess I got over my hatred. I love the story telling and the games. But I doubt I'll ever have children of my own."

"What makes you think that?" Domingo couldn't imagine her childless.

"None of the men in San Ildefonso give me a second glance. They're the ones who shunned me when we were kids." Francesca shrugged. "They still regard me as half savage."

"You must be mistaken. Or the San Ildefonso men are louts." As he spoke, he wondered about his own feelings. Francesca seemed a different woman now that he knew she was half Apache. Still, he tried to assure her. "Has your father," he stammered, "my cousin's husband—has he never received a go-between?"

"No. But he's the one man who made me feel welcome in San Ildefonso. It made no difference to him that his wife had been raped by Apaches. He treated me like his own daughter. He's the kindest, most understanding man in San Ildefonso." Her eyes glittered from near tears as she spoke. The gold specks took on a fascinating sheen.

"I lost my mother when I was young," Domingo said. "Your mother took her place—until she married."

"I know. She speaks of you often." The familiar grin reappeared. "What a brat you were." As she ran down the path, she called over her shoulder, "Mother had little hope that you'd ever run like your father, but she'll be disappointed to learn that you can't keep up with a girl."

She disappeared down the path while Domingo leaped to his feet and started after her.

The sun was nearly down when they approached a clearing, and the smell of smoke greeted them. Domingo anticipated seeing Cristina. He'd forgotten about her while racing after her sister. The few times he had gotten close to her, she was running backward, letting him catch up. When he did, she tossed a new insult at him.

As he searched for ranch buildings, he was taken aback. It was a pueblo, not an *encomienda*. It was San Ildefonso. Francesca jogged in place, awaiting him with a sheepish grin.

"This is not an *encomienda.*" Domingo squawked.

"The Bacas don't have an *encomienda.* They're nothing but squatters."

"You know all I wanted was to see your sister." Anger filled Domingo's words.

"All I promised was I'd show you where Cristina lives." Francesca swallowed her grin.

"Then why didn't you?" Domingo burned with anger.

"Remember when I showed you the meadow? I pointed twice. Didn't you see the sheep grazing? Couldn't you smell the stink of Spaniards? The ranch house was in the valley. I glimpsed it twice." She spoke rapidly so Domingo could not interrupt. "I guess your eyes are no better than your legs." She giggled.

"It's a terrible prank." Domingo felt more humiliation than anger. He'd have to retrace the way tomorrow, not sure that he remembered all the twists and turns.

"I'll take you back tomorrow. Honest. There's a shorter way." Her tone was serious.

"But why did we waste today?"

"My father told me to bring you back tonight. Remember he invited you to the kiva?"

Domingo recalled the invitation. Even at the time it was made, he was dreaming of spending the night with Cristina.

"Would you have returned?" she asked.

Domingo looked away. "I could have been welcomed another night."

"It's more than a welcoming dance." Her words were sharp. "Much more."

SEVENTEEN

Francesca's mother was tending a small pot. She welcomed Domingo and Francesca with a nod and poured a bowl for them to share. The aroma of venison appealed to Domingo so much that he could have gulped it all, but he sipped and handed it to Francesca. A bit of meat teased his stomach while the unfamiliar roots and leaves danced on his taste buds.

"What is this root?" Domingo pointed to a yellow piece. "I've never tasted anything so good."

"Francesca knows a mountain ravine where it grows. An old woman showed her." She half grinned. "I think the woman's a witch. Could be my daughter's an apprentice."

"That's right," Francesca said. "I bewitch men from other pueblos with it." Domingo shivered at the thought of witches even though he saw Francesca hiding a laugh. "They love it when I bully them."

Juan joined them from the other room. He carried a gourd rattle under one arm. Francesca offered him a sip of stew.

"No," he nodded. "Your mother and I ate earlier. You two need the meat after your run." He looked at Domingo. "Did you see Cristina?"

"I saw where she works," Domingo frowned at Francesca. "But I didn't see her."

"Humph," Juan glanced at Francesca. "That's good. I was afraid you wouldn't come back if you saw her."

"I'll take him tomorrow. I wanted to be sure he was here for his welcoming dance."

"Good. It's important." Juan turned to Domingo. "We'll go to the kiva when you finish eating."

Domingo took a bit of venison and handed the bowl to Francesca. "I'm ready," he said.

On the way to the kiva, Domingo said that San Juan would not have a welcoming dance for a young man such as himself. Juan replied that San Ildefonso wouldn't either. Domingo should expect more than a welcome.

Domingo hesitated as the two entered an ordinary room. Juan explained. "We pretended to fill in the kiva to satisfy the priest. After covering the top, we dug a new entrance from inside this room and hauled out the dirt.

"Doesn't the religious ever probe into your homes?"

"This priest honors our privacy. It's the best thing I can say about him."

"What about informers? No one in the village has told him?"

"If anyone in the pueblo tells, he'll be banished."

Domingo drew a sharp breath. Banishment was the extreme sanction the pueblos employed against one of their own.

Juan lifted a wooden platform covering the kiva entrance. He and Domingo climbed down a notched log and crawled through a tunnel. When they reached the kiva, Domingo found its walls covered with bright designs. He recognized a few of the painted motifs from kachina figures, but most were a mystery. The lower half of the walls, once a glowing red, was badly marred from the fill dirt.

No one was drumming or singing. Small groups of men huddled along the benches lining the walls. They were so intent in their conversations that no one paid attention to Domingo. Juan told him to wait while he went to speak with Little Pot, the Summer Chief. When he returned, all the men took places on the benches, staring toward Domingo. The room fell silent.

The Summer Chief didn't have the looks of a leader. His short, squat figure revealed how he got his name. He motioned Domingo to him. A drum beat started in a corner, and four elders approached Domingo. They asked him what instructions he had received at his finishing ritual. After he told them, they reported to the Summer Chief, apparently satisfied that he was qualified to stay. They danced him and Juan to the bench, swaying from side to side in routine steps.

Little Pot called two other men to approach. His deep, rumbling voice echoed, as if issuing from a small-mouthed vessel. Juan whispered to Domingo. "These two are the War Chiefs. They've heard about you and have questions."

What have I done? Do they think I'm a traitor? His mouth went dry, he touched his deer fetish without thinking.

Red horizontal lines across the forehead highlighted the somber features of the first War Chief. His shoulders were unusually broad. He towered above Domingo. "We hear you have met Po-pe. Is that true?"

"Yes. Briefly." Domingo couldn't fathom how they had heard of his chance encounter at Taos.

"Do you consider yourself loyal to him?"

Domingo felt his underarms go sticky. "I guess. I'm not sure what he expects of me."

The red marks wrinkled under the War Chief's scowl. "Are you friends with the Spanish?"

"I hate the Spanish!" Domingo stood more erect. "I'd never be their friend."

"Why is that?"

"The priest at San Juan beat me." Domingo pointed to his eye. "Here is where his whip almost took my sight."

"Let us see your back."

Domingo turned and lifted his tunic.

"Only two scars? Why is that?" The second War Chief, a squat little man with a squeaky voice, ran his finger over the red welts.

"He gave me the rest with willow rods."

"Humph," the man chortled. "I guess that's what they mean by Christian compassion."

The first War Chief spoke. "We don't understand why you went to Taos after your beating. Didn't you hate all the Spanish after that?"

"It was Father Lucas' idea to send me there, to separate me from my beloved." He nodded at Juan. "His daughter. But I would never have gone just because of that."

"Why then?"

"My cacique wanted me to learn all I could about the priest's relations with Santa Fe and the surrounding ranchers. My cacique is Po-pe's lieutenant."

"What did you report to Po-pe?" The red marked War Chief asked slyly. Domingo wondered if the man meant to trap him.

"I didn't. I reported to my cacique."

The two War Chiefs turned to each other, a look of surprise on their faces. They stepped over to talk with the Summer Chief. When they returned, they asked for details. When Domingo told them how the Martinez ranch could be overrun, they grinned, clasped his shoulders and led him before the Summer Chief.

"You serve the cause well." Little Pot suppressed a burp, but the sound echoed from his stomach. Domingo wondered how the stout little man ever raced as a youth. "Po-pe insists we investigate everyone who has the potential to join us. We'll need every person we can recruit, but we know some of our people have betrayed us. You must understand our caution."

"I suppose it will be another year before we drive the Spanish back to Mexico," Juan said.

"It won't be long." The Summer Chief offered a wry smile. "It may be only days away."

"But the other pueblos can't be ready." Juan blurted. "Do the Hopi or Zuni even know?" His face drained of blood.

"Po-pe has sent word to all the pueblos. They'll be organizing warriors for a battle in Santa Fe. Even some Apaches will join us. But before we destroy Santa Fe, we'll kill every priest in our villages, then attack the settlers on the way to Santa Fe." His rumbling voice carried a conviction that reminded Domingo of Po-pe. "The Spanish can only survive if they flee to Mexico."

"It is still arrows and spears against guns. We're going to pay a high price for freedom." Juan's lips went dry.

"May we kill all the Spanish." Domingo hissed his wish, but both War Chiefs beamed their approval.

Little Pot said, "Po-pe knew the winter snows would flood the Rio Grande. His spies have returned from El Paso del Norte to report that their wagon train is stalled. The stinking beards are so short of ammunition the governor has banned hunting." The Summer Chief pounded his fist into his other hand. "Po-pe knows there will never be a better time to strike!"

Domingo's insides flooded with elation. He saw Catholic churches burning. He'd see Lucas whipped, then beheaded, his remains thrown to the dogs. He imagined a spear in Nicolas' belly, his gluttony spilling forth in a river of blood. He had a harder time imagining the death of the Martinez family until he remembered Cristina. He pictured her in the hands of a rancher. *All the Spanish must die.*

"Po-pe wants you in Santa Fe as soon as the revolt starts." The Summer Chief put a hand on Domingo's shoulder.

Domingo gasped. "Why me?"

"You're fluent in Spanish. You'll read every document we find in Santa Fe. And Po-pe can use advice on how to sow confusion." His grip tightened. "Will you do that?"

Domingo spoke with determination. "I'll do everything I can. I swear."

"Good. You must get ready now. Do you know where Nambe pueblo is?

"I can find it. I know it's just north of Santa Fe."

"You must be in Nambe three days from now. Do not let the cacique know why you are there. We don't trust him. In fact, we count on him to supply the governor with misleading information." He laughed bitterly. "Take some trade goods with you. Blunder around as if you are looking for trading partners. Don't ask for Po-pe, one of his men will find you."

Domingo was awed by Po-pe's organization. But in a moment, he recalled Cristina. "I'll start the day after tomorrow."

"Why not tomorrow?"

"I came here to ask Juan's daughter to marry me. I can do that tomorrow and still reach Nambe in time."

The elder War Chief cleared his throat as if to protest, but before he could speak, Juan said, "He can get to the Baca place and return in one day. He'll have time to reach Nambe."

"Po-pe can be as relentless as the Spanish when his orders are disobeyed." Little Pot stared at Juan, his eyes unblinking. His words reverberated so Domingo couldn't miss what he had to say. "He ordered his own son-in-law killed when he suspected him of revealing our plans." A chill shot through Domingo despite the warmth of the kiva. Po-pe's son-in-law lived at San Juan.

Domingo sucked in a breath. He must see Cristina to proclaim his love. Then, he'd leave for Nambe. As long as everything went according to plan.

EIGHTEEN

The kiva cover rattled. Everyone fell silent. A muffled "must be the priest" came from a corner. Instead, two young men of the pueblo scrambled down the notched log. They dashed to the War Chiefs to report nearby Apaches in the western mountains. Two other guards had stayed with the enemy to track their movement. The youths had counted a dozen savages and suspected more.

"Are they headed here?" a War Chief asked.

"They might be going to the Baca ranch," one youth said.

"Or the Keres pueblos to the south," the other added.

Several men spoke at once, urging patience to see if the war party would bypass San Ildefonso. They argued the Keres people could defend themselves. Everyone agreed it would be even better if the Apaches attacked Baca. That would save them the trouble.

Domingo gritted his teeth, his mind scrambling for an argument to alert Indians at the ranch. Luck was with him. A War Chief chastised the men for turning their back on the Keresan pueblos, urging everyone to remember that all the pueblos were now allies. The other War Chief, in his squeaky voice, argued that it was wishful thinking to believe the Apaches might attack Baca. The rancher had fended off Apache raids twice in the past three years. The last time, the Spaniards had pursued their enemy and killed half a dozen in the retreat. The muttering that ensued showed a consensus with the wisdom of the War Chiefs. The men of the pueblo had to face the Apaches. Everyone went home to prepare. They would assemble in the plaza before the sun rose.

On the way home, Juan told Domingo that he should stay in the pueblo. A San Ildefonso war party depended on its teamwork, and the War Chiefs could not work him into their organization on short notice. When Domingo protested, Juan insisted that he was needed to guard the pueblo in case a few Apaches snuck by to raid the town. Domingo's shoulders sagged, but he agreed to stay.

That night, he went to the rooftop but could not sleep. He descended the ladder as soon as he heard stirring below. Juan had a bow and full quiver on one shoulder with a stone knife strapped to his side. He had slung the water flask over his other shoulder. His wife held a half finished tortilla for him. Francesca was straightening the feathers on one of his arrows.

Juan finished his tortilla. "Domingo is staying to protect you," he said as he left.

Francesca and Domingo followed him to the plaza to see the men off. "Why aren't you going?" she asked Domingo.

"Your father told me I'd upset the pueblo's teamwork."

She laughed. "The only teamwork they know are kachina dance steps. They're in as much danger of shooting each other as being shot by an Apache." She shook her head in disgust. "One thing they have going for them is that the Apache are no better organized."

"How would you know? You've never seen them in action."

"I followed a war party three years ago. They avoided an Apache ambush only because they stopped to argue among themselves about what to do next." She shook her head. "When they did fight, the Apaches turned and ran because their leader was killed by a lucky shot. Our men could have killed more, but they started quarrelling over who had rights to what honors."

"That had to be an exception. I can't believe they aren't better prepared."

"The last time was just as bad," she shrugged. "According to what my father told me."

"You mean you didn't follow them?" Domingo laughed, "I can't believe you stayed home." He intended the remark to be sarcastic.

"The War Chiefs, who are also Hunt Chiefs, made me promise I wouldn't follow the war party if they allowed me to hunt." Her tone showed her exasperation.

"Well, then, you can't go now, or you'll break your word."

"My promise was for the last battle, not this one." Her tone allowed no response. As they entered her home, she said, "I'm getting my bow. Are you coming?"

"What about protecting the pueblo? The War Chief told me I was needed here. You'd be helpful here, too."

"A dozen young men have been assigned to protect it. Besides, there are two warriors who had their feet cut off by the Spanish. They've become more proficient with the bow than most of our so-called warriors. There's more than enough protection here without us." She turned toward the house. "But go on up to the roof if you're going to stay. I'll throw you a bow and arrows."

Domingo chewed on his lip. *I was ordered to stay. Do they need me here? What will I tell Cristina if Fransesca goes and I stay?* By the time Francesca returned with the weapons, Domingo had decided to join her.

"You're still down here?" She raised an eyebrow.

"I'm going with you."

"You ever shot a bow?" Her lips curled in a lopsided grin as she handed him one and slung another over her shoulder. "We've only got a dozen arrows between us. My father filled his quiver."

She handed him a quiver while slinging her's. "He also took the flask. Drink all you can, now."

They both drank from the olla beside the door. They were about to leave when Domingo's cousin appeared from a neighbor's home. "You promised not to fight if you were allowed to hunt. Have you forgotten?" Wrinkles etched her forehead.

"I promised for the fight before. Don't worry. I have Mingo to protect me. Besides, we're only going to watch."

"I know you better than that." Her mother sighed. "If you were only going to watch, why do you need bows?"

"They're for defense, mother. I promise we'll stay behind."

"Do what you can, Mingo, to keep her safe. Her father will beat me if she's killed."

Francesca hugged her mother and turned to run. Domingo promised to watch after her and raced to catch up. At the edge of the pueblo, they slowed to a trot, their way illuminated by the first rays of the sun.

They soon found the pueblo war party strung out along the path to the western mountains. Francesca slowed to a walk.

Domingo licked dry lips. "When do we find Apaches?"

"How should I know?" Francesca gave him a sideways glance.

"I need to go to the Baca ranch tomorrow. If I don't get Cristina away from there, she could be killed by her own people." The thought raised a sour taste. "I can't let that happen."

"You going to be able to get to Santa Fe and also save her?" Francesca asked.

"How did you know that?"

"My father told my mother. He thought I was sleeping."

"Santa Fe can wait for me. Po-pe will have found plenty of persons who read Spanish just the way he recruited so many spies."

"The rumor is that Po-pe can be vicious when his orders aren't obeyed." She made a gesture with her finger as if slitting her throat.

"He's fighting for our freedom. He'd understand how I had to be late because of Apaches,"

"Going out of your way to see your lover is not exactly fighting Apaches." Francesca raised her arm as she halted.

"What is it?" Domingo asked needlessly. He could see that the pueblo war party had halted at the mouth of a shallow canyon. Its sides were the height of three men, but the ridges were lined with large boulders that made ideal hiding places. It was a perfect place for an ambush.

"It's too obvious for an ambush," Francesca said. "Unless an idiot's leading them—which could be."

The two War Chiefs were gesturing wildly between themselves and with those men gathered around them. Eventually, two men scrambled up the west side of the canyon while three scaled the east side. Domingo and Francesca watched their slow progress.

Suddenly, at the peak nearest them, an Apache rose in clear sight of Domingo but sheltered from view below. Domingo touched his fetish while unslinging his bow. He fumbled to retrieve an arrow. The Apache had his bow notched and started to draw the string. Domingo drew his bow. An arrow whizzed by his ear. The Apache still held his bow string when the arrow caught him below the shoulder and half turned him. Its point stuck out a finger's length from his back. He dropped forward. His fall dislodged a small avalanche.

The pueblo war party looked up, then stared behind them. Francesca had slid into a crevice. "Raise your bow and wave it," she said. Domingo did so without thinking. The San Ildefonso men roared their approval. Then, amid war cries, they split into two groups and started up both sides of the gorge. Domingo counted ten Apaches crawling from hiding places and retreating toward the far end of the canyon.

When the pueblo men saw them flee, they shouted victory cries while scrambling up the rocks. Their advance was not as fast as the Apache retreat.

"Let's go," Francesca urged, heading down the canyon floor.

Domingo raced to her side. "Why did you let me take credit for killing that Apache?"

"No man would have forgiven me if they knew I killed the first enemy." She snickered. "Or the last, or ones in-between."

"So where are we going now?" Domingo panted.

"We can get to the end of the canyon before the Apaches." A look of glee spread over her face. "Maybe even you can get a shot in. They'll have slung their bows and be running like rabbits."

The run wasn't far. Domingo was so elated that he no longer thirsted although his mouth had never been drier.

At the end of the canyon, Francesca pointed up. Two Apaches were attempting a short cut. They had to descend slowly, their fingers pressed into the walls, their faces against the canyon sides. "Take them," she whispered.

On the other side, an Apache faced her but knelt on a narrow ledge. He struggled for his bow. She had hers at the ready. Her arrow whizzed into his throat. The Apache tumbled onto the canyon floor so close that Domingo could see his eyes. One of the dead man's hands grasped the arrow shaft below his jaw.

Domingo aimed at the Apache closest to him. At the last moment, his target moved. Domingo's arrow struck his thigh. The Apache dropped a man's height onto the canyon floor. His companion raced past the wounded man into an open meadow at the canyon mouth. Francesca's arrow dropped him. He sprawled on the ground, his arms outstretched. The wounded man hobbled up to him. He stopped to feel his companion's breath. When he straightened up, he was dead. Another of Francesca's arrows had struck.

Domingo took two arrows from his quiver to give her, but she darted behind him to hide. “When our war party gets down from the cliffs, give them the victory wave. Distract them so they don’t come in here. I don’t want them to find me.”

Domingo felt utter confusion. He’d never lied to other Indians. Now Francesca wanted him to take credit for killing three Apaches when all he did was wound one.

What would the War Chiefs expect of him now?

NINETEEN

"Go join them," Francesca hissed from behind a boulder. "Otherwise, someone will come to get you. You're a hero." She snickered. "A leader of men."

"I've got no idea what to do," he hissed back.

"The Apaches will wait in the woods. They'll slaughter anyone crossing that open meadow. The War Chiefs will realize that much. Whatever you do, stall as long as you can."

"Where are you going?"

"If I get there, you'll know."

Domingo turned to argue, but all he saw was Francesca's back as she headed down the canyon the way they had come.

Domingo faced the San Ildefonso warriors. They were motioning him forward, waving their bows overhead. He massaged his leather bag with its deer fetish.

When he reached the battle line, the War Chiefs clasped both his shoulders and congratulated him. They then fell into an interminable dispute about what to do next. The squeaky voiced War Chief cautioned restraint. He believed the Apaches must be hiding in the pine forest at the meadow's edge. The other War Chief wiped a hand across his forehead in exasperation. His red paint smeared into a solid swash. He argued that the Apaches must have retreated after losing four men. The pueblo war party should pursue them.

His words convinced Domingo until he recalled Francesca's warnings. When the first War Chief asked for his opinion, Domingo gulped. "They may lie in ambush. The forest makes great cover. Especially that dense growth along the ground."

"Someone should make a foray. To draw them out if they plan an ambush." The War Chief looked at Domingo.

"It's not his fight." Little Pot scowled at the War Chief.

Before the dispute could escalate, two young men charged the forest, yelling insults at the woods. They stopped and waved their bows. An arrow shot out, landing between them. They backed away.

Another arrow followed. It nicked the closest youth. Both turned and ran back to the war party.

A line of Apaches stepped from the shelter of the woods. The tallest had black stripes down his cheeks. The vertical lines looked as if they continued onto his chest, his sweat having made the paint run. He appeared to be wearing a black vest. The man took half a dozen steps forward and screamed a curse at the San Ildefonso warriors.

"Where is Jacaba?" the Summer Chief said. "He can translate for us."

A boyish looking man stepped forward to stand by the chief. "I didn't understand him. It's been a long time since I heard Apache."

"You spent five years as a captive. You must know what he's saying."

"I'll do my best," Jacaba blanched.

The Apache screamed again. Everyone looked at Jacaba. He shook his head. Once more the warrior screamed.

Domingo looked around puzzled. "Isn't he shouting something in Tewa?"

Little Pot yelled for the Apache to repeat what he'd said, if he dared.

Domingo could see the man looked disgusted even from an arrow's flight away. He howled each word slowly. "I'm going to cut off the balls of the dirty dog who killed my brother." He drew a knife and sliced the air in front of his groin. "Who was the coward who shot him in the back?"

The men turned to look at Domingo. He hoped the Apache couldn't see everyone staring at him.

A young man who had made the initial foray stepped forward. "How can we shoot you cowards anywhere but in the back. You're always running from us." The Summer Chief guffawed. A chorus of whoops from the San Ildefonso men showered their approval of the insult.

"You won't be in any mood to chase us after we've burned your corn fields and raped your women," the striped giant yelled. The War Chief with the red forehead turned livid. He stepped to the front, drew an arrow, and aimed it high. It fell two men's length from the bellowing Apache who laughed his disdain.

Other Apaches stepped forward. One shouted at length. The pueblo men looked at Jacaba. "He says if we bring them our corn, they won't rape our women," he blushed. "They don't want them anyway because their sweet spots have all been stretched too far from using corn cobs as a penis."

Half a dozen of the men ran forward, notched arrows and let them fly. They were barely in the air when Apache arrows rained down on them. One ripped a warrior's tunic, so spent it only scratched the skin. The warrior yelled his own curse.

"No more," both War Chiefs warned. "The wind comes from behind them. We must shoot into it."

The Apaches must have realized their advantage and moved farther out from the tree line. The puebloans moved back among the rocks. The enemy launched a few more arrows. Although the wind helped, the arrows fell without effect.

The Apaches continued to taunt. The black striped one challenged any two San Ildefonso warriors to a knife fight. Domingo's hand gripped his knife handle, but he smelled the sweat of his fear. When no one responded to the dare, the Apache yelled one incomprehensible curse after another. His fellow warriors backed up his threats with a shower of arrows. When they fell short, the younger pueblo warriors shouted that women must be shooting at them, young women that they'd soon rape.

Domingo wondered if the day would ever end. *We'll be here all night and tomorrow. How will I ever rescue Cristina?*

The thought of his love made him ask himself where her sister was. His question coincided with the smell of smoke. It rose from behind the enemy line, the stiff wind barreling it along. The Apaches looked over their shoulders. They couldn't see the blaze, but Domingo watched flames sprout in the pine tops, exploding sparks into the air. A few embers reached the meadow but fell without igniting the grass.

When the crackling of the fire reached the puebloans, a shout went up that caused Domingo to tremble. He had never been in the midst of such blood thirsty lust.

The Summer Chief smiled cruelly while rubbing his belly. "The kachinas have sent lightening to burn out our enemies."

"From a cloudless sky?" An old warrior spoke without considering whom he confronted.

"How else would you explain the fire?" The chief scowled at him. The old man shrugged.

The War Chiefs shouted instructions. The war party spread along the edge of the meadow as flames engulfed the forest. The Apaches had no choice but to attempt escape through the meadow. One ran parallel to the woods but was felled by an arrow in his thigh. He dropped to his knees. Another arrow found his ribs. He gave an agonizing cry before he dropped.

The line of San Ildefonso warriors moved out into the meadow until they were within arrow range of the enemy. Sparks lighted fires in the grass near the trees. Domingo readied himself for a slaughter. The first Apaches to break from cover were all killed or wounded as they raced along the meadow's edge. The striped warrior yelled at the rest to charge straight ahead, but his companions cowered in the woods, glancing back at the forest fire, then forward to see where the meadow was free from flames.

Domingo decided he'd kill the black vested man before he could convince the others to charge. He crawled forward through the grass for a close shot, raising his head now and then to track the enemy. As he got closer, smoke chocked him and his eyes blurred. He could no longer make out the forest edge. The Apaches disappeared in the shroud.

A spark landed nearby igniting the grass. Domingo leaped into retreat. Others of the pueblo ran to the shelter of the bare canyon. As everyone gathered, the War Chiefs asked men to report what they achieved in the confusion of the smoke. A dozen claimed they were certain—or almost certain—that they had shot at least one Apache. When Little Pot said they'd count the corpses after the fire burned out, a few men admitted to greater uncertainty.

Domingo wondered how many victims Francesca could claim.

TWENTY

Domingo was so eager to tell Francesca about the success of her fire that when the war party reached the edge of the pueblo, he raced ahead. At the door, she was washing ash from her face. Domingo wiped grime from the back of her neck. Soot filled her hair. He whisked flecks away and chuckled. She hastened to brush away more, not bothering to hide an impish grin.

Her mother hurried from across the plaza when she saw her daughter. Juan left members of the war party and called a greeting to the three of them. Domingo admired all that Francesca had done, but a rush of warmth swept over him because of their shared secret.

Juan was the first to speak, his words tumbling out. “You’ll never believe what a hero Domingo is,” he said to his wife. “The pueblo has never seen such a warrior. He was killing Apaches right and left.”

“You can’t mean little Mingo,” she said.

“I do. We saw him kill four of the scum.” He held up three fingers of one hand and a fourth one with his other hand. “San Juan warriors must be the best marksmen in the world.”

Francesca’s lips curled in mock surprise. “Tell us all about it, Mingo.”

Domingo could have kicked her. “It was luck.” He thought to play her game. “I had help.” He stared at Francesca until she turned away. Then he fingered the sack at his neck “My fetish gives me special strength when I need it most.”

Francesca covered her mouth with her hand.

“Whatever it was, it will be a long time before those savages raid us again. The ones we didn’t kill had their asses scorched.” Juan explained the outcome of the battle to his wife while Francesca finished washing her face and arms.

“You deserve a victory dance, Mingo.” His cousin beamed at him. “Sorry, there’s no chance for a feast. I used the last of the venison to welcome you. But you and Juan deserve a celebration.”

"We must honor the kachinas, too," Juan said. "They sent lightening to start the fire. The Apaches we didn't kill have burns they'll remember the rest of their life."

Francesca burst out laughing. Juan stared at her with upraised eyebrows. His wife glanced at her daughter and frowned, then urged them all inside to eat.

After such a day Domingo couldn't keep his eyes open. When Juan yawned, Domingo retreated to the rooftop. He laid on his back, recounting the day's events, saw a shooting star, and considered it a good omen. Cristina would be in his arms tomorrow. If not tomorrow, then the day after. He rolled to his side, welcoming sleep, when he heard a hiss at the ladder. He looked up and Francesca crawled to his side.

"I brought you a bite of venison I saved."

"What?" Domingo fought sleep.

"Open your mouth, Mingo." She stuck the venison to his lips. He opened his mouth, and she tucked the meat inside. He chewed slowly savoring the flavor.

"You want to talk?" Francesca stretched out beside him.

The stars gave just enough light that he could see the way her eyebrows flared. "What about?"

"Anything."

He could think of nothing. He made no reply except to snort a snore.

When Domingo awoke the next morning, he heard rustling below. He got up, stretched and went to the ladder. A wisp of smoke curled up to the roof. He climbed down to find his cousin spreading tortillas on the stone grill. The sizzle awoke his taste buds. He watched the cakes bubble. Francesca was pounding nuts or herbs in a mortar, adding them to a pot of corn mush. Juan lay on a mat, facing the wall, worn out from the day before.

His cousin smiled a greeting. Francesca glanced at him but turned away before he could smile at her. He recalled the morsel she had brought him the night before. He flushed. He was so tired then that he didn't realize she might have more than food on her mind. Would he ever know?

He looked at his cousin, but his question was meant for Francesca. "What's the shortest way to the Baca ranch?"

His cousin frowned. "Francesca will show you." She turned to her daughter. "You are taking Mingo to find Cristina? Then, you can all come back here."

"Sis and Mingo will go where they want to, won't they?" Francesca's question sounded like an invitation for Domingo to leave San Ildefonso.

"You could bring the priest back with you," Domingo's cousin said. "When all the men left yesterday, the fool thought they meant to rebel." She laughed softly. "The women who cook for him couldn't convince him otherwise." She shook her head in disgust. "He scurried off to the Baca ranch for protection. Maybe you can convince him it's safe to come back."

Juan had rolled over and was listening. "Yes. Get him to come back—alone."

"What do you mean by that?" his wife asked.

"Never mind." He stared at Francesca. "You take Domingo, then convince the priest it's safe to return."

Francesca went to get her moccasins without saying anything. Domingo's cousin continued to ask why it mattered if the priest returned by himself. She got no answer from Juan. Francesca returned with her bow, quiver, and the flask.

"What do you need that bow for?" her mother asked.

"Maybe I'll see a rabbit on the way. Or a porcupine. One can get close to a porcupine." She threw the word, close, at Domingo. Her sarcasm irritated him, particularly since it must have alerted her mother.

"It's time we go," Francesca spoke curtly. "You got everything you need; Mingo?"

"Shouldn't I take a bow?" he asked.

"Did you bring one of your own?" Francesca mocked.

"He can have one of mine." Juan glared at his daughter. "Fetch the war bow I made. These are dangerous times."

Francesca went into the back room. When she returned with the bow, she tossed it to Domingo without a word. He tested its strength. It tested his arm.

"Remember the priest," Juan said. "Bring him back alone."

Francesca nodded and started at a trot. Domingo followed. The path was nowhere near the one she had used the first day. It followed a dry stream bed, fairly level, but its sharp rocks bit at Domingo's feet.

They ran for a long time before Francesca stopped. Domingo was parched. She uncorked the flask and handed it to him. He swallowed four times before realizing they must conserve water. He handed her the flask with a sheepish grin. She took a short swallow, eyeing Domingo with contempt.

"Must you always prove you're superior to men?"

"Would that men accept me as an equal," she retorted.

"What would you do if they did?"

"I'd be in the midst of a revolt. If the men ever get around to rebelling. How much more do we have to endure from the Spaniards?"

"It won't be long." Domingo gritted his teeth. He had been sworn to secrecy.

"What do you mean?" Her eyes burned into him. "What do you know?"

"I guess it's safe to tell you now. The revolt is coming in a few days. Can you keep it secret?"

"Like you did?" she jeered.

"Let up, will you?" Domingo regretted that he'd told her about the uprising although he had no doubt she'd keep it secret.

"Why did anyone tell you, anyway? You're no warrior."

"I'm needed to read Spanish documents. Po-pe will use the knowledge I provide to spread confusion."

"Who is Po-pe?"

"It doesn't matter who he is. Just know that the revolt is close. We must save your sister from Baca. No telling what the Spanish will do to their servants in an Indian uprising."

"And what will you do with Cristina? Hide in the mountains to protect her? Instead of helping to confuse the enemy?"

"I'll take her to San Juan on my way to Nambe. She'll be safe with my father. Or she could go home with you."

"Why are you going to Nambe?"

"It's where I'm to report."

"You'll be going out of your way if you go to San Juan."

"I know. It means I won't have much time."

"Then why are we standing here?" Francesca spurted away like a deer. Domingo touched his fetish before racing after her.

It was early afternoon when they left the cottonwooded path to enter a pasture. Domingo heard a stray sheep bleating for its herd. On a rise before them, a ranch house overlooked the valley. Numerous out-buildings flanked it. A wisp of smoke rose from the ranch chimney, but the place was strangely quiet.

Francesca stopped, looked all around, then walked to the house. "I've never seen it like this," she murmured. "They may be expecting an attack if they listened to the priest, or they may have fled."

Domingo's stomach crept toward his throat. He scrutinized each window for an harquebus, expecting a roar any moment. "Why don't we leave our bows here."

"Good idea," she said.

Domingo gasped. It was the first time she had agreed to anything he suggested.

"They're sure to think something's wrong if they see a woman carrying a bow." Francesca pushed her bow and quiver under an agave. Domingo added his.

They walked slowly toward the ranch house, talking nonsense to each other so people in the house would hear their approach. At the porch, Domingo called a greeting. Moments later, he yelled one. No one answered. The door was locked, but a side window remained open. Domingo called through it in vain. He peered in the window. The furniture was in tact, but drawers were opened with papers and clothing strewn on the floor. He crawled through the window calling out again. The scattered contents of a bedroom made it obvious the inhabitants had packed in haste.

Francesca joined him. "Never been in a Spanish home before. Can't believe anyone would want all this stuff. It's suffocating." She looked at the bed and two chairs. "Don't they know how comfortable the floor is?"

"Their bones have gotten soft after generations of using furniture." Domingo entered the kitchen, followed by Francesca. The embers of a wood fire warmed the oven. A hint of baked bread lingered in the air. "They haven't been gone long, but it'd be dark before we could overtake them." His shoulders sagged.

"How do they make all these things?" Francesca lifted a large skillet on the stove. "They're to cook with, looks like."

"It's all made in Mexico and hauled up here." Domingo shook his head. "You'd think they might learn to use our pottery."

"What about this?" she lifted a small pan by its handle. "Do you think my mother would like to cook with this?"

"Not much of a substitute for her daughter," Domingo said. "Her other daughter." He wrinkled his nose at Francesca. Cristina's absence was sinking in. Baca must be on his way to Santa Fe but might stop to assist priests at one of the pueblos. Or he could detour to help other ranchers. Domingo sat at the kitchen table and put his head in his hands.

"I'll go get the bows," Francesca said. When she returned, Domingo had regained his composure. She pulled back a chair, tested its strength with her hand, and sat gingerly. "I can pick up the trail to Santa Fe. We sleep overnight along the river and get there before noon."

"Let's wait here till morning. We can easily track them. Probably got a loaded wagon. Driving sheep. They can't be far. Except…" He sobbed from more than exhaustion.

Francesca reached a hand to his shoulder. "What is it, Mingo?"

"I'll never find Cristina. After the priest at San Juan whipped me, my cacique sent me to Taos to spy." Without thinking, he touched the scar near his eye. "There I had to work for a stinkin' priest who gloated over detaining me. When I thought I was finished, they sent me to an *encomienda* for more spying." He lifted his head to look at Francesca. "By the time I got home, Cristina was here." He sighed.

"If you had led me here that first day, I would have found her. Or if the Apaches hadn't attacked the next day..." His anger got the better of his frustration. "Let's go kill the filthy devils, every one of them."

Francesca gripped his shoulder tighter. "We need to rest. Let's find something to eat. We can be off at first light. I promise you'll see Cristina tomorrow."

A little hope ignited in Domingo's heart—until he remembered she'd promised that once before.

TWENTY ONE

"Well, you won't have to lure your priest back to San Ildefonso to be killed." Domingo hadn't remembered the religious last night, but when he awoke his first thoughts were about Lucas. How could he kill Lucas if he went to Santa Fe?

Francesca was sitting on the floor by a window where first light crept inside the house. She gave Domingo a sideways glance. "I never liked our priest, but I couldn't have killed him." She rose and started slicing a leg of lamb that had been half cooked when the Bacas fled. The two had feasted on it the night before. This morning they finished it. Their hands were blood stained and greasy. Domingo wiped his hands and mouth with a cloth hanging by the stove, then threw it to her.

"You don't want any blood on our hands?" she snickered.

"Not sheep blood but Spanish blood. Your priest's and Baca's. Above all the blood of Lucas. He's the priest who flogged me. I hope he makes it to Santa Fe so I can kill him there. Some long drawn out death," Domingo's nostrils flared.

"What happens if Po-pe keeps you at Nambe translating, and you miss out on all the killing?"

"I'll kill my share one way or the other." Domingo never felt so positive about anything in his life.

"Then we better get going." Francesca threw him a flask. "Take this. You may get thirsty for water as well as blood."

They started at a trot. Baca had made no attempt to conceal his tracks. The wheels of an over-loaded cart had gouged the way to mark even its rockiest parts. A blind man could have tracked the sheep herd that followed. Domingo urged Francesca to a faster pace, but she stopped often to scrutinize the trail.

"We can't miss where they went." Domingo frowned his impatience. "Why are you holding back?"

"I want to know how many people we're chasing." She pointed to a boot print. "I've counted three horses and eight Spanish men on foot but only two women. Don't you'd think there'd be more women?"

"The wife will be in the cart. Maybe other women, too."

Francesca stopped at a patch of soft dirt to examine moccasin prints. "I count ten to twelve Indians. Not sure which are men and which women."

Domingo stooped to look. "The sheep have trampled the tracks. How can you be sure how many Indians there are?"

"The moccasins all differ. Pretty easy to tell one from another. But I have trouble with the boots."

"Some of the Mexican Indians may be wearing boots. I'd guess there are not as many Spaniards as you think."

She shrugged. "What are you planning on doing once we catch up?"

Domingo had been thinking about it since they left the ranch. "We catch Cristina's eye. She sneaks off to join us. We may have to wait until tonight for her."

"Why don't I just walk in and tell her I'm there to take her home? Baca doesn't have any need for her now."

Why can't she ever agree with anything I say. Baca's not about to let such a beautiful woman go. He said, "We can't take chances. They may shoot any Indian they see. Even a woman. Once we spot her, we can easily get to a place where she'll see us, given how slowly they're going."

Francesca picked up the pace. In late morning, they found a shattered chest with its spewed contents. Farther on, they came across a mattock head and iron bars. Midday, Francesca paused over the trail. She walked its periphery, scratching her head.

Domingo's impatience grew. "What is it?" he said gruffly.

"They've split up. Two of the horses with the wagon and sheep are headed for Santa Fe. Most Indians going with them. The others went that way." She nodded to the east.

"What's over there?"

"Nambe pueblo." She screwed up her nose. "Or if they detour a little, they'll reach a small Spanish settlement."

"Why would they go there?" Domingo's heart raced. *If the party with Cristina heads for Nambe, I can rescue her and report to Po-pe's lieutenant at the same time.*

"If Baca's the hero type, he'll go out of his way to warn the Spanish farmers." Francesca tilted her head. "Coming back he could rescue priests. Your guess is as good as mine."

"For once, I think you're right. And he'd take Cristina with him."

Francesca stared, her mouth agape. "Why would he do that?"

"He'd insist on keeping such a beautiful woman by his side. He may have already used her."

"I wonder sometimes if we're talking about the same person. She may be a great lay, but you're the only one who thinks the whole world wants her."

Domingo was so angry he couldn't speak. He started off in the direction of Nambe without a word. Francesca trotted behind. At a rocky part of the trail he paused to study it.

"They went that way," Francesca pointed with her chin.

"I know that. But don't you see this track?" He knelt as if in worship, outlined the footprint with his finger. "The moccasin of a delicate woman."

"Or a young man—unless you're a lot better at reading footprints than I am."

"You don't care if we find your sister, do you?"

"Of course I do. But she can take care of herself. She doesn't need a hero to rescue her. What you ought to be doing is reporting to Nambe."

"If you want to turn back, why don't you?" Domingo countered. "I can find my way to Nambe—after I've found my Cristina."

Francesca turned and walked away. Domingo started back on the trail, but before he'd gone more than a few steps, he felt a tingle in his stomach. *If Baca isn't gong to Nambe, how will I find it. What will I do with Cristina in Nambe? I'll have to take her home first—won't I?* He turned and called to Francesca. "I thought you wanted to be in on the revolt. You won't have to hide yourself in this battle."

She shook her head in disgust but ran to his side. "It'll be dark soon. This group's made good time since it split off. If we want to catch up while we can still see them, you'd best keep up." She set off at a full run.

They had reached the top of a ridge when Francesca stopped so quickly Domingo ran into her. "There they are," she said. The two were so close that they dropped to the ground to watch. The party was in clear view, and no women were among them. Two boys who might be Baca's sons were trotting close beside a Spaniard on horseback.

"So do we take on all ten?" She taunted. "Or can you wait till later to kill Baca?"

Domingo gritted his teeth. If Baca's other party hadn't reached Santa Fe already, they would before he could overtake them. There was nothing to do except head for Nambe.

The last rays of the sun caught the gold flecks in Francesca's eyes as they stopped to look down on Nambe pueblo, nestled along a tributary of the Rio Grande. The stalks in its fields had turned brown. They could see ears of ripened corn. The beans spiraling up the stalks looked ready to harvest.

As they neared the town, an eerie silence greeted them. Two dogs barked at each other, but no children made sounds, and the few people in the plaza scurried to wherever they were going. Young men on roof tops looked in all directions while keeping Domingo and Francesca in sight.

"What kind of trader are you?" she asked. "Coming in with no trade goods?" She giggled and shook her head.

"I'm going to see what I can get for you?" he mocked. "You might be worth one of those barking dogs—if you can keep your mouth shut until after I've traded you off."

She gave him a dirty look. When they reached the plaza, he said, "We stick to the truth. Well, more or less. You explain you're looking for your sister. I'll pretend to trade in San Juan pottery. Wouldn't bring my wares until I found a market."

When they entered the plaza, Domingo nodded to a man crossing it. He gave a furtive glance behind him and to both sides when Domingo spoke to him.

"I'm a trader from San Juan. I've got to unload a lot of pots. It wouldn't take much turquoise to make a good deal."

The man shook his head. "No speak Tewa." The man tried to maneuver around Domingo. Out of the corner of his eye, Domingo saw one of the young men from the roof tops descend a ladder. He tried Spanish with the man before him, almost shouting for others to hear. The man slipped by him and ran to a door of the pueblo. Francesca covered her mouth with a hand.

Domingo looked for someone else to solicit. The young lookout was approaching fast, and Domingo guessed the youth would try to escort him from the pueblo. He approached an elderly man tottering in his direction.

"Grandfather, you look as if you'd be a shrewd trader or know someone who is. I'm looking for turquoise or silver. I've got fine San Juan pots to exchange."

"What's that?" The old man cupped his ear. "Sounds like you want to trade, but you're too young to be a trader."

Domingo backed away muttering that traders have to start out sometime. He backed into the youth he had seen on the roof top.

"Where you from?" the young man asked, his words a hoarse whisper.

Domingo frowned, mumbling an answer.

"Would you trade with Po-pe?" the young man asked.

Domingo was taken aback. He hadn't expected anyone so young to be part of the revolution. "Yes! With him or for him."

"Come with me." He glanced at Francesca. "Is she your wife?"

"No," his emphasis shocked not only the youth but also himself. In a moment, he regained his composure. "But you might help her. She's looking for her sister who fled from an *encomienda*. She's probably in Santa Fe, but her sister thought to ask here first."

"You can stay with my family," the young man said to Francesca. "I'll show you after I take him to Tupatu. Tupatu is in charge."

"Not Po-pe?"

The youth's lips curled in disdain. "Po-pe has too much to do to bother with the likes of us. Tupatu leads us. You're lucky to serve him."

Domingo and the youth went to a room near the center of the pueblo. No one was about, but the young man looked in all directions before he led Domingo inside. A candle burned in a silver holder atop an ornamented desk. A pile of papers was stacked to one side, on the other laid a red ledger book.

A man sat in the shadows behind the desk. When he rose he had to stoop because of his height. Domingo wondered if he was Indian. The man put his hands on the desk to lean forward, his face full in the candlelight. Domingo gasped. Nothing remained of his left eye. The socket looked scarred although Domingo couldn't be sure. Otherwise, the man's features were Indian.

"Lean close," the man said. His voice resounded in low tones. He reached across the desk to touch the scar near Domingo's eyes and asked in rapid Tewa what had caused the mark. Domingo guessed the man tested his knowledge of Tewa and answered in detail how he had been whipped.

"We will kill the brown robe dog, rest assured." The man came out from behind the desk. "Po-pe has a list of the worst offenders. They're to be executed. If the rest choose to leave, they can. Otherwise, we'll kill them all."

"Do we kill other Spaniards?" Domingo's insides churned. If Baca had to be killed, Cristina would be in danger.

"We want to be rid of the Spanish. If they leave in peace, the soldiers and ranchers can go. The priests that must pay with their lives desecrated our gods or tortured us." He pointed his lips at Domingo. "Lucas is one who must die."

Domingo felt a warm glee at hearing the death sentence although for the first time he realized how little chance he'd have to be the executioner.

"Sit," Tupatu said. "There's pen and ink in the drawer."

Domingo got them out. He fingered the soft leather covering of the ledger book before he opened it to glance over the first few pages. The entries were those of an *encomendero*, accounting for expenses and income. He explained the contents to Tupatu.

"Tear them out," he said. "We'll begin our accounting fresh. Are you ready to write?"

Domingo dipped his pen into the ink and nodded. Tupatu squatted and began to dictate. "August 10, 1680, in the Spanish way of keeping the date. We will begin a pueblo chronology with this day." He rubbed his finger along his upper lip. "This morning a priest came out to Tesuque from Santa Fe accompanied by a mounted warrior. He mouthed the usual line about taking care of his children. It's clear that governor Otermin has learned of the revolution, but he may have fallen for the misleading date we fed him." He waited until Domingo looked up. "Our man at Tesuque assumed the priest's so-called guard was a scout sent to determine how many Indians had taken up arms. The Tesuques killed the priest and wounded the scout, but the horse carried their warrior off. He likely made it to Santa Fe."

"I'm getting behind," Domingo interrupted.

Tupatu smiled at him. "I'm not used to someone writing down my words. I'll go slower. There's not much more to tell."

Domingo blotted a few places and filled in others where he had run short of ink. He looked up in anticipation.

"Scouts in Santa Fe report many refugees arriving from the south. They move in with people in the town. A few have gone to the fortress beside the plaza." He paused to watch Domingo finish. "Not many refugees are from the north. Seventy Spaniards around Taos were killed. A scout here saw three mounted men race past from the north. Their horses were frothing." Domingo stopped writing. He pictured warriors occupying the Martinez fort, lying in wait when others burned his ranch. It wasn't as satisfying an image as Domingo imagined the day he reported to the San Juan cacique.

"Warriors from Tesuque and Nambe are waiting for the northern army to join them. They killed three Indians loyal to Otermin. They ambushed settlers at the nearby settlement, but many of the enemy fled earlier. Indians burned the houses and surrounding ranches." Tupatu wore a self-satisfied smirk.

Domingo swallowed, his insides aflame. The whirlwind waited to be mounted.

TWENTY TWO

The next day Tupatu told Domingo to stay within the plaza. He expected news and when he had anything to document, he'd need Domingo's help. Domingo paced in front of pueblo entrances until Francesca joined him at a doorway. She had found a distant relationship to the wife, and they spent the night exchanging news about relatives before discussing rumors of the impending revolt.

Domingo asked if Francesca planned to stay. She looked at him with raised eyebrows. When he failed to reply, she said she had no choice but to return. Her parents would be worried, and if the San Ildefonso men joined the revolt, she'd be needed to harvest and to protect the village from vengeful Apaches.

Francesca touched Domingo's shoulder and urged him to be alert. He told her to be on guard, took the fetish from his neck and started to put it over her head. "This will help you sense danger." The gold flecks in her eyes sparkled more than usual, and he wondered if her sight were as unusual as her eyes. He stammered, "It helps you run, too."

"You can't be serious," she said, raising her arm to block his. "If anyone needs help running, it's you." She laughed her teasing laugh, then turned serious. "It's you who'll be in the midst of danger."

Domingo replaced the fetish, felt a surge of warmth. "Once I find Cristina, we'll come to San Ildefonso."

"She can make it back on her own, Mingo. Stay and help free the pueblos."

Won't she ever stop telling me what to do? My Cristina is worth more than scribbling down records. He nodded as if to agree. Francesca jogged to the path north, stopped to wave, then dashed away.

Domingo returned to Tupatu's room to see if any Spanish documents waited for him. None did. Usually, he could sit with nothing to do and dream of Cristina, but anxiety made him restless. He picked up his war bow, tested its string, then put it back in a corner. He left the room to pace the plaza. A child came out of a door to stare at him. He motioned the little girl toward him. She came, head down. He picked up a pebble and played his guessing game with her. Another child slipped from a room. The two were soon laughing at how Domingo hid the stone, then found it in their ear or in his mouth. Their laughs drew the girls' mothers who called their children inside.

Domingo started back to the headquarters room when Tupatu entered the plaza. His easy walk made Domingo guess he'd have no work. The two entered their room without speaking. Tupatu sat on the floor leaning against a wall. Domingo followed his example.

"The word is the army from the south will enter the outskirts of Santa Fe today," Tupatu said. "The northern army arrives tomorrow. It's been clearing out settlements along the Rio Grande. There'll be no Spaniards left when they finish."

"So we sit all day?" Domingo couldn't conceal his impatience.

"We'll get reports off and on I suppose, but we can stay out of the sun much of the time."

Neither spoke. Tupatu appeared to doze. When he stirred, he asked Domingo to tell him more about the scar near his eye. Domingo down-played the whipping since he had but two scars on his back to show for it, but his hatred of Lucas renewed in the recounting. Tupatu nodded sympathy.

"And what did the hairy chins do to you?" Domingo asked.

Tupatu pointed to his eye socket. "One season my family starved. I wasn't big enough to help farm. So my father sent me to an *encomendero.* I earned enough food to send my family a little. The rancher had me work in the house. The Spanish language came pretty quickly, but I was slow to learn their ways. They did everything so differently." He rubbed his brow above the missing eye. "One day the master sent me to tell his wife he'd be looking for missing cattle. I found her in the bedroom putting on her clothes. She didn't have anything on her breasts." He shrugged. "They aren't anything Indians don't see all the time." His laugh was cynical. "In fact, she had very little for me to see. I just stood there relaying the message when she started screaming. I looked around to see if there was a snake in the room. Her daughter came in and saw me standing there. She went to the porch and screamed. Before I knew it, the *encomendero* knocked me down and a servant dragged me off to the root cellar." He rubbed his finger over his upper lip and grimaced. "The next day the ranch hands built a fire like they do for branding cattle. But instead of a branding iron, they heated a poker. The master waved that iron around my face threatening one eye and then the other. I thought he'd put out both. That torture seemed to last forever, but the iron was still red hot when he shoved it into my eye." He shuddered as did Domingo. "You know what?" He paused as if recalling the scene. "The pain must have been terrible, but what I always remember is the terrible stench."

Domingo sat speechless, drenched in cold sweat.

In late afternoon, Domingo sat outside the room with his back against the wall, unable to forget the image of a burning eye. Tupatu was inside, probably dozing. A runner crossed the plaza, one shoulder slumped from a pouch bulging with papers. The man demanded to see Tupatu. The two spent a long time inside talking in low tones. Domingo caught only snatches of their conversation. After the stranger left, Tupatu summoned Domingo.

"My nephew brought me papers from the church in Picuris."

"Are you from Picuris?" Domingo asked.

Tupatu nodded that he was.

"Yet you speak Tewa without a Tiwa accent." Domingo had worked hard on his Tiwa pronunciation but knew his accent identified him as an outsider.

"My mother spoke Tewa. My father thought I could trade if I learned both languages."

"Did you trade? Is that why I was told to pose as a trader when I came here?" Domingo believed he was beginning to think like a master spy.

Tupatu shrugged. "No, I spent my life farming. I have a field of corn that's only half harvested. Don't know if my wife can finish it without me."

"Oh," Domingo said, crestfallen.

"My nephew found these letters in a box buried behind the altar when they tore it down. Just before they set fire to the church. He guessed they'd be incriminating since the priest had taken such pains to hide them."

Domingo began reading. Tupatu lit a candle and stood watching him. Domingo sweated over the correspondence a long time, muttering curses under his breath. Tupatu waited without saying a word.

"There's a lot here to record. I hope that filthy dog of a priest at Tesuque is on the execution list. He was a thief of the worse kind!"

"Tell me what the letters says."

"I'll sum it up for you before I begin recording." Domingo took a deep breath. "The correspondence is among the priest, neighboring ranchers, and the previous governor. The governor's letter accuses the priests of moving the church land markers onto Indian owned land.

"The priest denies the charge in his reply. Then he writes to two neighboring *encomenderos* asking them to support his claim. One Spaniard refuses because he knows that the priest really did move the markers. The other rancher doesn't know anything about the boundaries but says he'll support the priest if the church assigns him more Indian labor. He claims the pueblo sends him only old men or children to fulfill their levy. He's beaten one of the old men, but it didn't do any good. And he complains that the children steal food from the fields.

"The priest replies that he'll get able-bodied men. Then there's some Spanish I'm not sure about, but he seems to suggest he'll include a young girl, too. He describes her beauty at length."

Tupatu did nothing more than nod. Domingo wasn't sure if he should start writing or report on the correspondence of other *encomenderos*. He rubbed his fingers while staring into the candle flame. The fire reminded him of Tupatu's torture. He shuddered. The uneasiness he felt led him to break the silence. He related another case.

"This rancher wanted more irrigation water. When he marked off his land, he knew he'd have to depend on rainfall, but he wrote the governor to ask permission to connect to the Indian irrigation ditch. The governor must have denied his request. So the rancher writes to the priest arguing how heathens don't deserve so much water. The priest doesn't want to hear that argument, of course. The Dominicans have been making good Catholics out of us for eighty years."

Domingo looked at Tupatu. "The correspondence covers three years. The rancher's next ploy is a bribe. He promises to supply the priest with wheat and beef if he convinces the Indians to let him have their water. So the priest twists the arm of the Little Governor until he grants permission. But can you believe this?" Domingo threw up his hands. Tupatu waited. "He insists that the Indians dig the irrigation channel to his fields. And in his last letter, he complains the Indians harvest their fields before his." Domingo looked up at Tupatu, but the big man simply shrugged. "He promises the priest peaches if he can get the Indians to harvest his crops first."

Tupatu rocked on his heels, his chin in his hand.

"Shall I record what I've summarized tonight? What should I do with the letters?"

"You can burn them." Tupatu's face was impassive.

"What? Why—?"

"We know the Spanish did these things all the time. To all the pueblos. That's why were rebelling."

TWENTY THREE

"It's time to see for ourselves what's going on in Santa Fe," Tupatu said. "Maybe we can figure out how the devils mean to defend themselves."

Domingo blinked himself awake, ashamed that Tupatu had risen well before him. He took two tortillas that the tall man offered and bolted them. He made sure his knife was secure at his side and reached for his bow and quiver. "I'm ready to kill my first Spaniard. You think we'll get a chance?"

"Not if we're lucky." Tupatu wore a grim smile.

"What do you mean?"

"Po-pe wants the Spanish to return to Mexico. It'll cost many Indian lives if we have to go against guns and armor."

"You think they'll leave without a fight?" Domingo felt a flood of disappointment yet mixed with a trickle of relief.

"If Governor Otermin knows how many Spanish have been killed in the north, he may want vengeance. On the other hand..." Tupatu stared at Domingo. "You must not say a word of this." His good eye flared. "I'll kill you myself if you do."

The chill that hit Domingo was like the one he experienced when he first met Po-pe.

"We've planted rumors that the Spaniards to the south have retreated. If Otermin believes that, he may volunteer to leave Nuevo Mexico, given safe passage to Mexico." Tupatu scratched his upper lip with a forefinger. "Po-pe's shrewd. He figures if Indians suffer many losses, one of the pueblos will back out—and the rest will be right behind them."

"I can't argue with that." Domingo rested one hand on his knife. "But I hope the San Juan priest is killed." He took a deep breath. "Maybe he's dead already."

"Very few Spanish in the northern pueblos have survived. Odds are he's dead. Unless he snuck out early."

"The Baca *encomendero* was headed to Santa Fe the day I got here. Do you know if his party made it to Santa Fe?"

Tupatu hesitated. “Do you think your priest joined them?”

“I don’t know. A relative of mine from San Ildefonso was with Baca.” Domingo flushed. Calling Cristina a relative wasn’t exactly a lie, but neither was it the truth.

“I’ve got agents who’ll be observing what the Spanish are doing for defense. Doubt they know anything about individual Indians.” He chuckled. “But you know how Indians are. Relatives always come first. So if anybody recognizes someone, they’ll be bound to remember.”

The two started at a trot. As they settled into a faster pace, Domingo exerted himself to match Tupatu’s long legs. He was winded when they reached a hill looking down on Santa Fe.

On the far side of the city, a dozen columns of dense smoke snaked upward. The burnt wood smell irritated Domingo’s nose. It was a crisper smell than the forest fires he had experienced.

“What’s burning?” he asked.

“Looks like it’s Spanish houses scattered around the town. Maybe some Indian homes, too. A lot of Pueblo people think the Mexican Indians are no better than the Spanish.”

“You think Indians set all the fires?”

“I’m not sure. The southern army trickled in last night. Probably flooded the place this morning. If the Spanish resisted, the Indians likely set fires wherever they could. I should hear soon.”

“How will anyone find us?” Domingo asked.

“I sent out scouts before you woke. We’ll meet them on the hill north of the fortress. As soon as they find out anything, they’ll report.”

Domingo looked at Tupatu with awe. He had never known anyone so well organized. Unless it was Po-pe. When they reached the hill, he found a rock and mounted it. Given the distance and the smoke, it was impossible to identify individuals. Domingo sat. Below him, Tupatu squatted.

Two more columns of smoke bellowed up before anyone reported to Tupatu. When a young man finally arrived, he was panting so hard he had to catch his breath before speaking. Domingo scrambled down to overhear.

"I found someone from Sandia so I could understand him. He was with the Keres when they stormed the town. At the first shot, they started burning homes. Almost all the pueblo Indians came over to our side. The women and elders headed for home. Only the Mexican Indians resisted."

"Did they start more fires?" Tupatu asked.

"That would be my guess. If there were any Spanish there in the first place, they got out early. The Mexicans might have come over to our side if they had been given the chance. Or they would have fled."

Tupatu sucked at his lips. "Where did they go?"

"Many were killed. The survivors joined the Spanish in their fortress."

"That means they'll have more strength," Domingo spoke on impulse. Immediately, he feared Tupatu would send him off, but the man only gave him a curt nod.

"Should we try to keep everyone from the fort?" the young man asked.

"No. The Spanish won't share ammunition with any Indians." His smile was sardonic. "But they will have to feed them." He rubbed the brow above his empty eye socket. "That much of the plan was my idea."

"It's sure to work." The young man nodded and left.

The smoke hid everything in the valley so Tupatu and Domingo headed down the trail the young man had taken. They were met by a tall man. His appearance surprised Domingo. "He looks like you do," he said to Tupatu.

Tupatu wore a broad grin. "No, he doesn't. He looks with two eyes."

Domingo guffawed, more because Tupatu could joke about his handicap than at the wisecrack.

When the man reached them, his smile matched Tupatu's. "So you're still alive, Old Fart." He placed his hand under his armpit and swung the arm down to explode an ersatz fart. "You been hiding from the Spanish all the time Po-pe has been killing everyone in sight?"

"How'd you know the northern army's been so successful?"

"I don't, but lots of rumors say it's so. You got more reliable news?"

"Po-pe wiped them out for sure. A couple got away to warn Otermin, but he's had little time to prepare."

"The southern army has been just as successful. Most warriors at Isleta and Sandia pueblos slipped north before the Lt. Governor knew anything was going on. The Sandians held us up some, but we stayed on schedule more or less."

"How about the Keres pueblos?" Tupatu asked.

"They were ready when we got there. Must be more than five hundred of us all together."

"How's their discipline?" Tupatu said.

"Three Keres war chiefs are taking charge. For a time, I thought they'd gone crazy. Killed everything in sight that isn't Indian. Horses, cattle. They crucified the Cochiti priest on an upside down cross so anyone passing by could piss in his mouth."

"Did that make the urine holy water?" Tupatu quipped.

"If it did, that priest must have floated up to his heaven."

They all laughed, the crucifixion vivid in Domingo's mind.

"So how's everything with you? Been ten or twelve growing seasons since I've seen you. You ever satisfy those wives of yours? Or are they still calling you, Limp Dick?"

"I'm down to one. The old one so malnourished last year she didn't survive the winter."

"So are you potent enough now? Or does your wife have to find someone at Sandia to satisfy her?"

"She's more satisfied than your wife. With that one eye, I hear you find her sweet spot only half the time."

Tupatu tried not to laugh, but he held back so long that he bellowed. When he half regained his composure, he turned to Domingo. "Limp Dick, here, is my little brother. One of my father's brothers' sons. None of the Picuris women would have anything to do with him. He had to go all the way to Isleta to find a bride. Smart move. He pretended he was a trader so he could go off a month after sex in order to regain his potency."

It was the other man's turn to laugh. Domingo asked him if the part about trading were true. The man answered. "The part about us being brothers is true. But I left because everyone started called me Tupatu Two since we did look alike. I sure didn't want to be reminded all the time how ugly I was." Tupatu Two pursed his lips in Tupatu's direction. "Now all he looks like is a one-eyed old fart."

"Let an old fart sit while we catch up," Tupatu said.

The three found a rock out-cropping where they could rest their backs and watch the path to the valley. The two Tupatus interspersed reminiscing with humor until dusk when a red haze filled the night. Domingo forgot the battle below them until a cannon blast rumbled from the fort. His hand went to his knife. He gulped, thinking how useless it would be against an harquebus, let alone artillery. He rose with his two companions, and they looked over the valley although they could see nothing. When no further volleys reached their ears, Tupatu Two said he should return to track the southern army and to pry into Spanish defenses.

"Do you have any spies inside the fortress?" Tupatu asked.

Tupatu Two glanced at Domingo. "I don't know how long the siege is going to last."

Tupatu nodded agreement with his brother's evasion. "You probably know we've planted rumors that the Lt. Governor's force has retreated to El Paso del Norte. If you should get a spy inside the fort, Po-pe needs to know if Otermin believes our propaganda."

Tupatu Two only shrugged.

"If we know he's misled, it'll figure into our bargaining tactics," Tupatu said. "He's not likely to hold on if he thinks there's no chance of a relief force reaching him."

Tupatu Two rose stiffly, rubbed the small of his back with both hands, and waited for Tupatu to get up. The older brother struggled a little more with a stiff leg, then stretched. The two brothers looked at each other nodding ever so slightly, their lips barely betraying their good humor.

"If the hairy faces fight, we'll going to see a lot of Indian blood," Tupatu Two said.

"Too much," Tupatu said. "You be careful or more than your dick will go limp."

"Watch out for that artillery. You get a white hot cannon ball up your ass, and it'll end any new fart as well as Old Fart."

TWENTY FOUR

The next day, Domingo and Tupatu paced outside their room awaiting word from Po-pe. No messenger came all morning although armed arrivals flooded the pueblo, eager for battle, and vowing to kill any Spaniard they met. Each would-be warrior brought his own rumor as to Po-pe's whereabouts. The speculation had him commanding ten armies instead of one although two rumors had him fleeing to the mountains.

"I hope Otermin is no better informed than we are." Tupatu grumbled. "If he finds out he's facing only half our force, he's apt to lead a foray into the town."

"That'll make it easier to kill Spanish," Domingo scowled.

"No telling what those Keres war chiefs will do against Spanish artillery," Tupatu said. "A couple of cannon blasts combined with cavalry, and they may take off for Hopi country. We need Po-pe to inspire discipline. A thousand more warriors won't hurt either."

"Then he should be here with his troops," Domingo groused.

"And we need his patience." Tupatu growled his advice.

Domingo answered sheepishly. "And we need his patience."

The two sat sweating. Not a single cloud disturbed the militant blue sky. Tupatu rose to stretch when a messenger came from the north. Domingo brought a flask for him. He gulped water while he reported. Po-pe had assembled the northern warriors, taking extra time to fill his chain of command with competent men.

He instructed Tupatu to tell the local caciques they must be ready to feed a thousand warriors. An advance party, scheduled to arrive that night, would help with logistics. The messenger accompanied Domingo and Tupatu as they carried out orders.

The Nambe cacique shrugged at the request. Despite hundreds of secret caches in a decades long struggle to hide supplies from the avaricious Spanish, the pueblo women could provide sufficient supplies for no more than four or five days. The cacique guessed at the quantity neighboring pueblos had. If the siege lasted more than eight or ten days, the army would have to depend on whatever food was stored in Spanish warehouses. No one knew how much that would be.

Tupatu returned with Domingo to their office where they recorded estimates. When Domingo finished writing, he and Tupatu headed for their overlook on the north hill. Most fires had died down giving them a better view of the siege.

Indian warriors ringed the plaza facing the governor's complex. It was built like a pueblo but stretched far longer than anything Domingo had ever seen. Two watch towers dominated the ends of the fortress. Thick walls surrounded a large courtyard behind the row of houses and offices. Countless sheep and cattle grazed in the open area. Domingo guessed that a row of buildings constituting the back wall sheltered equipment and ammunition.

Indian archers shot an occasional arrow at the narrow slits in the fortress. Most bounced off the thick adobe. The Indians hurled insults at the Spanish in so many different languages that Domingo made no attempt to remember any of them.

He was getting bored with the seeming futility when the young messenger from the day before found them. He nodded to Tupatu as he caught his breath. "Juan, I don't know his Indian name, is going to give the Spanish a chance to surrender."

"No!" Tupatu's eye widened, his eyebrows shot up, and he shook his head in frustration. "Otermin can't know that Po-pe's army is arriving. It's too early to discuss terms. Who's the idiot that dreamed this up?"

"Juan is the son of one of the medicine men the Spanish hanged. He had been a servant of the former governor and one of our best spies. He left the fortress only a few days ago. The governor probably hadn't missed him."

"So why is Juan delivering an ultimatum? Otermin will take it as an insult to have his servant demand his surrender." Domingo shivered at Tupatu's show of anger.

The runner looked at his feet. "I heard that the Keres' chiefs thought it up to humiliate the governor."

"Oh, no. My brother must be right. The Keres chiefs are out of their minds."

The three stood without speaking. An ominous silence encircled them as they edged closer to the plaza.

Tupatu turned to Domingo. Deep lines wrinkled his forehead. "I've got to stay here. The two of you get closer to hear what's going on. Remember every detail. Po-pe needs to know it all."

Domingo and the messenger scurried closer. The quiet among so many people was eerie. Domingo wondered what effect it had on the Spanish. A horn blast made him jump. "One of the Keres," the messenger said. "Took it from a Spaniard he killed. He blows it whenever he thinks anything important is about to happen."

From scanning the crowd, Domingo was about to conclude the sound was premature, when he saw a mounted Indian heading toward the fortress. The blue-gray steed was an imposing beast, its saddle trimmed with silver. The diminutive Indian riding it seemed out of place. He wore a purple sash decorated with silver letters that Domingo couldn't make out.

"Got any idea where he got that sash?" he asked his companion.

"It's that cloth they put in the Bible to tell them where to read. The Bible was gigantic."

"I'd like to see it," Domingo said. "Where is it?"

The young man laughed. "Two altar boys shit all over it before the cacique chased them off. Then the women burned it. They resented all the work they did for the church with nothing in return."

"Why'd they save the book mark?" Domingo asked.

"Guess it appealed to someone's fancy. I heard Juan found it on a trash heap."

"If the Spanish recognize it, they'll be even angrier." Domingo shook his head at the turn of events. "Juan must know that since he's lived with them."

"Yeah, that's one reason he was chosen to ask for their surrender. He speaks fluent Spanish."

"Let's get closer. There's more noise."

Juan's horse pranced. He took a few moments to control it, obviously uncomfortable on horse back. He nudged its ribs, but the horse didn't respond to his soft moccasins. He slapped its flank and the horse started forward. The crowd grew silent. Young Indians edged onto the plaza.

The fortress gate opened, and Otermin led forth an armed party. When he got close enough to identify Juan, he roared his question. "What do you want, you traitor?"

Juan attempted to be equally haughty, but when he replied his words faltered. Domingo felt sure the man must have rehearsed his lines. "I have two crosses for you." He held a white cross and a red cross high, waving them for everyone to see. "Chose the white cross and you can leave for Mexico in peace. We want no more fighting."

Otermin glared contempt. Domingo wondered if his grimace caused his horse to rear. The governor tugged its reins to calm it. His control contrasted with Juan's fumbling. Juan groped at the crosses in his hand lifting up the other one.

"Chose this red cross and you chose to fight. You and your women and children will be killed." His horse tossed its head. "I'll return for your answer shortly." He wheeled his horse around. It whinnied at the biting bridle. Juan kicked hard, let up on the reins, and the horse responded.

Otermin and his soldiers wheeled their horses in unison.

It seemed an eternity to Domingo, but the sun had not moved much when Juan rode into the plaza again. He shouted, "I am ready for your answer."

A musket ball whizzed over his head. Spanish curses followed. The young men who had filled the plaza fled to the safety of the homes lining the plaza. Juan raced his horse to their shelter also. A few musket shots rang out from harquebuses captured by the Indians. Chunks of clay flew from the fortress wall, but the lead balls did no more than pockmark the thick adobe. The Indians settled for screaming threats.

Domingo climbed the wall of a home crumbled by cannon shot. The scattered possessions of the interior suggested former wealth. He brushed off adobe fragments on a flattened section and sat to watch. The messenger with him decided to leave after checking with Tupatu.

The fortress gate creaked. Three times as many Spanish soldiers filed into a line facing the Indians. The cavalry flanking the infantry carried banners and flags. Their sashes and uniforms offered a colorful display. The armor of the infantry gleamed white in the sunlight. In a bluster of dust, half a dozen other soldiers dragged out a cannon and positioned it. From the fort, enemy insults turned into challenges. A few arrows flew at the line, most falling short. The Spaniards waited. Domingo thought of Tupatu's caution to be patient. If Indians accepted the Spanish challenge and charged across the open plaza, they'd be slaughtered. None left the protection of the wrecked houses.

Domingo decided to inform Tupatu. He headed to the hillside where he found the man talking to three others. As he neared, he heard Tupatu give rapid fire orders to two while listening to the third. Domingo waited until the men left. He came in on Tupatu's blind side. Tupatu jumped when Domingo spoke. "Otermin tried to provoke an attack. No one responded."

"I know. Two of Po-pe's lieutenants conferred with me after I left you. When I told them about the Keres chiefs, they rushed over to impose discipline. I assume they've taken control of the southern army. Or at least their chiefs are listening to them."

"I suppose there'll be no more Juans."

"It's going to take a genius to get a surrender now." Tupatu threw up his hands. "I don't know if even Po-pe is up to negotiating a peaceful way out."

"Seems to me all the governor has left is bluff. Like his foray this afternoon," Domingo said.

"He must have known Juan was bluffing, too, with that hocus pocus of the crosses." Tupatu's frown registered disgust.

"What are the chances Otermin will think Po-pe is bluffing when he negotiates?"

"If Po-pe can't convince him that he doesn't have a chance, then he's chosen the red cross. Santa Fe will be drenched in blood."

May most of it be Spanish!

TWENTY FIVE

A young woman hissed a greeting to Tupatu. She carried two ears of corn and chunks of meat. The roasted corn smell made Domingo realize he had gone all day without eating, not once thinking of food.

Tupatu hardly chewed his meat. "It's good. Not venison. Is it beef?"

"Horse," the woman said. "There are dead horses everywhere. We're feasting."

Domingo savored another chunk before he bit into his corn. "Did you think Spanish meat would feed the army?" He grinned at Tupatu.

"Po-pe said we'd have Spanish livestock only if they didn't leave for Mexico." He laughed as he chewed on a chuck of meat. "No one mentioned eating horse."

The girl grinned. "It's not as good as venison, but we all like it. First meat I've had in more than two seasons."

"You should be leaving," Tupatu said. "Can you find your way in the dark?"

"I'm to guide you to Po-pe's new headquarters."

Domingo hurried through his corn while Tupatu gnawed the last chunk of flesh. Then, the three threaded their way through the ruins. Every house facing the plaza had holes in its roof, if a roof remained. On streets farther back most homes were charred or torn half to the ground. Doors were ripped from hinges of intact homes, shards of ceramic ware were scattered inside and out. Shredded cloth hung from splintered window frames. The acrid smell of burnt wood made Domingo forget the roasted corn.

On Santa Fe's outskirts the three broke into a trot. The girl set a fast pace, obviously on familiar ground. They soon reached a home hidden along a small watercourse. Domingo sensed cottonwoods from their rustle in the evening breeze. He glimpsed their dim silhouette when they stopped. The girl pursed her lips at the house and nodded farewell.

Two guards blocked the graveled path to the entrance. One recognized Tupatu and waved him forward. At the house, two more men guarded the arched doorway. Domingo froze for an instant. He mistook them for Spanish because they wore chest armor and steel helmets. One guard kept pushing his headgear back clearly unaccustomed to its weight. Both held steel lances with strips of bright red ribbon tied below the gleaming points.

The guards crossed their lances to block entry. Tupatu grinned recognition at them. "I'm the one who's half blind," he said. One of the guards laughed and raised his lance.

The other held his pose with no trace of a smile. "You must be cleared by Po-pe," he announced in a loud voice.

The words brought Po-pe to the door. His hair was held in place by a purple, silk scarf tied across his forehead. The ends dangled to his waist. He wore a silver necklace with a red stone pendant over his tunic. Po-pe acknowledged Tupatu with a nod but looked askance at Domingo. Tupatu reminded Po-pe that he had recommended Domingo to record the revolution. Po-pe turned his penetrating eyes toward him. Their glint acknowledged recognition. "Have you killed any Spanish yet?"

"Not yet," Domingo muttered. He hoped he hid his disappointment with Po-pe's adoption of Spanish adornment.

"You'll get your chance. But you have more important work to do. We must be sure every priest is killed or expelled. We want none of their witchcraft left behind. Do you understand?"

Domingo nodded his agreement.

"You trust him completely?" Po-pe asked Tupatu.

"Completely."

"Then come in. A runner from El Paso brings good news. The wagon train remains blocked by flood waters."

"Just as you planned!" Admiration filled Tupatu's words.

"Of course. Now tell me what you saw today."

Tupatu reported and said Domingo had seen more. Po-pe looked at Domingo. He started in a low voice, but Po-pe's eyes commanded him to speak up. He described how Juan had demanded the governor's surrender and how Otermin had responded.

When Po-pe showed no anger at the premature demand, Tupatu asked if Juan shouldn't be banished from the battlefield.

"We'll have to put up with him, but I have ordered the Keres chiefs to keep him under control."

"He could be dangerous," Tupatu said.

"When the Spanish threw me into their dungeon, his father was there. So beaten and starved he was out of his mind half the time."

"He was a medicine man?" Tupatu asked.

"He practiced a little curing. But he had a powerful vision." Po-pe closed his eyes. He waited so long, Domingo thought he had finished, but Po-pe opened his eyes to resume in a low voice. "Jesus came to Nuevo Mexico carrying a white cross. He started in the northern pueblos, and the priests followed him south. Also the ranchers. When Jesus reached Santa Fe, the governor led them all down the Rio Grande. According to the vision, every Spaniard left the colony."

Po-pe bowed his head for a moment, then looked up. "When the priests learned about it, they became incensed. They informed the Inquisitors. Juan's father was put on trial. The judges condemned him without listening to a single Indian."

"Why did he use a red cross, too?" Tupatu said.

"Who knows?" Pope said. "Juan went crazy for a while after his father's death."

"We must kill them all." Domingo spoke in a flush of anger.

Po-pe scowled at him. "We don't kill them if they leave peacefully. Too many Indians will die if we seek revenge."

Tupatu placed a hand on Domingo's shoulder. "We have a lot to record tonight." He faced Po-pe. "Do you have anything for us to add to the record?"

"No. I have a boy with me who's recording what we've done. We can compare notes later." Po-pe nodded a dismissal.

On his way out Tupatu asked for orders.

"Observe what's going on in the courtyard. Find out how crowded the fortress is. We'll have to starve them out if they don't leave in peace."

Back at their office, Domingo's handwriting went from bad to worse. Tupatu dictated steadily and the dwindling stub of a candle hardly broke the darkness. By the time Domingo laid down to sleep, his puffy eyes shut tight.

In the morning, he dreamed he was riding a horse, struggling to control it. He had it almost calm when a soldier grabbed his leg to pull him off. He pushed and pulled to free himself, muttering a curse.

"Come on. It's light. You want to spend all day in bed?" Tupatu's voice was gruff, but Domingo recognized a teasing gruff.

He rubbed at his eyes wondering how much grit they could hold. "Didn't we record everything last night?"

"Yes. Now we've got to go out again and find more for tonight." Tupatu gave a final tug. "Aren't you eager to kill a Spaniard?"

Domingo wondered if he was. He thought of Lucas and his father's amputation, of his forced separation from Cristina, and clenched his teeth. *The Spanish must be killed. But at what price?* Yesterday's scenes of destruction troubled him. He followed Tupatu outside without speaking. They went to a ramada near the plaza where women were boiling meat. Two warriors ahead of them picked up the last tortillas. The young woman who had guided them the night before served them bowls of the soup. "It isn't venison," she laughed.

Domingo chewed the stringy flesh. There wasn't much taste to it, but he relished the morsels. When he finished, he handed the bowl to the girl. "Sorry, I can't give you more," she said. "There are hundreds to feed." She gave Domingo a second look and smiled. "Perhaps you can feast on mule tonight."

He and Tupatu returned to the hill overlooking the royal houses. They had a clear view of the compound in the late morning light. Animals crowded the courtyard. They clustered around a trickle of water that branched off an irrigation ditch outside the fort. The livestock had eaten every blade of grass. Children chased each other among the animals, women trying to keep them away from the cattle. The braying of a mule momentarily drowned out the bleating of the sheep.

In one corner, half a dozen men were butchering two cows and a couple of sheep. Domingo noted their number, realizing that most of the men must be manning posts inside. He watched the butchers collect the blood in leather buckets, paying closer attention to it than the hides and sheep skins they hacked away. "That's enough meat to last them to winter, if they aren't packed elbow to elbow inside." Tupatu grimaced. "We underestimated how many animals they'd crowd in there. Must be thousands of sheep, hundreds of horses and cattle."

A dozen Indians approached the clearing on the hillside. Domingo didn't recognize them. Tupatu didn't acknowledge anyone. Three of the arrivals carried harquebuses. They set up tripod stands and steadied the guns, taking aim on the courtyard. Domingo's mouth went dry. His hands sweated. Cristina could be among the women in the court yard. "Wait," he called.

The men scowled at him.

"There are Indians in the courtyard."

"They're traitors if they're there."

"You can't know that about the women and children." Domingo shouted his anger.

"We won't shoot children," one said. "We'll not aim at any women," another said.

Tupatu grabbed Domingo's arm. "You mustn't interfere. They've been ordered to shoot up the compound."

Two of the harquebuses belched fire. Dirt shot up by the butchers, and they dived inside the living quarters. A cow bellowed and fell to the ground, bleeding from its mouth. The harquebus of the third gunner failed to fire. He fiddled with it and took aim. It fired prematurely, and the gunner screamed. The explosion set his hair on fire. He rolled on the ground to put it out. His two companions roared with laughter. Undaunted, the other gunners reloaded, aimed their guns, and fired. A sheep went down. A geyser of water erupted from the trickle.

Domingo noted with relief that the women had herded the children inside. Not a person remained in the courtyard. Several more Indians arrived with harquebuses and tried their luck at shooting livestock. They soon ran out of powder. A few others tried arrows but gave up in frustration when a spent arrow bounced off a cow. Still more Indians crowded onto the hillside, but they were reduced to being on-lookers.

"You think we could storm the courtyard and drive out the livestock?" Tupatu was thinking out loud. Domingo stopped thinking of Cristina and tried to imagine breaking through the walls at one end and opening the other end for the stampeded animals. "If we shoot all the animals, that just saves them the trouble." Tupatu sat with chin in his hands.

Domingo's mind went blank as he watched cows crowd out sheep at the water. Their bleats said they were still thirsty. "That's it," he yelled. Indians close by stared at him.

"What's it?" Tupatu said.

"The water! We cut off their water supply. We don't have to starve them out."

Just as Tupatu turned to congratulate Domingo on his brilliance, they saw Tupatu Two ambling up the hill side. A streak of white scarred his forehead. One eyebrow was missing.

"What happened? You trying to look like I do?" Tupatu said.

"Shit. I could lose both my eyes and never be half as ugly as you are."

"I guess some woman got tired of waiting for you to get it hard. What'd she do? Burn you with a poker?" Tupatu brushed a hand across his forehead.

"Some turd fired an harquebus at me. Would you believe it was an Indian?"

Tupatu laughed but with a grimace.

"I ask you. Do I look like a Spaniard?" Tupatu Two nodded his disgust.

"You better sit out the siege," Tupatu advised. "Since both sides want to kill you." He covered a laugh with his hand.

Tupatu Two gazed at the compound. "There are things to do. Tonight we're going to divert the irrigation channel. That courtyard will be desert dry tomorrow. We'll see how long the furry faces last without water."

Domingo was crestfallen. His face must have shown it because Tupatu Two asked what the trouble was. His brother explained. Tupatu Two claimed that he had just thought of the tactic on his way up the hill. Domingo felt a little better.

"Did your spy ever learn if Otermin believes his southern force has retreated?" Tupatu asked.

"If I ever find out, you'll be the first to know."

Tupatu patted at a place beside him for his brother to sit. "Po-pe's learned that the wagon train's been stalled in El Paso. No way it can reach Santa Fe in time."

"Now if we can convince Otermin of that. And that the forces of his Lt. Governor have fled." Tupatu Two leaned to his brother and whispered but Domingo still heard. "Garcia has left Isleta." He chuckled. "Not much of a Lt. Governor, if you ask me. He believed our rumors about how we wiped out Otermin."

Tupatu Two motioned Domingo to join them. "You keeping tabs on how many furry faces are in the compound?"

Domingo gulped. *How could he know my assignment? But then everyone must want to know how many enemy we face.* "We've seen half a dozen. Before the shooting. How many do you think?"

Tupatu Two shrugged. "I don't know how we'll ever get an accurate count. Besides, there are still Spanish hiding in the city. Ones who didn't get inside the fortress yet."

"How could that be?" Tupatu said.

"The scavenging parties are more interested in looting than searching," Tupatu Two said. "But they'll find them sooner or later." He ran his finger across his throat to signify what would happen when they did.

Domingo's heart stopped. The Baca party might not have reached the fortress. Cristina could be killed by Indians scavenging Santa Fe.

TWENTY SIX

Domingo tossed all night on the hillside imagining dangers to Cristina. He'd turned in early because Tupatu had little to record, and Po-pe had no time for them. For once, it was Domingo who woke Tupatu at first light. They saw the fine plume of a cook fire and headed toward it, arriving early at the serving line. An old woman heaped chunks of meat on a red pottery dish and plopped a half-burned tortilla atop the steaming pile.

"Am I going to start whinnying soon?" Tupatu asked her.

"No," she said sternly, cupping her lips with a hand to hide her smile. "You may start braying though."

"You Nambe people are famous for your beans," Tupatu teased back. "When are you going to share your beans instead of hoarding them?"

"When you help us harvest." A frown crossed her face. "If we don't start soon, we're going to lose our corn as well as our beans."

"At least you won't have to feed any Spanish lords." Tupatu's voice showed his concern.

He and Domingo squatted under a ramada to eat. Thoughts of Cristina filled Domingo's head. *How do I get away today? I hate to lie to Tupatu, but I must save Cristina.*

"Let's go see if my brother stopped up the irrigation ditch," Tupatu said. "If they've blocked it, the Spanish may be ready to negotiate."

As they approached the hill overlooking the fortress, two shots rang out. Indians with an harquebus were scurrying to higher ground. In the courtyard, three soldiers were dipping up muddy water from a disappearing trickle. Two others, in body armor, covered them with their harquebuses. Farther down the ditch, a cow was bawling, its front legs mired in black mud. Other cows trampled her. Pitiful sheep stood helpless at the end of the ditch where it exited under a wall. Their bleating matched the bawling of the cattle. As more Indians gathered on the hillside, the soldiers gave up scooping water and scurried inside to take cover.

Tupatu sat cross legged. His lips curled in a sardonic smile. "I hope my brother gets here to enjoy this sight."

"I'll go look for him," Domingo said. He darted away before Tupatu could answer. He hadn't exactly lied. If he saw Tupatu Two while he searched for Cristina, he'd tell him his brother wanted to see him.

The homes near the plaza had been reduced to rubble. Wood smoke curled up here and there. The smell blended with the stench of dead animals. Indians in ragged dress looted the ruins. One had draped himself in crimson velvet curtains; another paraded with a sword that dragged on the ground. The looters didn't concern Domingo, but he came across a squad of Indians going house to house ignoring booty. Their leader gave him a quizzical look but said nothing.

Farther from the plaza, homes were scattered. A few were well hidden and hardly touched by the conflict. Others laid in ruin. Domingo searched a few intact homes and found no trace of habitation. He turned onto another street where white-washed walls were smudged with black. Numerous, mutilated bodies laid around the houses. He paused at the prone body of a soldier, an arrow through his throat. He turned him over. A swarm of flies buzzed from the corpse's face, its puffy cheeks a lifeless white. A streak of dried blood trailed from lips to chin. Domingo gagged.

But his eyes riveted on an harquebus under the body. Domingo had not seen one so close since Martinez had shown him his collection. *If Lucas lives, I'd love to kill him with it. How ironic a death, killed with a Spanish weapon.*

He was about to reach for the gun when a short, darting figure scampered from the ruins on his right, dashing toward the corpse. Domingo reached for his knife. The figure looked up at him, his eyes beseeching. He wore only tattered pants, a few sizes too big for him. An unraveling rope held them in place.

Domingo spoke in Tewa. The response a blank stare. He resorted to Spanish. "Where are you from?"

"Mexico," the man stammered. "My tribe is Mixtec."

The name meant nothing to Domingo. "Where have you been living?" Domingo guessed he must be a slave.

"I'm a servant of Señor Baca. We fled here from his ranch."

Domingo gasped. He almost blurted out questions about Cristina but decided to approach her whereabouts with round about questions. Besides the man's rotund figure, his eyes bulged like those of a frog. A dullness in them suggested the man might not be too bright. *He may be loyal to Baca. Or maybe not bright enough to run away now that he could be free.*

"The señor sent me to see if I could find Gustavo." He pointed at the dead soldier with his toe.

"And what is your name?" Domingo asked.

"It's Mixtec. No one can pronounce it. Everyone calls me Bullfrog."

Domingo had never heard a more appropriate nickname. The man's deep voice contended with his eyes for the appellation.

Bullfrog continued in his deep monotone. "The señor told me to bring back the harquebus if Gustavo was dead." He reached down for it.

Domingo stepped on the gun and drew his knife. Bullfrog backed away. "I'll tell the señor I couldn't find Gustavo."

"Do you want the harquebus to help the Spanish?"

"It makes no difference to me who wins. Baca says the Indians will kill me or make me a slave."

"Do you know how to fire an harquebus?" Domingo asked.

Bullfrog swallowed, narrowed his eyes. "They showed me once, but it's hard to remember things after Baca beat me."

Bullfrog turned his head to show a huge scar running through his black, tangled hair. Domingo winced. He pointed to the scar above his eye. "A priest almost blinded me with a whip."

Bullfrog nodded in sympathy.

"How does one use an harquebus?" Domingo picked up the weapon and looked it over.

Bullfrog knelt over the body and rummaged in its belt and pockets. He showed Domingo two lead balls and a small powder horn. "Smell the gun," Bullfrog said.

Domingo wrinkled his nose at the burnt offering of gun powder.

"I'd guess he's fired it," Bullfrog said. "So you have two shots." He handed Domingo the balls and powder. "Here's how you load it."

He loaded the weapon slowly, explaining each step with gestures as best he could. Domingo nodded understanding. Bullfrog went through half a dozen warnings, repeating himself often, screwing up his forehead in recall. Finally, he handed the weapon to Domingo.

Domingo held it in one hand and the powder horn and remaining ball in the other. "Where do I put these?" He held up the hand with the ammunition.

Bullfrog pointed at the dead soldier's belt. Several pockets were attached to it. Domingo stooped to struggle with the belt fastener. Flies buzzed around him. A tremor went down his back. He handed the harquebus to Bullfrog as he struggled with both hands to free the belt. When he put it around his own waist, he felt the weight of death from the leather. Bullfrog handed him the gun and wished him luck.

"Wait, friend," Domingo said. "You said you served Baca?"

Bullfrog nodded he did.

"I have kin who are with him." Domingo could not bring himself to say that Cristina served Baca.

Bullfrog looked up, waiting.

"My cousin. A beautiful woman from San Ildefonso. Long black hair, smooth complexion, about this tall." He held his hand at chin level.

"There were three women from San Ildefonso. They all were beautiful. They all wore their hair long."

"Her hair is luxurious." Domingo breathed deep, relishing his image of Cristina.

Bullfrog stood with mouth open, waiting.

"She came to the Baca's recently. Surely you remember her."

"It couldn't be Juanita. She's been there a long time."

"It's Cristina." Domingo tried to hide his impatience.

"I don't know the last two women. They came recently."

"Are they both alive?"

"Yes, but it's been very hard on them. When we left the ranch, a supply wagon turned over. We unloaded only a little of it. Señor Baca was in such a rush. The priest from San Ildefonso had come to him claiming the Indians were on a rampage." Bullfrog became animated at the memory. "The women tried to pack everything. The señor kept yelling that we had to leave. I've never seen him in such a state. He yelled at the Indian women to go home. The señora yelled at them to stay."

"Sounds like your señor is a coward."

Bullfrog shook his head. "Just before we got here, he went out of his way to warn a friend. It delayed us a day so we didn't get into the fort."

"What happened then?" Domingo wiped sweat from his brow.

"Everyone stayed together after that. Even when we ran out of food. The señora has a cousin here. When we found her home, she took us in. But she has no food."

"What have you been living on?"

"We've chewed leather. I've scavenged a few dead chickens from the streets. Bones of a horse that had been butchered."

"Did you try to go into the fortress?"

"We got here too late. Anyway, the señora's cousin thought the family would be better off outside. She believed her Indian friends would protect her."

"Have they?"

"They all disappeared," Bullfrog croaked.

Domingo's mind raced. *How do I get him to take me to Baca? He must have been instructed to make sure no one follows him.*

"If Señor Baca is hiding, why does he want the harquebus?"

"He doesn't tell me such things, but I think he'll try to get into the fortress."

"Does he have far to go?" Domingo tried to sound nonchalant.

"Not far." The hesitation in his answer confirmed Domingo's suspicion that Bullfrog would not reveal where Baca hid.

He quit being cautious. "Take me to where you stay. I'll convince my cousin to leave. It'd be one less mouth to feed!"

Bullfrog gave a furtive glance behind him. "The señor would kill me."

"I'll give you the harquebus. You don't need to take me inside. Just show me the house. Baca will never know." Domingo pleaded. "My cousin needs me."

"There's a second priest there to protect her." Bullfrog whined.

"Why should he help her? He doesn't know her." Domingo stepped toward Bullfrog, a scowl on his face.

"He knows her. She was in his pueblo. San Juan."

Domingo's mouth opened wide. *That stinking Lucas. What's he done to her?* Hatred filled his guts. He pictured himself aiming the harquebus. His lead ball smashed Lucas' skull, brains flew in all directions, followed by a fountain of blood.

A rustle of footsteps interrupted his reverie. A search party surrounded him. Two men grabbed his arms. Another notched an arrow and shot at Bullfrog who scampered unharmed into a nearby alley.

TWENTY SEVEN

A tall man with broad shoulders leered into Domingo's face, a scant finger's length away. "Why are you here?" His voice whipped at Domingo's ear. "Who's your friend?"

Domingo thought fast. "He's no friend. We were fighting over the harquebus." He pointed to it with his toe.

"You didn't look to be fighting."

"He backed off when I reached for my knife." Domingo pointed at his hip. The two Indians holding his arms gripped them harder.

"You haven't said what you're doing here." The words racheted up a notch, but the man stepped back and averted his eyes. He seemed uncomfortable acting like a Spaniard.

"I assist Tupatu, a rebel leader from Picuris. He sent me to find his brother."

"What's his brother's name?"

"Tupatu."

"You said you worked for Tupatu." The man scowled and thrust himself into Domingo's face again.

"Both are named Tupatu. His younger brother is nicknamed Tupatu Two."

The tall man repeated the nickname under his breath and chuckled. Domingo relaxed a little. He studied the leader of the search party. His build made Domingo wonder if he were a Comanche. They often allied with pueblo Indians, especially when they felt the Spanish had cheated them.

Yet, the man spoke Tiwa without an accent and Domingo looked over his tunic for familiar markings. Domingo half choked, aghast at the man's necklace. Half a dozen ears, strung loosely on a thong, decorated his chest. They were so encrusted with black, dried blood that Domingo couldn't tell their natural color. When he looked at the man's face, he saw that his left ear was gone, a hideous scar running from his cheek into his hair line.

"So why do you think your Tupatu Two is in this part of Santa Fe?"

"In all this rubble who knows where anyone is?" Domingo was thinking of Cristina's whereabouts, not Tupatu's. *If I could get away, I might still be able to follow Bullfrog.* "I must tell Tupatu to report to Po-pe."

"You know Po-pe?" The man's tone was dubious but showed awe at the same time.

"Yes. I record events of the revolt for him." Domingo mustered his resolve to speak with authority. "He gave me work to do only a day ago."

"Then why are you running errands in the middle of a battlefield." The men holding Domingo's arms squeezed harder. His interrogator leaned closer into his face.

"It's not an errand. It's an emergency. Tupatu Two blocked the irrigation ditch yesterday. His dam has broken, and it must be repaired. Without water, the Spanish will have to surrender."

The big man hesitated, mulling over Domingo's lie. Domingo realized the man might know the condition of the dam. He fought to keep calm.

"Alright. We have more important things to do than question an errand boy. Go find your Tupatu Two." He motioned to his followers, pointing to the alley where Bullfrog had disappeared. "Let's question the other one. If we can find him."

Domingo knew he must return soon to Tupatu, but he could not give up his own search when he was so close to Cristina. His instinct was to follow the search party down the alley. No. *Bullfrog might not be the brightest, but he seemed shrewd. With people after him, he'd run in the opposite direction from where he meant to go.* Domingo had two choices of streets. The first was lined with houses built close to the cobblestones. Smoke came from many of their windows. Roofs had collapsed on a few of them. The houses on the second street stood farther back, protected by walls. Thick bushes offered further protection. The best choice of a hiding place.

Farther along the street, shade bathed the homes. They looked untouched. He clambered over the wall of one, tried its door, and found it locked. He circled the house peering in windows, most of them shuttered from inside. In a garden at the back, roses bloomed.

The beauty of a yellow blossom proved irresistible. Domingo bent to smell its fragrance. *Who can believe beauty in such a time and place?*

The walls between adjoining houses were low. Domingo jumped one and proceeded from house to house. None of them showed any sign of occupancy. At the last one, the street intersected a boulevard. He stepped into it looking up and down, having no idea which way to go. His shoulders sagged.

He couldn't give up. Cristina might be in the next house. He cursed himself for letting Bullfrog get away. His only link! He had to keep searching. Yet the longer he spent exploring empty homes, the greater Tupatu's wrath would be. Besides, he might be needed if Pope decided to attack the fortress.

A new urgency overtook him. Domingo shaded his eyes and scanned the nearest homes. Four houses to his left, a woman screamed. A harquebus roared, and pandemonium followed. Domingo hesitated only a moment. The house might be where Cristina was hiding.

He dashed half-way to it when four Indians burst from the front door screaming victory calls. The first man waved a scalp above his head. Blood splattered onto his shoulders. Domingo couldn't see what the next two carried although their arms were full. The last man held a head aloft in his right hand, a long black mane flowing down over his arm. Whatever he waved in his left hand couldn't be identified.

Domingo blinked, shook his head, and squinted to make certain what he saw. The last man was Harelip. The head he held still dribbled blood. His left arm was also soaked in blood dripping from whatever it was he held in his left hand.

Harelip squelched his scream when he saw Domingo. He glared at him. Then his lips broke into a vicious grin. He stomped a mock war dance in a circle waiting for Domingo to reach him.

"You want to kiss a Spanish bitch—like you kissed my wife?" He lowered the head to jab it in Domingo's face.

Domingo blanched and turned away in horror.

"Maybe you'd prefer to suck Spanish tit?" Harelip thrust his left hand toward Domingo. Domingo guessed it held a severed breast.

"See if you like it better than my wife's." His laugh that followed was maniacal. He raised both hands and danced another circle.

"I never touched your wife." Domingo could not have been more emphatic, but on second thought guessed he had touched her when she jumped onto his lap. He blushed. Harelip was too engrossed in his blood lust to notice. He kept jumping up and down with his trophies. Drops of blood struck Domingo on his face. He had to fight back the bile flooding his mouth. The first three Indians half danced, half trotted down the street.

Before Harelip joined them, he turned to sneer at Domingo. "You can go scalp the bitch's sweet spot. I've never seen so much hair." He snickered. "I won't tell anyone that you're too cowardly to kill." He screeched his maniacal laugh.

It felt hard to breath. Domingo couldn't shake the image of the head and bloody breast. *Is this what revenge is about? How many times have I thought of killing Lucas?*

Domingo tasted half digested horse. He spit out the vomit. He'd have to search the house for signs of Cristina.

Every drawer had been emptied. Clothes, papers, even jewelry were strewn about. When Domingo didn't find the corpse he dreaded to find, he thought the slaughter must have occurred elsewhere. Until he entered the room farthest from the door. A naked body stretched out on the floor. The head was missing and only a bloody mess oozed from the crotch. Domingo identified it as a man from the hair on its chest. In a corner the body of a woman was propped against the wall. He could tell the sex from the one breast that remained.

Domingo retched until every stomach muscle ached. He staggered into a front room, collapsed onto a sofa and passed out.

TWENTY EIGHT

Domingo lingered on his return to the hillside, the morning sun spreading its red to the wisps of clouds dancing on the eastern horizon. He couldn't believe he had slept most of a day and a full night. How could he explain his overnight absence and the harquebus he carried? Tupatu could banish him for desertion, he guessed. Surely, he'd not let him out of his sight again.

Tupatu was talking with half a dozen Indians. They laughed as they took their leave. Tupatu's wrath might not be so great. "I couldn't find your brother," Domingo said.

"He probably spent the day sleeping. I dozed a little myself."

"What's happened?" Domingo wondered if Tupatu was leading up to a joke or a rebuke.

"A dull day. Nothing to do but watch cattle die. The sheep are so weak they've stopped their bleating." Tupatu yawned.

"What do we report to Po-pe?"

"I got a message from him. He's making the rounds to encourage the troops so we can't get in touch with him."

"Is he setting a day for a new attack?" Domingo didn't expect an answer even if Tupatu knew, but he couldn't help asking.

"He's building morale. A lot of these men have fields to harvest. Without any action, they'll leave for home."

"So. Do you want me to look for your brother again?" Domingo felt his face flush.

Tupatu looked at him closely. "What are you really looking for?" He emphasized really.

Domingo stared at his feet. "My wife." *I can't lie to him.* "She's almost my wife. My father's sent a go-between." *It's not exactly a lie. Dad promised he'd send a go-between.* "Yesterday I ran into a servant of the *encomendero* she worked for. He was about to take me to her when a search party stopped us. The servant got away while they questioned me."

Tupatu grinned in sympathy. "I'd guess the fortress will hold out another day. Even when Otermin surrenders, there won't be much to do. Keep a record of whatever priests accompany them, I suppose."

Shame filled Domingo. Until now he hadn't realized the importance of what he had learned from Bullfrog. He relayed to Tupatu that he'd been told the priest at San Ildefonso had died and Lucas of San Juan lived. When he explained how he had found out, Tupatu said it was worth making a note of, but they'd need better confirmation than the word of a Mexican servant.

Domingo stood with his head bowed.

Tupatu barked at him in mock anger. "Get out of here. Go find your wife-to-be."

"I'll be back as soon as I do." Domingo dashed down the hill. It proved too much for his legs, and he took a tumble. The harquebus flew from his hand. When he stood up to shake himself off and adjust his bow, he heard Tupatu laughing. He picked up the weapon with a sheepish grin.

A block from the plaza, Domingo ran into a search party getting organized for the day. When he asked what they had found, the leader scowled at him but answered. An elderly couple had been hiding in a root cellar. They must have known where other Spanish hid. The leader had twisted the arm of the old woman until it broke. Her scream caused the husband to weep, but he refused to talk. The search party killed them.

Domingo's stomach turned. His tongue stuck to the roof of his mouth. *How can we ever be known as the gentle people after this? Or was it being gentle that cost us our freedom?* On the far side of the plaza, two groups of men sat on the ground throwing sticks. Domingo smiled. Even in a revolution his people took time to gamble. Farther on he could identify the smoke from camp fires that contrasted with the black plumes issuing from rubble. He stopped at one and was handed a chunk of meat. He couldn't tell if it once had brayed or whinnied.

He was getting his bearings on the street where he had encountered Bullfrog when horns blared from behind him. He twirled at the harshness of the sound just in time to see horses dashing from the fortress gate. The lead soldiers carried flags and banners. The silver tops of their poles glistened in the sunlight. Behind them two men in armor stood trumpeting ruthless calls to battle. More men on horseback poured out of the gate and fanned into a skirmish line. Behind them foot soldiers, armed with spears and maces, gathered. They glared toward their enemy while keeping an eye on servants around them armed with axes or knifes.

Domingo's mouth went dry. Other soldiers pulled two cannons from the fortress and wheeled them into position. While they scrambled to ready their weapons, the cavalry charged. Domingo ran to hide behind a thick adobe wall.

The cavalry reached the gamblers and other Indians on the plaza before they recovered from their surprise. Ones that weren't trampled by the horses were cut down by swords. Here and there pistol shots rang out. Domingo's heart pounded. He notched an arrow and shot at a horseman. It ricocheted off his armor. The soldier looked in vain for the archer. Domingo shot another arrow at the man's horse. It reared but managed to stand. It tried to shake out the arrow in its right front leg, limping as if hobbled.

The cavalry veered to the left, followed by the infantry. The Spanish had cleared the plaza when the two cannon fired their rounds. Domingo never heard anything like the thunderous roar that blasted his ears. He shook his head, convinced he was deaf.

He looked around. In the ruins with thin walls, half a dozen Indians lay dead or wounded, cut down by the grapeshot. Two were screaming for help. Another begged for someone to end his pain. The horse that Domingo had wounded was down, but its rider limped after his companions. The Spaniard stopped when he saw Domingo standing in a daze, drew his pistol and fired. Fragments of adobe struck Domingo in the face. He felt his cheek. When he drew his hand away, it was covered with blood. Domingo sat, held the bottom of his tunic to his wound and waited. His head spun. He dropped it between his knees to steady himself. Nausea replaced the dizziness.

He moved so he could prop his back against the adobe wall. *I've got to fight. I can't look for Cristina now.*

He staggered from behind the wall. The man who had shot at him was running toward the fort. The nausea left Domingo as he followed after the main force. The Spanish had headed toward the river. Indians lived on its south side. Following the tracks, he came to the ford. The water was muddy from all the horses which had crossed. He plunged in. At the middle, water came to his waist. He lifted the harquebus high, felt his belt for the powder horn, and lifted it.

As he struggled out on the other side, Domingo saw a cluster of huts made of wood scraps and whatever other materials were left over from Spanish construction. *How can my people live like this? Strange! I never thought of them as my people before.* The roofs were covered with branches, their leafy protection long gone. The smell of human waste was over powering.

Domingo noticed two naked toddlers in front of a shack. They were tossing dust in the air and batting it in each other's direction. A young girl came out, saw Domingo, and grabbed the children's arms to drag them inside.

He heard a noise behind him, turned and saw two near naked Indians running toward the Spanish with poles, topped by strips of cloth. He guessed the men were slaves, but had no idea what they carried.

The Spanish cavalry halted at the end of the Indian quarters. When the slaves reached them, each of the men on horseback took a pole. One of them did something with his pistol that caused a flash, and the end of the pole burst into flame. The other soldiers lit their poles and started torching the Indian dwellings.

Domingo dashed to the home where he had seen the children play. Inside, a woman, girl, and the two toddlers cringed in a corner. He grabbed the toddlers, hoping the girl and woman would follow. The girl struck him on his back. He grimaced. He pointed the mother to the other toddler. She followed him outside. Domingo motioned to the Spanish setting fires. The woman whimpered. Domingo released the girl, lifted the toddler to his shoulder and headed toward the river.

The toddler struggled on Domingo's shoulder, Domingo slipped, but stayed upright. At the other side, he set the boy down. In a moment, the girl stood beside him to take the child's hand. A cry from the far river bank made him turn. The woman stood quaking, the child in her arms. The girl must have explained that her mother was frightened of water, but there was no time to find out. Domingo crossed the river again, took the woman by the waist and pulled her along. She screamed alarm at the middle of the river but clung to Domingo with her free arm while clutching her child with the other.

On the other side of the river the girl and woman embraced, tears flowing. The woman kissed Domingo's hand. The toddlers stood quietly, their frightened eyes fixed on Domingo. As the crackle of the fire turned into a roar, they turned to watch the flames engulf the tinder dry homes of the Indians. Domingo would never forget the screams that followed. The odor of burning human flesh was even worse.

Domingo pointed the family to what he guessed was the safest part of the city, realized that the woman and girl knew more than he did, and set off at a trot to the fortress, expecting Po-pe to attack while the Spanish force pillaged and burned the Indian village.

When he reached the plaza, he found utter confusion. A handful of Indians had gathered, anticipating an attack on the emptied garrison. Other Indians were carrying off the dead and tending to the wounded. Scattered shots rang out from the Spanish headquarters to compound the chaos.

Domingo headed for the hill to rendezvous with Tupatu. Half way up the hill he encountered him, his good eye scanning in every direction. When he stopped before Domingo, he licked cracked lips. "I underestimated Otermin. Never thought he'd attack. I guess the lack of water made him desperate."

"He burned the homes of the Indians on the south side of the river. It was terrible."

"Doesn't make sense, unless he felt it was punishment for disobedience. At any rate, in the confusion every man and woman inside the fort rushed to the stream. They carried water in anything that'd hold it."

"How long will the supply last?" Domingo asked.

"Four or five days, I'd guess."

"What do we do now?"

"Right now, we get in position to watch who goes back inside. We can use an accurate count of their troops. They probably put every able bodied Spaniard into the foray."

The two found a house nearby the entrance. One crumbling wall offered adequate cover for their watch. Remaining walls on two sides offered further protection. It made a perfect outpost.

Domingo had just adjusted himself to a slot in the wall when he saw three Indian women fleeing inside the gate, half carrying a large Spanish woman. Despite her disarray she held her skirt high. It was more tattered than her blouse. A boy cowered behind her. His yellow coat had ripped at the seams, its sleeves stained and torn. An old Indian limped behind him, his hand on the boy's back to urge him forward. His tunic was torn down the back. He was missing one of his moccasins.

A tall, lean Spaniard without armor jerked the reins of a prancing horse, circling behind the entourage. The dust from the horse's hooves obscured Domingo's view. On the fringes of the dust cloud, a man in a tattered robe resembling a cassock, struggled with a Spanish girl who had collapsed against the fortress wall. He was unable to pull her to her feet.

At that moment, two Spanish boys dashed toward the gate from around the corner of the fortress. Water splashed from the buckets they carried. The man with the girl called to them, but they dodged him to rush inside. A pudgy Spaniard with a barrel on one shoulder followed. The man in the robe reached toward him. The man hesitated, then grabbed the girl's arm and jerked her upright while holding tight to the barrel. He jogged toward the gate without a backward glance.

Domingo cursed himself for being moments late to watch. Cristina could have been one of the women dashing into the fortress. From their backs, he had not been able to judge if the women were young or old. If he had been on watch before the mounted man stirred so much dust, he would have been able to tell whether or not the man in the robe was Lucas. And if he had not propped his harquebus against a wall, it wouldn't be out of reach. He held the back of his hand to his teeth and bit hard. Would he ever be able to kill Lucas? And was his beloved now inside or did she remain prey for some Indian search party?

TWENTY NINE

Domingo had retrieved his harquebus and taken off his bow. He scrutinized every street, each ally, the sides of the fort in case another family ran for the garrison's protection. He wiped sweat from his forehead. The battered building he and Tupatu occupied offered no protection from the sun but blocked the breeze that stirred a dust devil in the plaza. The wind sufficed to carry the stench of dead animals from inside the fort to Domingo's nose. He wondered when the dead bodies in the plaza would begin to stink.

"Can you stay awake?" Tupatu's question startled him.

"Sure. Why not?"

"I figured you might have found your wife-to-be. You'd have spent a sleepless night with her." Tupatu chuckled.

Domingo shook his head. "I didn't find her."

"Oh," Tupatu smirked. "Someone else then?"

Domingo didn't bother with an answer.

"Have you slept with her often?" Tupatu asked.

"A few times."

"Is she good?"

Domingo didn't like being distracted from his observation. His shrug was noncommittal.

"Be sure the sex is good. Don't marry not knowing that."

"It's very good." Domingo's answer was curt.

"These Spanish priests corrupted our youth. Urging chastity before marriage. If they don't enjoy a good lay, that's up to them, but they shouldn't force such a ludicrous idea on us."

"They forced many things on us." Domingo thought of the many churches his people had built while Spanish ranchers never lifted a hand to help.

"It will be a new land when we're rid of them." Tupatu leaned toward his observation slit. He wiped his good eye and blinked. "Do you see movement in that alley across from us?"

"Yes," Domingo hissed. He caught his breath. Bullfrog's head protruded from behind a house in ruins. His bug eyes peered in all directions. He retreated behind a crumbling wall. Domingo was about to chase him, but Bullfrog reappeared, glanced right and left, then crossed the street in a crouch.

Moments later, a man dressed in a dirt stained tunic, torn at the neck, followed. He wore a cloth over his head as if bandaging a wound. Domingo studied his unprotected face. It was smeared with soot, but a short black beard, badly cut, was obvious. The breechcloth he wore failed to cover his white legs. The man scanned the plaza and looked behind him. He clasped the hand of a preteen girl.

Her tattered buckskin dress reached to the ground. She could have passed for Indian except for the way she clung to the man's hand. *They've lived a lifetime among us yet never realized a girl would not hold her father's hand like that.* A humpbacked Indian hovered behind the father and daughter to protect their rear. The four walked slowly but deliberately toward the fortress gate. The man halted, turned and called in the direction of the corner.

Domingo reached for his bow, thought again, and retrieved his harquebus. *Surely Lucas accompanies them.* He crept to a part of the wall where he had knocked out a niche for the gun. He trained the weapon on the corner, waiting for Lucas to appear.

A tall woman turned the corner instead. He smirked at the tattered buckskin she wore. She carried herself in a haughty bearing to give herself away. *What a blow it must be to have to wear such a garment!* She limped but held her head high. Domingo couldn't believe that she carried a fan.

Tupatu snickered. "She'll need that fan inside the fort. It's got to be hot as their hell."

An elderly Indian woman caught up with the señora to take her arm. The señora leaned against her retainer. At that moment, Cristina rounded the corner, hurrying to the señora's other side. Domingo's heart leapt to his throat. He stood up to see better.

At that moment, Lucas rounded the corner, scurrying to join the entourage. He wore a stained tunic over his robe, but it failed to cover the cassock hem. The kerchief around his forehead would have fooled no one on second glance. Even from his post, Domingo could see profuse sweat on the priest's face. He was sure he caught the stink of a rotten onion.

Domingo was hardly aware of other Indians and Spanish bringing up the rear because his eyes never left Cristina and Lucas. Cristina's eyes never left the señora whose limp gave way to a stumble as she approached the gate. Lucas kept a mere pace behind the señora, his head down.

Domingo steadied the harquebus on Lucas. Before he squeezed the trigger, an arrow whizzed between Cristina and Lucas. When it struck the adobe wall, Lucas gave a shout that was mostly whine. He pushed Cristina forward and took her place beside the señora, holding tight to her arm. The señora lost her composure. She struck the priest's head with her fan, knocking away the kerchief and revealing a bald white spot among tousled black.

Tupatu guffawed. Domingo cursed, easing up on the trigger. The señor returned to his wife to urge her on, but she would not hobble any faster. The señor's glare forced Lucas back a step.

The party reached the shelter of a roof offering protection from arrows. It did not protect Lucas from a gun shot. Domingo leveled his weapon, aimed, and fingered the trigger. Lucas looked in his direction. Terror flooded his face. Domingo dropped the shoulder holding the harquebus. Its front end rose. The gun's blast knocked Domingo back two paces, but he managed to remain standing. Tupatu roared laughter.

Domingo rushed to look. His ball had crashed into the wall above Lucas's head. Dust from the adobe lingered in the air. Lucas clutched one arm. Cristina was screaming. She and the elderly Indian woman lifted the señora by her arms and ran. At the fortress gate the señor shielded them with his body. Domingo's mouth stayed open until the whole Baca party dashed inside.

Domingo dropped into a corner to sit, holding his head in his hands. His ears roared from the belch of the harquebus. He rubbed his nose trying to rid it of the foul odor of burnt gun powder. He sniffed his fingers. He'd never smelled such evil. His belch tasted of smoky vomit.

Tupatu came over and squatted before him. He took a strip of dried meat from his belt. "Chew on this. Real meat, venison. No braying or whinnying."

Domingo's hand went to his throat to finger the leather pouch. He had come through all the combat without a scratch. He must remember to tell his father what power the fetish held.

He chewed reluctantly until the meat brought saliva to his mouth. It reminded him that he had nothing to drink all day, but his mouth began to feel refreshed. He'd wait until nightfall when they could slip away from their outpost.

Tupatu's smile was infectious. Domingo grinned back. "Where'd you get venison in the middle of a war?"

"Off a dead Indian. He looked like he just arrived—clean tunic, new moccasins. Not a scratch on him except for a gash in his forehead. I'd guess grapeshot. But I haven't seen many grapeshot wounds."

"You going to ask why I didn't kill that priest?"

"You'll tell me if you want. Otherwise it's not my concern."

"I don't know why." Domingo's voice was plaintive.

"You don't know why you couldn't kill him, or you don't know why it's not my concern?" Tupatu forced a straight face.

Domingo giggled at his friend's play on words. "I've seen too much killing. Too much lust for killing. I couldn't do it."

"It won't matter," Tupatu said. "We'll starve the villains out." He stood to stretch. "Was your wife-to-be part of the group?"

"Yes. She was propping up the señora. She dashed through the gate after I shot." He looked at Tupatu. Anxiety gnawed at his belly. "How will she survive the siege?"

"She'll get food inside. But the water supply won't last long. They couldn't have carried much." Tupatu was interrupted by the sight of the man with the barrel, running for a refill. "Gimme that gun."

Domingo handed him the gun. He unbuckled the heavy leather belt with its powder horn and last ball, glad to be rid of its evil weight.

Tupatu loaded the harquebus and threw the belt into a corner. He went to another part of the wall and carved out a niche to position the gun. "They can't have enough containers for more than a few days. Thirst will drive them out."

Before the water carriers reappeared, a trumpet blast made them both turn. Otermin was returning from the south side of town. Domingo saw why he had been gone so long. He led a line of Indians being prodded forward by Spanish soldiers. They were tied to each other at the neck like slaves.

"Get a count," Tupatu told Domingo.

Domingo's face burned. *Where is Po-pe? Why aren't we attacking them?*

As if he had read his mind, Tupatu said, "No one expected him to take prisoners. He ought to be satisfied with the couple hundred Indians he burned alive."

Domingo noted the first twenty. The twenty-first was a boy who hadn't reached puberty. When he was directly opposite Domingo, the lad dropped to his knees and bowed his head to a soldier. His actions choked the men in front and behind even though they bent to give him slack. He clasped his hands as if in prayer. Tears ran down his cheeks. The soldier gave no sign of listening to him. Instead, he kicked him in the face. The blow knocked the boy's head back. At the same time the soldier grabbed the rope and pulled him upright. The jerk muffled a scream of pain.

Guards at the front were whipping their prisoners, not realizing why they were being held back. With the boy in place, the prisoners jogged forward. When the line ended, Domingo had counted forty-seven captives.

"Why do you think Otermin took prisoners?" Domingo asked.

"He wants to know what's happened to his relief force. It's not likely any of those Indians could know, but each of them will have a rumor to report. Let's hope most of them have heard Garcia retreated to Mexico."

Domingo licked at cracked lips. "When can we leave to get a drink?"

"We could use a little food, too." Tupatu rubbed his stomach.

For the first time Domingo noticed how gaunt his friend looked. “I’ll go see what I can scrounge.”

“No. It’ll be dark soon. Safer then. Besides Otermin might try to surprise us again. No telling what’s going on in that crazy head of his.”

Domingo fingered his bow while he sat. His mind raced with thoughts of Cristina. What was her fate inside the governor’s quarters? As he slipped into a light sleep, he wondered if Francesca was alright.

Tupatu’s whisper awakened him. He didn’t know how long he’d dozed. It was growing dark. He started to rise, but Tupatu put a hand on his shoulder to keep him from standing.

“They’ve brought the prisoners out. Still tied.”

The Indians were strung out in a line. They stood on the edge of the plaza facing the fortress. The boy had regained his composure, staring fixedly at the fifty soldiers who faced them. The soldiers lifted their harquebuses. The boy spat in their direction, a gambit he must have learned from the conquerors.

At the end of the line, a soldier raised his sword and yelled “fire.” The volley knocked down all the prisoners but one. He trembled, started to run, but the rope around his neck stopped him. The man with the sword ran to him. He almost decapitated the Indian with a single blow. He finished the job with a second slash as the corpse dropped to its knees. Another soldier raced to the bodies and stabbed one corpse after another. Two of his companions rushed to drag him away. A rain of arrows came from Indians on the far side of the plaza. One caught a soldier in the leg, but most fell short or ricocheted off armor.

Domingo stood frozen. Sweating like he had never sweated before, yet a chill raced through him. Tupatu put a hand on his shoulder. “Let’s find Po-pe. Maybe he can make sense of this.”

THIRTY

Po-pe was not at his headquarters, but an aide gave Tupatu and Domingo directions as to where he might be. They lost their way in the dark a few times but eventually found him. He was seated at a desk under a ramada, finishing a plate of beans and meat. The remains of two pears lay beside the plate. Three candles in a candelabra flickered over his meal. Domingo's nose twitched at the aroma of venison. Po-pe dismissed the three men with him when he looked up to see Tupatu.

"You have news?" Po-pe's eyes were as piercing as ever.

"We watched the Spaniards burn the Indian village on the south side of the river. No Indians resisted the attack." The accusatory ring in Tupatu's last sentence startled Domingo.

"The Keresans did not follow my orders. They were responsible for protecting that side of Santa Fe." Po-pe's eyes bored into Tupatu. Domingo felt Tupatu's loyalty was being questioned.

Tupatu glared in return. "No one did anything later when the Spaniards executed forty-seven prisoners on the plaza."

Po-pe hesitated. Domingo thought one eyebrow shot up, but in the wavering candle light he couldn't be certain.

"Tell me what you saw," Po-pe said. "I've had varying accounts."

Tupatu described the event in detail, including Otermin's wounds. Domingo stood in awe at his friend's mastery of recall and vowed to follow his example.

"That confirms what I knew," Po-pe said.

He sounds as if he's bluffing. Is he only pretending to know about the executions? Domingo shuddered. Maybe Po-pe wasn't the omnipotent leader he had believed him to be.

Tupatu must have had doubts, too. "Are we ready for any future forays? Who's responsible if Otermin attacks again?"

Po-pe spoke with reassurance that he controlled everything. He named pueblos responsible for certain sectors although he filled in few details.

"What do you want from us?" Tupatu asked.

"Go back to your outpost. Our first priority is to learn what Otermin believes about Garcia's southern force. If he thinks it's retreated, he'll surrender soon."

"Do we execute him then?" Tupatu asked.

"We'll let him go, if he goes in peace. We don't need any more deaths among ourselves. Freedom is our revenge."

The answer seemed to satisfy Tupatu. He said nothing more. They had turned to leave when Po-pe called them back to share his meal.

Po-pe's confidence infused Domingo until he and Tupatu had returned to their outpost. Domingo curled up in a corner and tried to sleep but his mind raced. *How can Po-pe coordinate so many different pueblos? Is he pretending to know much of what he claims to know? Is he shrewd or is he devious?*

Shortly before dawn, Domingo awoke from a nightmare. He, Cristina, and Francesca stood in the plaza tied together. Lucas was aiming a harquebus at them. Domingo wanted to tell Tupatu about the dream, but his friend was nowhere about. He reached for his bow and rose to study the fort. Absolute stillness reigned until broken by a footstep. Domingo swung around.

It was Tupatu. He carried a large jug of water and a basketful of tortillas. "We'll be better prepared today."

"How did you find tortillas?" Domingo laid down his bow as he squatted to eat.

"I saw wood smoke at first light. Guessed it must be a cook fire. Sure enough, half a dozen women were making tortillas."

"They're selling tortillas in the middle of a battle field?"

"You should know better!" Tupatu growled. "They know there are men to be fed. Half were speaking Keresan, the others Tewa."

"They have anything besides tortillas?" Domingo thought of the meat he had enjoyed the past few days.

"Lot of gossip. Except I fear most of it is hard news. They removed the bodies of the executed last night. They couldn't find relatives for five of the dead." He sniffed. "The horrors of war. No relative around to bury you."

Domingo took a deep breath. That was a horror he hadn't considered. In his pursuit of Cristina, he never thought about the absence of relatives.

"One woman was in Indian town when it burned. More than two hundred died. When people fled the fire, the Spanish slaughtered them."

"How did she get out?"

"She had diarrhea. Had gone extra far to relieve herself. When she returned, the Spanish were burning everything in sight."

Domingo broke the silence that followed. "I hope Po-pe has inclded women in his spy system."

Tupatu rubbed at his eye socket, nodding agreement.

"Maybe they can do our work for us here." Tupatu went to a corner, took off his bow, and squirmed to find comfort in the rubble. "Another long day with nothing to do but wait."

Domingo watched while Tupatu slept, glad that his friend could nap. He looked up. Not a single cloud dotted the liquid blue sky. Domingo scanned the plaza and the fort once more before lifting the jug to his lips. The water was warm but satisfying.

He had just returned to the wall when a shot exploded around the corner of the fortress, followed by a grunt. He looked in vain for an explanation. A second shot rang out inside the building. Tupatu had leaped to his feet at the first explosion and stood beside Domingo watching.

"We'll have to wait until dark to find an answer. Why would any one fire an harquebus inside the fort?"

Curiosity got the better of them shortly after sundown. They crawled from their post to an alley to see down the eastern wall. The body of an Indian dressed in rags laid near it.

"We'll never know what happened," Domingo said.

"Wait. He moved."

"He is alive."

"They may be using him for bait. Don't make a sound."

The two crawled to the prone form lying face down. They lifted him by his arms and dragged him to cover. When they got him into a sitting position, Domingo gasped. The man's guts leaked from his belly. Even in the starlight he saw the ash stained face was drained of blood.

Tupatu sobbed. "Little brother."

A chill swept Domingo. He dropped to his knees beside Tupatu Two helping cram intestines back into his wound. Tupatu Two gasped in spurts.

"What were you doing at the wall in daylight?" Tupatu asked his brother.

"Poor Indians are selling the Spanish water. I tried to pass as one to contact my spy." His eyes had a film on them.

"Did you talk to him?"

"Her," Tupatu Two lisped between labored breaths. "Otermin's servant. You can tell Po-pe the governor is convinced his southern force has retreated. She heard him cursing Garcia for cowardice."

"What took him so long to be convinced?"

"It was the prisoners he took. Most said nothing, but those who did claimed they knew Garcia's force was fleeing to El Paso."

"Po-pe will want to reward your spy. How will we know her?"

"It was his niece, Teresa. They shot her after they shot me. I heard her scream a curse at them."

"I'll go for a medicine man," Domingo said.

Tupatu Two wriggled into a sitting position. Domingo grabbed for more intestines that oozed from his stomach. "No need to," Tupatu Two said. He looked at Tupatu. "It's time big brother. Repay me for all those women I lined up for you."

Tupatu notched an arrow. "A few weren't half bad looking, either."

"Get me upright." Tupatu Two spit up blood.

Domingo never felt so chilled in his life as he realized what was happening. He muttered a "no" under his breath as he saw Tupatu draw his bow.

"I hope you shoot straight, you old one-eyed fart."

Tupatu must have been prepared for his little brother's quip. The point of his arrow didn't waver. Domingo felt its impact before he heard the bow's twang. He sprang back from the body, ran to a wall, and choked on sobs. When he returned, Tupatu had his brother's body in his arms to carry up the hill. The soul could watch the Spanish retreat.

Who will bury me if I'm killed here? When I'm killed here?

THIRTY ONE

When Tupatu and Domingo reported the deaths of Tupatu Two and Teresa to Po-pe, he told them that Teresa was his favorite niece. Yet a dry swallow after the word niece showed his only sign of remorse. Immediately, he questioned them about what Tupatu Two had said, demanding to know his exact words. When Tupatu stumbled on a phrase, Po-pe turned to Domingo. Domingo gave a word for word account. Only after Domingo repeated what he had said, did Po-pe seem satisfied.

Domingo felt a black shroud descend. Was so little feeling the price of freedom? But who was he to condemn Po-pe? Hadn't lust for revenge choked off his own feelings? He hung his head until Po-pe told him he had work to do. "We have Spanish documents signed by Otermin. Copies of past orders. You will compose one to Lt. Garcia from Otermin saying his force verges on collapse, he is about to surrender, and expects to be imprisoned. Order Garcia to return to Mexico to save Spanish lives. You must convince Garcia that the Spanish cause is hopeless."

"But Garcia may be dead," Tupatu interjected.

Po-pe glowered at him. "Whoever is in command will read our forgery. That's all we need."

Po-pe ushered the two of them to a desk with two chairs. He sat at one and directed Domingo to take the other. Tupatu stood. The three composed in a style based on the captured documents. Po-pe dictated a general outline, Tupatu added an idea here and there, Domingo worked their thoughts into Spanish style. When they finished, Domingo admired their shrewdness.

As he read back the copy, Po-pe added a few phrases, deleted others. Domingo flexed his fingers as he read aloud what he hoped was the final copy. Po-pe and Tupatu smiled their satisfaction.

Domingo practiced a forgery of the governor's signature. The paper and quill Po-pe provided were the best he'd ever held. Even though his fingers ached, he was tempted to begin with an illumination. He shook off the thought and reached for a page of poor quality paper.

He practiced a dozen times. Po-pe frowned. Tupatu asked, "Why use more than one signature?"

"Each Spaniard writes in a different style. Otermin's officers will recognize his style."

"It all looks like scratches to me," Tupatu said.

"It's like our pottery," Domingo said. "You can tell your mother's pottery from your wife's, can't you?"

"Sure. Anyone can." Tupatu fingered his chin. "You mean the writing is like an art?"

"Something like that. A few write clearly, others with a flourish."

"What about Otermin?" Po-pe asked.

"A lot of flourish."

"He should have become an artist," Tupatu said. "Maybe he would have stayed in Spain instead of dying here."

Po-pe laughed but admonished Tupatu. "We want Otermin out of our country. He can live if it means saving Indian lives."

Domingo rubbed his knuckles. He had filled a page with practice signatures. He took the orders he had written. At the bottom he signed Otermin's name with a flourish. He was ready to return to his outpost to watch for Cristina.

"I need a courier to convince whoever commands the southern force that this is Otermin's order." Po-pe's eyes tunneled into Domingo's. "One who won't gag at the Spanish stink."

"We should have a Spaniard deliver it," Tupatu said.

"I've thought of that," Po-pe said. "But there's no one we can trust. It must be one of us. One who can convince the vultures he sympathizes with them."

Domingo's stomach tightened.

"Someone who speaks fluent Spanish. Understands their religion. Could swear an oath on their Bible and be convincing." Po-pe fingered the fetish around Domingo's neck. "Someone who'd wear a cross instead of a fetish." He and Tupatu chuckled.

"I've just found my wife-to-be." Domingo's words were frantic. "She's inside the fort. I can rescue her from my outpost. Surely, you can find another messenger."

"No one better than you." Po-pe put a hand on Domingo's shoulders, but it was his eyes that Domingo felt.

Domingo begged. "From the outpost I can rescue her—soon. Can't the message wait?"

"Go to your outpost. You don't have to leave until morning."

"But it's dusk now." Domingo hated the whine in his voice.

"You'll be rested for your run." Po-pe's tone left no room for compromise.

"But I've never been down river. I don't know where Garcia's force is."

"No one does right now." Po-pe's tone showed impatience. "They'll be scavenging food from either Sandia or Isleta Pueblos while they wait word from Otermin. Indians along the way will have a good idea where they are. You speak the language of the Sandians. That's another reason you're the perfect messenger."

Domingo's eyes appealed to Tupatu. He turned away. When Domingo started to protest, Po-pe draped a necklace with a cross over Domingo's head. "Put your fetish away."

Domingo's arguments were exhausted. Po-pe's logic overwhelmed him. He stifled his feeling for Cristina. So close and yet so far.

When Domingo awoke the next morning, Tupatu was gone. He studied the fortress, but only a trace of wood smoke rose from the courtyard. He examined the soles of his moccasins. Both were worn through. *I can't run three days in these. And how can I scrounge food? I've got to wait here for Cristina. But I have the orders that will convince Garcia. Jesu Cristo.* He closed his eyes and shuddered. *Why am I swearing by a Christian god?*

Before despair could enshroud him, Tupatu crawled over the wall at the back of their outpost. He tossed Domingo two tortillas. They were still warm. Domingo was about to take a bite, when Tupatu motioned him to stop. He offered him a small pot filled with warm shredded meat in a sauce. Domingo wrapped the meat in a tortilla and devoured it.

"Figured you could use these, too," Tupatu said. He slung a Spanish canteen from one shoulder and a pouch from the other. "It's full of dried meat. Pretend it's venison."

Domingo sniffed. The putrid smell could have been anything. At least, he didn't see any green on it. The canteen he valued. It was vital for a run in unknown country.

"You probably can use these, too." Tupatu took three pairs of moccasins from his belt. They showed little sign of wear.

"Where did you get them? They're almost new."

"There were a lot to choose from." Tupatu nodded in the direction of the burned out town. "I had to guess at your size."

Domingo tried on a pair. They were barely large enough. He held the other two pairs to his feet. The match was close.

"Will you keep this for me?" Domingo gave the deer fetish to his friend. He felt a loss of warmth. The cold metal cross only added to his anxiety.

Tupatu seemed to read his mind. "I'll have it for you when you return. And I'll watch for your bride-to-be." He put the deer around his own neck. "I didn't get a good look at her, but if she's with that priest, I'll know them."

Domingo nodded his gratitude. "I'll count on it little father." It was the first time Domingo had used a kinship term for his friend. He wished the relationship had been a real one, the feelings certainly were.

"Be careful, little son. I know you'll convince the hairy devils to retreat. I'll meet you here afterwards."

Domingo fell into an exhausted heap that night. He was close enough to the Rio Grande to hear water lapping at pebbles. The sound lulled him to sleep.

A moaning awoke him before sunrise. He roused himself to investigate. In a clump of brush, he found an old woman tossing in her sleep. Her moaning no doubt came from the scratches on her face and arms. Pus oozed from a deep one running from her ear to her chin.

Domingo used his tunic to wipe the wound. The old woman opened her eyes, but Domingo couldn't tell if she saw him. She licked her lips and motioned with fingers down her throat. He guessed she was both thirsty and hungry. He lifted her to a sitting position and held the canteen to her lips. She gagged after the third swallow. He offered her a piece of dried meat. Since she didn't have any teeth, he thought the gesture futile, but she grabbed the morsel and gummed it. Domingo found a small piece, chewed it thoroughly, took the first piece from her mouth and replaced it with the one he had chewed. Her eyes shone in gratitude as she swallowed.

Her words that followed were incomprehensible. He guessed she spoke Keres. When she saw his blank stare, she gestured. From her motions, he assumed she had been left behind by a party of Spaniards. Possibly she was near her home. She signed that they were near a ford, and she wanted to be taken to the other side. *This is the last thing I need. How can I take time to help her? The revolution depends on me.* Domingo helped her to her feet while he argued with himself. She walked with his help.

She waved a finger at the water crossing, made him think she could swim, and the two hobbled to the river. Perhaps she had swum in her youth, but now she was helpless. Domingo put every effort into swimming when they no longer found a footing. It wasn't far to the other side, but Domingo emerged exhausted. He reached to his neck to finger his fetish. The cold cross chilled his spine. He checked to make sure his knife was intact. The doeskin scabbard reassured him. He shook his bow dry and hoped the water hadn't softened his bow string.

The woman gestured again, pointing down river. Her pueblo must be close. She tried walking alone, stumbled and fell. He helped her to her feet. It seemed forever, but the sun was still low when they reached a campfire where youngsters roasted a bird of some kind. The smell brought water to Domingo's mouth. The thought of his own meat made his stomach turn.

One of the youngsters darted forward, exclaiming what must be a term for grandmother and took the old woman's hand. Two older boys ran to help. The woman nodded at Domingo to be on his way. He smiled at her and turned to go, but another boy ran to him with the roasted bird, insisting he accept it. Domingo smiled his gratitude. He almost finished the bird with his first bite. Three or four bites later, he was trotting, pausing only a moment before plunging into the river.

Back on the river's east side, Domingo became conscious of what the trail told him. It was a well travelled route in ordinary times, now its traffic overflowed. Discarded clothing, tools, and religious relics marked the way. Many Indians traveled the route, too, judging from the pottery shards.

Domingo's mind wandered as he tired from the hurried pace. He had replenished his water numerous times when the trail led close to the Rio Grande, but his food supply was almost gone. His mouth watered at the memory of the roasted bird the boys gave him.

He ran into three Indians along the trail. They sought word about what was happening in Santa Fe. Domingo's conscience twinged as he lied to them that Otermin had surrendered.

That evening a smell of smoke told him that he neared the Spanish encampment outside Sandia Pueblo. He pictured a decent pallet after two nights spent wrestling rocky ground. He reached for his last bit of meat, held his nose, and chewed. His stomach growled in protest. He promised it he would find Indian hospitality near the Spanish camp.

The sun was low on the horizon when he came upon three soldiers who had butchered a pony. Strips of meat simmered on green sticks over a wood fire. A few pieces blackened, others oozed blood. The pungent smell of charred roast tantalized Domingo's nose.

The three men stared with contempt when Domingo hailed them. He slipped the cross from beneath his tunic. He couldn't interpret their grunts when he approached. In his best Spanish, he said, "I carry a message from Governor Otermin to Lt. Garcia. Would you be so kind as to direct me?"

"And I have a message for your cursed Po-pe." The tallest man turned, bent, and farted. The other two snickered.

"I wish I could carry the message to him. Perhaps something heavier." Domingo's humor eluded the three, but they quit scowling when they heard his fluent Spanish.

"What are you doing with a message from the governor?" the tall soldier said.

"I serve a priest, we made it inside the fort. The governor knew that only an Indian could penetrate the Indian barricade. Father Lucas guaranteed my loyalty to the governor."

"Let's see the message." The shortest of the three leered at Domingo, obviously skeptical.

"I've been instructed to give it only to the highest ranking officer here." Domingo's insides churned. He felt it'd be effective if he challenged their authority yet they were armed and looked ready to kill him without compunction.

The tall one must have been impressed. "I'll take him to Rodriguez," he muttered to the others. He stripped the meat from one stick and crammed it into his mouth. "I'll be back for the rest of my share. I'll kick ass if it's not roasting when I return." He gripped Domingo by an arm and pushed him forward.

The camp headquarters skirted Sandia. Its one tent had a guard. A dozen other men loitered nearby. The tall man spoke to someone in the tent, his voice rising. "All I know is he speaks Spanish better than me."

A small man with a nervous tic appeared. Domingo recognized sergeant's insignia and asked for Garcia. The sergeant said he was in command and demanded to know what Domingo wanted. The two sparred for some time until the Spaniard convinced Domingo that he was indeed in charge.

"I'll go on to Isleta, then. Otermin insisted I deliver his message to Lt. Commander Garcia."

"You won't find him there either."

"But Otermin is depending on me."

Rodriguez wrinkled his nose. He asked about conditions in Santa Fe. Domingo described how Indians blocked the fort's water supply, how the crowded animals died, and how desperate the Spanish were. He mentioned Otermin's foray, describing it as a hapless venture. As Domingo realized that Rodriguez admired his command of Spanish, his confidence grew. He depicted the sufferings of Spanish families in Santa Fe in vivid terms, implying their safety if Otermin surrendered.

Eventually, Rodriguez explained that he commanded only a squad of men. Lt. Commander Garcia had heard so many reports about Santa Fe's fall that he left for El Paso a few days after the revolt began. When rumors reached him that Otermin survived, he had sent Rodriguez north to learn what had happened.

"You can read for yourself." Domingo handed Rodriguez the forged document.

Rodriguez read the document half aloud, sounding out many of the words. He wiped at a tear. Without thinking whom he addressed, he said, "The order confirms everything I've heard."

Domingo turned to leave, but Rodriguez said, "Stay and eat with us. You must be hungry"

Domingo took a deep breath. He had hoped to leave for Santa Fe immediately. But if he refused the invitation, the sergeant might suspect him. Domingo repressed thoughts of Cristina and thanked Rodriguez profusely. Under his breath he cursed every Spaniard in the province of Nuevo Mexico.

THIRTY TWO

Domingo tasted little of Rodriguez's meal despite its flavoring of beef. Rodriguez steered the conversation toward conditions at the Santa Fe fort. Domingo invented details of Spanish suffering to convince Rodriguez that Otermin would have been foolish to hold out. When a servant appeared with a second offering of food, Domingo made an excuse to leave. His host insisted he stay. By the time Domingo left it was too dark to continue.

The next morning, he stood in the foothills watching the Spanish squad leave for the arduous down river trip. The soldiers made half hearted attempts to drive a few cows into a herd. Two vaqueros started them south. The one wagon the squad managed to load became mired in sand at the first rise. The soldiers cursed the driver, then the two oxen. A handful of Indian women and children passed the wagon without a second glance. Domingo committed the scene to memory. Po-pe would enjoy his account.

Domingo neared the end of his first day's run when he encountered an Indian settling down for the night. With gestures, he offered the man water, then asked him for food. The man offered a little half dried meat, its edges green. Domingo chewed slowly remembering Rodriguez's beef from the night before. Domingo tried Tewa and Tiwa on the Indian. The man answered in Spanish, explaining he was from Mexico. "Are you escaping to Mexico?" Domingo asked.

"It's so far I'd never make it." The man shrugged, his dull eyes suggesting he'd be at a loss without someone to direct him.

"Where are you going, then?"

The man's eyes glazed over. "I'm just avoiding the fighting."

"Why not stay in Santa Fc? Otermin is about to surrender." Domingo suspected the Mexican was hiding something.

"What have you heard? Weren't you coming from the south?"

Domingo thought fast. "I ran into my cousin fleeing Santa Fe. He probably passed you a while ago. He told me Otermin has surrendered. The city is in chaos."

"What am I to do?" the man beseeched Domingo. "My master sent me to tell Garcia to come north." The words were no sooner out of the man's mouth than he seemed to regret having spoken.

"I've come from Sandia," Domingo said. "The last Spanish troops headed south three days ago." A few days extra ought to discourage the Mexican.

"My master will kill me if I don't find Garcia." The threat did nothing to relieve the Mexican's exhaustion. He curled into a ball. In moments he was snoring.

Domingo dropped beside him, but sleep wouldn't come. He wondered how the man had found new moccasins yet carried no vessel for water. He looked incapable of a hard run, but there must be no chance for his message to reach Garcia. Domingo sucked in his lips, knelt silently over the snoring figure, and unsheathed his knife. His hand went high in the air, he put his shoulder into driving it down. The blade plunged into the Mexican's chest three times. Domingo sobbed, gagged, vomited. He stared long and hard at his blood covered hands refusing to believe what he had done.

Once his gagging stopped, he busied himself looking for rocks to cover the corpse. In the dark he found none. *I can only leave him for the scavengers. His body's just one more stick in the revolution game.* He bent over the corpse to take the man's moccasins, reached for the pouch with the putrid meat, crammed dried strips into his mouth and chewed. When he awoke in the morning, the stench of rotten meat in his mouth mixed with vomit. His head swirled in revulsion.

At mid-morning, Domingo had run exhausted, trying to forget the man he had murdered. Only an encounter with Indians coming down river brought him to a stop. His gestures to the Keresan speakers led nowhere, but Tiwa speakers followed them. Their accounts varied, but they agreed that Otermin was not far behind. The governor had surrendered to Po-pe and abandoned Santa Fe. The war was over.

Domingo was free to find Cristina.

He reached to his deer amulet to give him swiftness. The touch of cold metal soured his mouth even more. He jerked the cross from his neck and stomped it into the ground. The pause made him think. *Baca will retreat with Otermin. I can wait here for Cristina, spy on the party, and plan a way to rescue her. I'll be with her in no time!*

He climbed a nearby hill to look upriver. More Indians came into view followed by a dust cloud. Soon, horses pranced into sight. One rider carried a banner. Others held spikes. Po-pe had allowed the Spanish to keep their weapons for the retreat.

Oxen pulling wagons followed the horses. Spanish women and children struggled on foot so the column proceeded snail-like. In the middle of the confusion, Domingo saw ragged Indians sneaking in to steal baggage from the wagons. The drivers were so demoralized they raised no alarm.

Despite the chaos, Domingo glimpsed Lucas. His cassock was coated in dust as was the rest of him. He hobbled along using a cane. Even from a distance Domingo could see he gasped for breath. Domingo smelled his onion breath. He had a harder time picking out Cristina. Her hair was wrapped in a scarf covered with dust. Even more grime and dirt coated her face and dress. She tottered, often holding to the side of a wagon for support. Two streaks ran from her eyes creating channels in the dust.

We'll flee tonight. No one's in shape to pursue us. And why would they want to?

The column halted before him. A soldier at the rear encouraged stragglers to catch up. The looters struck again. When one neared the Baca wagon, a bearded man on horseback charged, swinging a sword. Domingo guessed him to be Baca. He slapped the blade on the Indian's back. The man shrieked and fled.

Baca looked around, shrugged his disdain, and shouted at his followers. They broke from the column and headed toward the river. Cristina struggled to keep up. Domingo didn't know what Baca had in mind, but he descended from the hill to mingle with the dusty crowd. Soon he had his own grimy disguise.

Once past the column, he caught up with the Baca party. No one said anything to him although two women eyed him with suspicion. He dropped back from the party, then crept along a ridge line to follow. He was close enough now that Cristina, Lucas, and Baca were easy to spot. Cristina limped and grasped the wagon for support.

Several times Baca rode to the river to scrutinize the shore line. Once he rode his horse into it. When water rose to cover his saddle, he turned back. *He's disgusted with Otermin's progress and is striking out on his own. I wonder how the trail is on the other side.*

At noon Baca stopped at a wide part of the river. He dismounted to remove his chain mail vest, shirt, and boots, then waded in. He was half way across when he began to swim. In a few strokes he found footing on the other side. Baca returned, shouted orders, and the party unloaded the wagon.

Workers lashed parts of it into a raft, adding drift wood logs provided by the flood waters. Domingo guessed that a good number of Baca's party could not swim. By late afternoon, two of the Spaniards were goading the oxen across. A few of the Indian men swam behind with switches.

Domingo's throat constricted when he saw Cristina crawl onto the raft with two older women. Three swimmers took the side of the raft and waded with it to the deep part. They struggled in the current. Water lapped over the raft. An old woman screamed. Cristina hid her face in the woman's skirt. The third woman fingered beads. When they reached the opposite side, the older women crossed themselves.

After the swimmers made three more trips with the raft, they looked at the setting sun and crossed themselves. Their shoulders drooped, they sat, Baca yelled at them, and they struggled to their feet. Domingo had crept close enough to hear their curses. Only Lucas and a soldier remained for the final trip. The priest argued with the soldier to remove his chest armor. The soldier refused saying it belonged to his father. The muttering of the swimmers showed their disgust.

Baca swore at the five men to get moving, then crossed on his horse while they dragged the raft into the river. One of the swimmers stepped on something and dropped to his knees, cursing. The two others laughed at him and pushed on. The wounded swimmer massaged his foot before struggling for the opposite shore alone.

In mid-river, the rope holding the logs to the wagon parts broke. The soldier pulled a tree trunk back to the piece of wood he held. When the water swirled him around, Domingo saw a face filled with horror. Domingo thought to help, but at that moment, the man lost his grip on the log. His armor sucked him under. A large bubble erupted on the surface.

The two swimmers reached the place where the soldier went under. One dived after him. He rose down stream far from the raft. One of the loosened logs struck the other swimmer in the throat. He went under, rising down stream holding a hand under his chin and screaming for help in a choked voice.

Domingo trotted down river keeping Lucas in sight. The priest clung to two boards, wrapping rope around them but failing to knot the rope. The river swirled him back toward Domingo. The religious lifted one side of his cassock, struggling to get it over his head. He went under. Domingo wondered if his pockets were filled with onions or gold.

Another swirl brought Lucas close to the bank. When the priest saw his pupil, he raised an arm and shouted. His head went under from the effort, but his hands held tight to the boards. He pulled himself up, looked for Domingo, pleaded for help when he saw him. Raw terror vied with strangulation in his desperate call. Domingo viewed him with contempt. *Why is he calling on me instead of God? Why should I help him? Why?*

THIRTY THREE

It didn't matter how much he hated Lucas. Domingo plunged into the river to save him. He recalled the times his playmates went swimming while Lucas drilled him on use of the Spanish subjunctive; nevertheless, he swam on. The current proved to be stronger than he thought, he glanced about to dodge large chunks of driftwood, then stroked harder.

The raft swept beyond Domingo's reach and swirled toward the deep center of the river. Forced to retreat to the shore, he ran down the river bank to a point well below the raft and waded to mid-stream to await Lucas.

In the moments he had, Domingo willed Lucas to lose his grip. He visualized the priest going under. The second time, the image was so strong Domingo turned toward the shore, but Lucas' hapless look persisted in Domingo's mind. He had to watch the approaching raft. Terror filled the priests' eyes. His plea for help was even more nerve wracking.

Domingo lunged for the raft, grasping a board. A wave caught him and splashed water in his mouth. He spit it out, in Lucas' direction. Terror turned to panic on the priest's face. Domingo said no reassuring words, but he pulled hard for the shore he had just left. Lucas pleaded with him. "Have pity." His voice cracked. "Take me to the other side."

"Too far in this current," Domingo coughed, more water lapping into his mouth.

"Baca will protect us from the savages." Lucas kicked his legs to propel the raft in the opposite direction.

"We can't make it." Domingo spat water with his words. "The current's too strong."

"I'm going down. Help," Lucas begged.

"Take off the cassock."

Lucas struggled with the heavy cloth, got half of it to his head. Domingo used one hand to tug at the garment. He had it almost over Lucas' head when a pistol dropped from an inner pocket. The thought of the priest carrying a weapon so stunned Domingo that he dropped the cassock. Its weight pulled Lucas under. Domingo dived, found the man's hair and pulled him to the surface. The priest's mouth formed a circle as if it searched for words. Domingo's loathing hit hard, yet he could not let go. He looked to the shore. The current spun them closer, but the river ran faster. Domingo sought in vain for a footing.

He pushed Lucas hard against the two boards that remained of the raft. The man's knuckles turned white from his desperate hold. Domingo kicked hard and pulled with his free hand. The rope tying the two boards gave way. The current sucked Lucas away from the board that Domingo held. Lucas screeched. Domingo let go the board and struggled toward the priest.

"No," Lucas shouted. "My board won't hold us both."

"I know." Domingo never felt so much disgust. "I'll pull you in while you hold on."

"Get away."

"I'll help you."

"You'll try to kill me." Lucas shoved a hand in Domingo's face. He pushed him under. Domingo emerged sputtering. He turned to swim to shore. Lucas beseeched him with a scream. His board shifted and the priest went under. Domingo swam back.

As he neared Lucas, the man kicked in panic. For a moment his body rose, and he lunged forward. Domingo didn't know if the priest grasped him in fear or if he meant to drown him. The thrust took them both under. Lucas let go, but Domingo's arm was trapped in the folds of the cassock. When his feet struck the sandy bottom, he felt saved. He pushed upward with all his might. At the surface, he sucked in air. Nothing mattered but the air. After two more breaths, he searched for the priest. The man was no where in sight. Domingo swam after the empty board but realized pursuit was useless.

After a few strokes, his feet touched bottom. He worked his way to the shore, turned to look for the priest. A shout from the other side of the river made him turn. The Baca party had followed on the shore watching Domingo struggle with Lucas. A woman was shaking her fist at him, her face distorted with anger. Two soldiers were yelling curses. One claimed Domingo had been mothered by dogs; the other condemned him to hell.

Baca jerked a harquebus from a soldier and aimed it at Domingo. Domingo stood dumbfounded, not understanding the anger. Baca must have pulled the trigger, but the gun belched no fire. He threw the weapon back at the soldier, turned and ran to his horse. He shouted orders for the party to forget such scum and make their way to Sandia.

Domingo searched the anguished faces for Cristina. He saw her leaning on the arm of an old women. Domingo shouted her name but got no response. He waved with both hands. Cristina seemed to recognize him. She lifted an arm to wave—or she staggered. Warmth flooded Domingo as he forced himself to believe she had waved.

THIRTY FOUR

The warmth flowing from Cristina's possible wave didn't sustain Domingo long. Desperation overcame him. How long would the old woman supporting Cristina nourish her? He imagined his lover suffering some Spanish disease as well as lack of food. After all, the pestilences the Spanish had introduced were beyond comprehension, and their only cures were interminable prayers. Domingo cursed every Spaniard who had defiled his homeland.

He decided to make his way down river, find a suitable crossing, and await his beloved. He'd carry her away that night. His hand went to his neck only to discover no fetish. Caution prevailed. Baca would watch for him the next day, even two days. He must delay his rescue. In that time he'd find food for Cristina. The thought made his stomach growl. His last meal was the putrid meat from the murdered Mexican Indian.

Domingo stayed along the east bank of the river for two days, retracing the way to Sandia. On the third day, a column of smoke rose from the west side. It looked to be a cook fire. He dashed into the river, found he had to swim a considerable distance, and was exhausted when he reached the far shore. He sat to catch his breath, then checked his bow and quiver, patting the knife at his belt. He dried his bowstring as best he could.

The smoke came from behind a hill. On the other side, five women and a few children were tending the fire. They looked to be harvesting the field of its beans and corn, even a few rows of chilies. He wondered why they were cooking during a harvest, but the smell of roasting chili and the sight of boiling corn made him forget everything except his stomach.

Domingo walked slowly to the group, his smile as wide as he could force it. He greeted them in Tewa, then Tiwa, but got no response. He tried Spanish. The women scowled. He cupped his hand and pointed with his fingers to his mouth. The women paid no attention. A young child ventured toward him with a half eaten tortilla in hand. A woman called him back. The other women scrutinized the hill, obviously expecting Domingo's comrades. He gestured that he was alone, but the women showed no interest. He gestured again that he was hungry.

An old woman approached him. She pointed to the boiling mush, then to the new moccasins at Domingo's side. *How do I make it home without them? But how else do I feed Cristina?* He nodded agreement to the trade, gesturing for a pot to carry the mush. The woman finally understood, pointed to his knife, but Domingo shook his head. His expression must have convinced her that a pot was included in the trade. She went to the fire, rummaged in a bag, and took out a small one, filled it with mush, then capped it. Domingo was overjoyed. The woman smiled and took two chilies from the fire. She juggled them in her hands, then tossed them to Domingo. A tear of gratitude welled in his eye. He'd save both chilies for Cristina.

He walked to the top of the hill and scanned the river bank. Baca should reach him that night. He found a gully from which to observe the Spaniard when he camped, and imagined a dozen ways to spirit Cristina away after nightfall.

Domingo must have slept. The sun had passed well overhead. He heard noises from the other side of the river. Half a dozen Indians were jousting with each other over a haunch of something they carved and ate while they walked. Domingo suspected they were a vanguard of the governor's party. Two men teased a third tossing a large bone over his head in a game of keep-away. The teased man finally stopped playing. The man with the bone threw it into the river. The group moved away.

Domingo left his bow and quiver, ran down steam and plunged in. Only a bit of bone showed above water, but Domingo latched onto it with the tenacity of a dog. While he waded from the river, he used his knife to pry at the bone's marrow, chewing as many bone splinters as he picked away. The bit of meat and marrow lulled his stomach.

He sat to await Baca, yawned, and dozed. Footsteps startled him. It was too late to hide. When Domingo rose, his visitor's bulging eyes looked around as if seeking to avoid an encounter. Domingo recognized Bullfrog immediately. Bullfrog gave no sign of recognition.

"How are you doing, friend?" Domingo mustered all the warmth he could.

"I'd doing well. And you?" The words were perfunctory.

"You don't remember me?" Domingo's words were more accusation than question.

"Yes, of course." Clearly Bullfrog was scrolling through his memory. "You are a friend."

"Yes, friend! And now you must know Cristina. How is she?"

A gleam in Bullfrog's eyes suggested he recalled his encounter with Domingo in Santa Fe. He stepped closer to eye the pot Domingo carried. "I haven't eaten in days. The smell of roasted chili is driving me mad."

Domingo took half a step back. He had no doubt Bullfrog would kill for food if given the opportunity. "My stomach has gone without, too. I've bartered for a little mush for my beloved Cristina." Domingo put his hand on his knife and moved toward Bullfrog. "You must tell me how she is!"

Bullfrog squinted. "I do not know her, I swear." His throat bulged when he swallowed. "Didn't I tell you that in Santa Fe?"

"That was more than a week ago. She's been with you ever since!"

"I never learn the young girls' names. Baca sends me on errands. Like now. I'm supposed to find food. The last we had was a little mule. Everyone is staving."

"Even my Cristina?" Domingo was about to say how recently he had seen her but thought better of it.

"Since we left Santa Fe two old women have died, several children, even two of the young women. We'll never make it to Sandia. El Paso is impossible." His eyes clouded over, a tear formed in the corner of one.

How can I find out if Cristina is alive? This simpleton has never learned names. That's it!

"You wait here. If you help me, I'll give you a chili." Domingo knew Bullfrog would wait from the way he licked his lips.

He ran to the river to search for drift wood. The first piece he found would do nicely. He discarded half a dozen others before he found two more that satisfied him. He returned to Bullfrog and gestured for him to sit.

Domingo unsheathed his knife and began to carve.

His first figure was of the old woman he had helped to cross the river. He had no trouble seeing her features as a youth, scratching them into the wood and giving her a smile to match Cristina's.

The second engraving was of Cristina. He cursed the grain that did not allow him to capture the beauty of her hair, but he fondled her cheeks and chin that felt alive to his touch. He lingered over the smile he engraved.

He hesitated over a third choice. He could not imagine his grandmother as a young woman. Then an image flashed before him. He carved with even more care than he had with Cristina. The features emerged as he wanted—except for the eyes. He concentrated, did as best he could with the wood but wished for a few flecks of gold. He knew he should engrave a smile matching those of the two previous figures, but his knife took over to carve teasing lips.

He held the tableau in both hands. His heart beat faster. He did not know why. With reluctance he turned the wood toward Bullfrog. "Was this one of the women who died?"

Bullfrog shook his head.

"Well, was she one of them?" Domingo demanded a full answer.

"No. I've never seen her." Bullfrog croaked.

"What about this woman?" Domingo held the carving of the old woman.

Bullfrog leaned closer to study the image. "No. I don't know her, I swear."

Domingo bit at his lip. He was reluctant to hold up the image of Cristina, but he did. "And her?"

Fear flushed out Bullfrog's expression. He glanced from the image to Domingo's face several times before answering. "Yes. That's one of the young women who died. She had beautiful hair." He dropped his eyes to the ground. "Everyone talked about it."

"How did she die?" As soon as Domingo asked the question, he realized he did not want to know.

"We never had enough to eat, even before the siege. Everyone was weak. Many had the cough."

When Domingo said nothing, Bullfrog rambled on. "It was the night the priest drowned, but Señor Baca said the proper words over her."

"Did she speak of me? Did you ever hear her say Domingo? What were her last words?"

Bullfrog pulled his head into his shoulders. "I was nowhere near until we had to bury her. The only place we could dig deep enough was in the sand by the river."

An image of his beloved being immersed in cold water flooded out reason. Domingo slapped Bullfrog so hard the little man fell on his back. Domingo unsheathed his knife. Bullfrog whimpered. Domingo sheathed his knife and offered Bullfrog his hand. The man scurried backwards and jumped to his feet well away from Domingo.

"You promised me a chili." Bullfrog held one hand to his lip to stop the bleeding while he extended the other.

Domingo threw him the chili, clutched the pot of mush to his chest, and ran into the river. His one-arm stroke edged him through the current, but it carried him far down stream before he found his footing on the other side.

He staggered to a wall of clay to protect his back, sat, and devoured the mush. Tears poured onto his chest. Life no longer had meaning. The river must have washed Cristina away by now. *I'll join her. Even if I have to share the watery grave with Lucas.*

THIRTY FIVE

The morning sun woke Domingo. His eyes were encrusted. He sat up, rubbing them, looked down. He found himself curled around the empty pot of corn mush. Memories of Cristina flooded his mind. The pit of his stomach tightened. The river's waves breaking on the bank invited him to join his lover. *Curse this revolution! It's turned me into a murderer, kept me from Cristina, and tempts me to kill myself.*

He contemplated the river's invitation until he remembered Francesca. She deserved to know what had happened to her sister. Her mother and father, too. He'd return to San Ildefonso. He picked up the empty pot, scraped its insides with his finger, and licked at a few grains of dried meal on the pot's lip. *I must take time to hunt.*

The wet bow string had stretched. A new knot restored the bow's strength. He called on the deer and its living representatives to rescue him. The climb out of river valley led to hills on the east. An unlikely place for deer but a rabbit or a porcupine had possibly escaped the fugitives scouring the territory.

The farther he climbed from the river the more he wondered if he had made a mistake. No trace of game showed all morning, and he thought of the progress he could have made up river. He decided to climb one more ridge. On the other side a ribbon of water shone in the valley. Domingo's hopes rose. He proceeded downstream until the vale opened onto a patch of lush vegetation. Movement in the tall grass riveted his attention. He crawled to within arrow range, took his bow from his back and rose to study the oasis, certain a deer hid in the dense vegetation.

He took a step forward. A burro snorted. Domingo whinnied as he approached his prey, then shot an arrow into its chest. The burro stomped and snorted before falling, then bawled after it fell to its back, legs kicking at the air. Domingo slit its throat and drank its blood.

He built a fire while the animal finished bleeding, cut open the donkey's belly to feast on its heart and liver, then hacked at a haunch. He roasted a few slices of meat, dried others, and decided to carry what was left, along with part of the other leg.

Late afternoon found him trotting back toward the river until his conscience struck. He could not leave so much meat for the coyotes and vultures when Indians were starving. He cached the meat he carried and ran back to the carcass. There he chased away a cloud of flies and finished butchering. He put more slices of meat on his roasting stick and settled in for the evening. For once, his evening meal roasted until tender.

That night hands waved above swirling waters begging for rescue, but Domingo stood frozen, bound by leaden feet. His last nightmare was so vivid that he stayed awake and rose with the morning star. He added wood to the cook fire's coals, heated a little burro to eat, then cut strips of skin for rope. He tied chucks of meat to a carrying pole. The sun warmed him as he shouldered his burden. The weight forced him to a walk.

He bypassed his cache, reached the river, and was tying the carcass to a tree when a band of Indians approached. It took only a glance at the tattered group to see protruding ribs.

"Good day, friends." Domingo used Spanish on the strangers.

"Good day," one answered. He approached Domingo with care while his comrades spread out, fingering their bows.

"I'm a messenger for Po-pe." He guessed the men were remnants of the southern army returning home.

"We are friends. We've helped burn Santa Fe and chased out the Spanish." The men with him stopped fingering their bows. They gathered around Domingo, eyes on his load.

"Let's get wood for a fire. It's time to celebrate our victory," Domingo said.

The men ran toward the river, returning in no time with loads of drift wood. They lighted a fire and fashioned roasting sticks. Two men dribbled saliva as Domingo sliced raw chunks of burro. No one asked what kind of meat it was. Except for Domingo, they roasted the meat only long enough to get it hot.

Even before they finished eating, two of the men started pounding a hollow log. The others chanted and started a dance, their eyes on Domingo. He could tell it was an honoring dance even though the words were incomprehensible. The dancers pulled him to the center of their circle. First, his feet took over, then his whole body responded to the beat. He forgot Cristina.

After bouts of roasting and eating, dancing and singing, racing and jesting, Domingo fell to the ground exhausted. The others scraped out holes in the sand to cuddle in the earth's warmth. Domingo crawled near the dying fire and gazed at the glow. For a moment he thought of Cristina, but the twinkling coals reminded him of her sister's eyes. *I must start for San Ildefonso in the morning.*

He awoke with a start, the sun already hot. He couldn't remember when he had slept so long. His comrades didn't stir. No firewood remained so he went to the river and returned with an armload. The Keresans were jabbing the last pieces of burro with roasting sticks when Domingo returned. They smiled shyly when they saw him. The meat soon sizzled over a blazing fire, and his companions finished the remains.

Their smiles were their only parting to Domingo. After he retrieved his cache, he started for San Ildefonso. His run didn't last long before his full stomach slowed him to a trot. A few dimly remembered landmarks made him think he'd have another night on the trail before it branched to Francesca's pueblo. He settled into a steady pace that allowed him to mull over the horrors of the revolution. Twice he heard the call of the river, but each time his obligation to Francesca and her parents kept him on the trail.

He stopped early to gather wood for a fire. His stomach dwelled on corn mush, beans, and squash, finished by a peach. Domingo heaved a sigh and took two strips of half-dried, smoky flesh from his belt. He heated one piece while chewing at a second; a sour taste added to the smoke and his own sweat. He imagined his father storing corn and beans while slicing squash into strips for drying.

Without Spaniards to feed we'll have enough—even in this drought. Perhaps I can help Francesca's family with their harvest. It'll be good to see my cousin. But his thoughts were of what he would tell her daughter.

He hung two more strips of burro over the coals and cleared a place of rocks for a bed. The sun edged down, and in the western sky a dozen shades of red wove patterns in the sky. A turquoise strata between the reds mesmerized him.

"Ho! You're dead." He winced at the jab into his ribs.

Domingo's heart did such a flip-flop he knew what an Apache knife must feel like. When he recovered his wits, he could only stare, his mouth wide open.

"Your spirit will escape if you open your mouth any wider." The gold in Francesca's eyes danced in mirth.

Domingo pressed his lips together, then opened them to ask an endless list of questions.

Francesca smiled, waited until he finished, then responded. "Hopis volunteered to guard our fields so I went to Santa Fe to find Cristina. I guessed she'd be with you. When I stumbled across Tupatu, he told me you'd return from Sandia along this trail. So here I am."

"I'm glad you're here." Domingo looked into her eyes. His chest tightened. He must tell her of her sister's death. His mouth went dry. "I found Cristina with Baca's party, but before I could rescue her… They had gone for days with nothing to eat. Even in Santa Fe, they had been starving."

"She's dead, isn't she?" Francesca's eyes moistened.

"Yes. Did you guess before?"

"Tupatu said you were pursuing a spirit. I wondered if he meant she was dying."

Domingo wondered what Tupatu meant, too. He saw Francesca shiver, not knowing if it was from the cold, but he added wood to the fire.

Francesca looked around, found a flat rock, and placed it at the fire's edge. She took two corn cakes from a pouch and put them on the rock. "Not much of a meal but better than nothing."

"I've got a little meat." Domingo took the last two strips from his waist and laid them alongside the corn cakes.

"Where did you get meat?"

"I hunted two days ago." Domingo regretted his words as soon as he spoke. The burro could hardly be considered game.

"I'm impressed," Francesca said. "Both Spanish and Indian refugees from Santa Fe must have gleaned any animal that moves. I haven't seen a trace of game." She looked at him with admiration.

He looked at the ground. "Well, you might not consider it hunting." *Why does this woman draw the truth out of me?*

"What do you mean?" Francesca's tone demanded an answer.

"Well," Domingo dragged out the word to cover his embarrassment. "It was a burro."

Francesca roared, then looked at him with affection. "I promise not to tell." She handed him the larger of the corn cakes, topped with a piece of meat.

They both ate slowly, savoring every bite. When they finished, Domingo asked if she were sleepy. She waited a moment, then brayed loudly, laughing so hard she had to hold her sides. Domingo guffawed nearly as hard. He couldn't recall the last time he had laughed.

"You can never stop teasing, can you?"

"Seriously," she said. "It's the best meal I've ever had."

"Me too. The company has a lot to do with it."

She smiled and curled up on the opposite side of the dying fire. Domingo studied her eyes to catch light sparkling off the flecks of gold. After the final flames sputtered, he crawled to lie beside her. Their kiss was long and passionate like the lovemaking that followed, so unlike the hurried climax he'd had with the fruitless dream he had pursued.

In the morning they were still entwined. Domingo felt so good he could find no words to express himself. Francesca brushed his hair with her hands, kissed him lightly, and sat up. Domingo sat beside her.

"It's time we went home. Your home," Domingo said.

"You must go to Santa Fe. Tupatu said it's Po-pe's orders."

"He can find another translator. Your mother needs to know what happened to her daughter." He looked at Francesca. "And we can tell her about us."

"What about us?" Francesca's voice carried its familiar tease.

"A go-between should ask for you, but in these times we don't have to wait. We can marry as soon as your mother arranges a wedding."

"What makes you think I'll marry you?"

For a moment, Domingo thought she was serious. Then he laughed and pulled her to him for a kiss. "I'm afraid we have to leave," he sighed. "If we start now, we can make San Ildefonso tonight."

"We must go to Santa Fe." This time Francesca did not tease. She pulled away from his embrace and stood over him.

"I've done my share," Domingo protested. "No more translating. No more killing. I'm ready to marry. To lead a normal life." He continued to lie in the sand.

"You mustn't cross Po-pe. He's executed Indians who disobey his orders."

"What executions?" Domingo was incredulous.

"He killed his own son-in-law at San Juan. The cacique suspected the man had told Spaniards the date of the revolt."

"Not Bua," Domingo gasped. "He was a friend of my father."

"That's the name, I'm sure. Instead of freedom, Po-pe is acting like the Spanish governor. At least, that's the rumor."

"But Po-pe wants to get rid of everything Spanish. That's another reason he doesn't need me to translate."

"You can make your excuses in Santa Fe. Report to Tupatu. Let him cover for you after that." She sat beside him.

"You always insist on your way!" Domingo rolled onto his back and contemplated the sky.

"I want you out of danger," she said.

"Do you?" Domingo's question was tentative.

"You know I do."

"And I know you're stubborn." Domingo smiled.

Francesca brayed, more like a mule than a burro.

They both laughed. She straddled him and pinned his shoulders. Looked into his eyes with passion. He stiffened. She lifted her dress, pulled away his breech cloth. Their love making was as ardent as the night before. Neither cared if a passerby saw them.

Afterwards she lay atop him. When their breathing returned to normal, Domingo said, “Santa Fe awaits.”

THIRTY SIX

"You've lost your stamina. Guess you shouldn't make love more than once a day." Francesca turned and trotted backward, licking her lips, her tongue suggestive of more than thirst.

Domingo didn't change his leisurely pace. Santa Fe had no appeal to him except for Tupatu who could give him details of the Spanish surrender. "When we stop at noon, look for a place where every passerby can't see us. I'll teach you about stamina."

Francesca chuckled. "I don't know if I can wait till noon." She turned and ran ahead, then stepped in place facing Domingo until he caught up. They locked arms when they met, their bodies welcoming each other.

"You'll just have to wait," he whispered in her ear.

The two resumed their jog, brushing shoulders as they went. At dusk, they smelled smoke before they saw it blanketing the valley of Santa Fe. Domingo felt repulsed. The two stopped at a high point to survey the black clouded valley. After reporting to Tupatu, he never wanted to see Santa Fe again.

"If we go on, we can find corn and beans." Francesca ran a hand along his arm. "If we camp here, we'll have our privacy."

Domingo took her hand and led her to a cluster of pinon pine. They crawled under low lying branches of a tree and cleared old pine cones to make a bed.

Francesca laughed. "There are still some nuts." She popped two of the cones and gave Domingo four nuts. The seeds were bitter but a welcome complement to the last of Domingo's meat.

An unseasonal cool breeze made them shiver. Domingo pulled Francesca to him. "You need a lesson in stamina, I believe."

"I do." She licked her lips. "But who's to teach me?"

Domingo lightly bit her neck and shoulder before he kissed her. She grasped him. They reveled in each other's warmth, their hands rubbing each other in comfort as much as sexual desire. Sleep proved stronger than stamina for both. They fell asleep in each other's arms without making love. Neither moved until first light.

"You snore," Francesca said when they awoke.

"You have bad breath," Domingo said.

Francesca's hand shot to her mouth. "I'm sorry."

Domingo laughed. "I'm lying."

"I was too." Francesca giggled. "But it wouldn't bother me if you did snore."

Domingo brushed a hair from her forehead. "Bad breath could never keep me from loving you."

It was the first time he had confessed his love. The words were like an aphrodisiac. Francesca thrust herself into his groin, kissed him so hard he struggled for breath. She rolled on top of him and massaged his manhood. He would have stiffened without her hand. She guided him deep inside her. Her love making was more passionate than he had ever known.

After she had lain on him until he regained his breath, she twittered in his ear. "Will you be able to stand up to Po-pe?"

"I'm not sure I'll be able to stand at all…maybe tomorrow?"

She laughed as she rolled off him. "Think of hot tortillas. Corn mush, beans. Even fresh squash."

He reached for the dried meat at his belt, found it coated with dust of pine needles and decided they could wait to eat. He kissed her lightly after they crawled from their hiding place.

Thoughts of mush and tortillas motivated their run to Santa Fe. When Domingo asked an Indian where to find Po-pe, she pointed her chin to the governor's palace. The tower at one end had been replaced with a makeshift second story. Banners flew from it. The first story gleamed in a coat of white wash. The rest of the building lay in ruin, except for an opposite end. It had been restored to resemble an armory. A ladder at the top suggested all the sides were solid.

As they approached the building, two guards called for them to halt. One carried an harquebus, the other grasped an upright halberd. Domingo wondered if the man had any idea how to use its spear end, laden with a hook and ax. At least, the weapon appeared threatening.

"Po-pe has sent for me," Domingo called to the two.

"Your name? Your pueblo? Your business?" The man with the harquebus lowered the muzzle in Domingo's direction.

"I'm Domingo from San Juan, scribe for Po-pe."

The man with the halberd ran to the door. The hook caught on the frame and tripped him. Domingo suppressed a laugh. Francesca's was loud. The harquebus guard glared and swung his weapon in her direction. Domingo stepped in front of her.

It took the second guard some time before he came out of the building, dragging the halberd. He told his companion that Po-pe expected Domingo. Domingo stepped forward, but the guard stopped him with a wave of his harquebus.

"No one sees Po-pe armed with any weapon."

Domingo slipped off his bow. "Where shall I put it?"

"She can hold it." The guard motioned to Francesca.

"She's with me." Domingo said gruffly.

"She doesn't see Po-pe." The guard shook his head.

"All right." Domingo stepped forward.

"Your knife!" The guard was riled.

Domingo stepped back to hand Francesca his knife. He couldn't resist stroking the soft skin of the scabbard to rid it of dust and a pine needle.

He walked briskly toward the door. "Stop!" The guard seemed about to fire. "Your arrows. You don't think you're going to see Po-pe armed with a quiver of arrows, do you?"

Domingo almost grabbed the harquebus from the guard's hand but took a deep breath to suppress his exasperation. He threw his quiver to Francesca and approached the guard.

The guard blocked his way. "Lift your arms."

Without thinking Domingo did as he was told. The guard ran his hands over Domingo's shirt, then asked him to remove his moccasins. The search was cursory but eerie. Not even the Spanish had been so wary.

"You may enter. Po-pe likes it if you bow."

"Bow?" The word exploded from Domingo's lips. "I've seen him a dozen times and never bowed."

"Best you bow. A tip of the head is enough." The guard tipped his head to illustrate.

Domingo scowled and walked toward the door. The second guard fell in behind him.

Po-pe sat at a long desk, shuffling papers. Two stacks at one end stood so high Domingo guessed they'd soon tumble.

Po-pe glared. The guard nudged Domingo with his elbow. Domingo tipped his head.

Po-pe stopped glaring but spoke gruffly. "I must leave tomorrow. There are hundreds of documents for you to record. You should have reported sooner."

"Much happened on my return trip."

"I haven't time for excuses." Po-pe scowled. "I've sorted the church records from the northern and southern pueblos." He waved at the two piles. "You will inventory the church property and make a record I can understand. Tupatu will oversee your work."

"Where is Tupatu?" Domingo asked.

"I haven't finished," Po-pe snarled.

Domingo took a step back. Po-pe's attitude reminded him of Lucas when the priest was in one of his worst moods.

"I suspect the priests hid their gold and silver. Or Indians have stolen it. You must determine what gold and silver existed before my revolution. It's all to be stored in my palace." Po-pe pointed toward the room resembling an armory.

"You were going to do away with everything Spanish!"

"Don't raise your voice to me." Po-pe turned livid. The guard seized Domingo's arm. Po-pe took a deep breath. "Those metals are worthless now…until I find a use for them."

Domingo's head dropped in disgust. Po-pe took the gesture as another bow. He said, "You can begin work now. I must prepare for my departure. You have permission to use my desk."

Po-pe's desk was a long dining table. Domingo suppressed a smile. The guard left with Po-pe. Domingo leafed through the stacks. Po-pe's division made no sense. He found no reference to any treasure among endless records of births and deaths. Domingo sorted other papers with a glance at the first few paragraphs, ignoring the flowery language priests used.

A number of papers recorded the days of labor performed by Indians. The amount astonished Domingo. *No wonder we were starving. We had no time to work our own fields.* He realized suddenly that he was thinking of all the pueblo people as *we*.

He was about to stretch when a letter marked urgent caught his eye. A priest at Sandia claimed an Indian in his pueblo warned of a revolt and revealed who the traitors were. Domingo found no response to it. He went through dozens more of the documents, sorting them and recording little. He yawned and decided he'd done enough. It was only when he stretched that he remembered Francesca.

At the door, the guards gave him a cursory look. "Are you finished?" one asked.

"I'm half through. I've got to eat before I continue."

The guard pointed toward the plaza. Francesca sat with her back to a tree, its branches shattered from the fighting. She munched a tortilla from a pile before her. He raced to join her.

"There are beans, too." The tortillas covered a pot, half full. "I've had my share."

Domingo rolled a tortilla and drove it into the beans. The mouthful he took was too much and a bean tumbled from his mouth.

"You didn't learn manners from the Spanish?" Francesca said.

Domingo wiped his lips with the back of his hand. "Not about sitting on the ground to feast." He dipped the rest of the tortilla into the pot to scoop out a slightly smaller portion. "You're a wonderful cook."

"I didn't cook," she said. "I traded your knife for it."

"What?" he exploded. "My grandfather gave me that knife. My grandmother the scabbard. Who the thunder has it?"

She burst out laughing and pulled the knife from behind her.

"You think Indian women are going to let other Indians starve?"

"I'll never learn your tricks. How did you know the knife meant so much to me?"

"I've watched the way you stroke it. I doubt you're even aware of the affection you show it."

"I don't," he said.

"You do. I'm jealous of it."

This time Domingo knew she was joking. Before he could retort, he spotted Tupatu walking toward them. He leaped to his feet. "You want a tortilla?" he called. "They're still warm."

"No. I want to hear about your success at Sandia."

The two men sat beside Francesca, Domingo taking another tortilla. He related how the Spanish had received him, what he told, and how he had watched the soldiers head south.

Tupatu congratulated him and asked about Cristina.

Domingo looked down a moment, then told how she had died.

Tupatu nodded in sympathy. "Have you finished Po-pe's work here?"

"Almost. There's very little to interest you. The reports don't mention church property. They do record all the work Indians did for the missions. And labor for the encomiendas. I've added it up."

"Good. We may use it some day. You ready to finish your work?" Tupatu smiled as Domingo ate the last tortilla.

"I'm ready." Domingo stood.

"You can come," Tupatu said to Francesca.

The guards were annoyed at her presence, but they didn't challenge Tupatu's judgement.

Domingo stood at the desk, ruffling the remaining papers.

"Put aside the accounts of Indian labor," Tupatu said. "We know from experience how they enslaved us."

Domingo scanned a paper, glimpsing Harelip's name. He read the paper twice, drawing a deep breath the second time.

"What is it?" Both Francesca and Tupatu asked.

"The priest at Taos reports that Harelip, the Little Governor, claims to know Indians loyal to the Spanish who will inform on Po-pe."

"You sound as if you know this Harelip," Tupatu said.

"Yes. He's a Spanish lackey."

"Whom does he name?" Tupatu said.

"No one. The priest says Harelip doesn't trust the paper scratches. He insists on seeing governor Otermin in person."

"What's the priest say?"

"He believes Harelip to be reliable and recommends that the governor receive him."

"That may explain Po-pe's trip to Taos and San Juan," Tupatu said.

"How would he know about Harelip?" Domingo asked.

"You're not the first to read these letters. Po-pe used two other scribes before you."

"You mean I've done all this for nothing?" Domingo screeched.

"Po-pe trusts no one. He'll likely have a fourth person go over what you've done."

"But why didn't you tell me sooner?"

Tupatu shrugged. "Distrust has become our way."

"What do we do now?"

"I'm ordered to go through San Ildefonso on my way to San Juan. Po-pe heard the San Ildefonso church still stood. He wants it leveled and its stones incorporated in kivas."

"Let's go," Domingo and Francesca said in unison.

"My legs aren't young any more," Tupatu said. "Let's wait until tomorrow."

"Your mother can arrange our marriage," Domingo looked at Francesca but spoke for Tupatu's sake. "While she's doing that we can go on to San Juan to tell my father." Domingo glowed with anticipation. Tupatu cocked his head and frowned.

"What a rush you're in." Francesca said. "I haven't even said I'd marry you."

"The revolt is over," Domingo said. "It's time to settle down."

"You're right," Tupatu said. "I wonder if Po-pe agrees."

THIRTY SEVEN

Domingo and Francesca spent the night in the Santa Fe outpost he and Tupatu had occupied. In the morning they had just finished making love when Tupatu found them. He chortled. "I suppose now I can keep up with you on our journey since you won't have any stamina left."

Domingo jumped up, too winded for a rejoinder. He offered a hand to Francesca. Tupatu put his hands on their shoulders. "We have work to do at San Ildefonso and San Juan. There may not be time for a wedding."

Francesca glowered. "What if we don't find many records? What is left for Domingo to do?"

"I must make certain the churches are razed. No trace is to be left of anything Catholic."

"You expect us to do all that?" Domingo flushed.

"No. We must persuade the people to do it. After we find what they've done with church property. Especially gold and silver."

"I doubt they'll want to send any here," Francesca said. "Po-pe is losing his authority, acting like a Spaniard."

Tupatu put a finger to his lips. "Don't say that too loudly."

"What else have you been ordered to do?" Domingo's brow furrowed.

"Well, we should encourage people to destroy the boundary markers. It's a necessary step toward returning to Indian ways."

"Is that your idea?" Domingo said.

Tupatu evaded an answer, asking if they were ready.

Domingo retrieved his bow and quiver, adjusted his knife. Before they could start, a furor arose from the far side of the plaza. They crossed over to it.

"I must see Po-pe," an Indian insisted. An elegant feather draped from a velvet hat hid his face, but the voice was familiar.

"Po-pe isn't here." It was the voice of the guard with the harquebus, his back to Domingo.

"Then I demand to see his lieutenant."

"State your business," the guard said.

"I'm here for my reward." The voice lost some of its authority. Domingo guessed the muzzle of the harquebus had weakened the speaker's bravado. As he, Francesca, and Tupatu wove through the gathering crowd, the man swept the hat and feather from his face. It was Harelip. He wore a white embroidered shirt over his frayed tunic as well as the fancy hat.

"I know the gold and silver are here. I want payment for what I did."

Domingo could think of nothing that Harelip had done except commit treason. *How can he make such brazen demands?*

"And what did you do to deserve an award?" Tupatu asked before the guard had a chance. The command in his voice hushed the crowd.

Harelip gulped when he saw Tupatu. "Do you act for Po-pe?" he said.

"No one acts for Po-pe," Tupatu glared. "But while he is away, I'll hear your claim."

Harelip brushed his lips with the back of his hand. "I claim...My claim is," Domingo realized Harelip was tipsy. "I killed the governor's wife...and her guard."

"What proof have you?" Tupatu asked.

"Hundreds of people saw me with her head." He blinked his eyes as if to clarify his thinking. "I cut off her breasts for good measure!" He did a second take when he saw Domingo. "That man saw the head and a breast. He can back up my claim."

"I saw a head. I have no idea whose it was," Domingo said.

"You saw the breast. Everyone knows what big tits Otermin's wife had."

"The breast is no proof." Tupatu did not hide his disgust. "Besides, few Indians ever saw the woman." His eyes glared contempt. "How do you know it was Señora Otermin?"

"She was dressed like the governor's wife. She wore a gold necklace. Silver rings. Even a silver comb in her hair. It had to be her."

"And what have you done with all that gold and silver?" Tupatu's tone brooked no nonsense.

Harelip's jaw dropped. Obviously he was too drunk to think straight. "I…I reported them to a guard of Po-pe's. I didn't know the man."

"I don't remember seeing any silver comb in the storehouse." Tupatu stared into Harelip's eyes.

Harelip dropped his head. "It could be lost. Or the guard stole it." Harelip began to stammer. "I didn't like the looks of the man I handed it to. Maybe he wasn't a guard."

"What about the silver necklace?" Tupatu was unrelenting.

"The guard said he'd put it in the storehouse," Harelip sniveled.

"You said it was gold." The crowd hushed to listen to Tupatu's interrogation.

"It was gold."

"But I said silver. You didn't question it."

"That's what it was," Harelip slobbered.

"Which was it?"

"Gold." The word sounded like a guess.

"And what did you do with it?"

"I've got it! I kept it for safekeeping. I knew not to trust that guard. Maybe he wasn't really a guard."

"You've done well to keep the jewelry safe." Tupatu nodded affirmation. "What else did you hide?"

"The comb. Her rings." Harelip sounded hopeful. "I found other gold and silver, too. I've hidden it all," he paused. "I mean I've kept it all safe for Po-pe." His words hung in the air, indicting him.

A voice rang out in the crowd, "Traitor." A dozen other cries followed. Harelip cowered.

Tupatu raised an arm. The mob quieted.

"You betrayed the revolution when you dismembered bodies. Beheading a person is Spanish custom, not Indian."

"But Po-pe is cutting off heads," Harelip cried.

"What are you talking about?" Tupatu said.

"When I was hiding the gold at Taos, he ordered two men beheaded for treason." Harelip spoke with assurance. "Other Indians fled in terror."

Tupatu hesitated. Domingo muttered that Harelip had betrayed the revolution by informing on loyal Indians, but he stood too far behind Tupatu to be heard.

Harelip edged back from Tupatu. The guard with the harquebus waved his gun at him. Harelip froze. The guard moved beside him.

Tupatu called out for all caciques in the crowd to join him. Three elderly men walked to his side. The four conferred at length.

"Here is our judgement," Tupatu said. "We suspect you have betrayed the revolution, but we don't have time to find witnesses and hear all the evidence. So we will not judge you guilty of treason."

Harelip stood straighter and took a deep breath.

The oldest of the caciques stepped forward. "However, it's clear from the way you hoarded wealth that you must be a witch." Harelip blanched. "Different pueblos have different ways of punishing witches so we must resort to Spanish custom." The elder spat out the words, Spanish custom.

The crowd's muttering indicated displeasure. The people clearly were in a mood for blood and uncertain as to Spanish punishment for witchcraft.

An old woman shouted. "The Inquisition burned my husband at the stake when they claimed he was a witch."

Harelip bolted, but the crowd closed in on him and handed him over to the guard.

The caciques didn't need to give orders. Two men were driving a stake into the middle of the plaza ground, and young men began hauling in firewood. Domingo didn't like the rush to judgement, yet Harelip deserved to die, if not as a witch certainly as a traitor.

Francesca took his arm. "In the old days, we knew people who didn't share their wealth were witches, but the Spanish taught us greed. Maybe he shouldn't burn."

Domingo nodded that Harelip might not deserve death as a witch, but he assured Francesca the man was a traitor. She grimaced to show her sympathy with Domingo's judgement.

The guard lashed Harelip's feet to the stake, using the rest of the rawhide cord to bind his body. Young women piled firewood all around Harelip to the height of his knees. Domingo remembered as a child how he and others had burned dried leaves in their hands to show their disdain for pain. He wondered if Harelip had played the game. He tried to imagine the agony engulfing the feet before shooting up the legs. His groin tightened.

A young man brought a dozen candles from somewhere, one lit. Other youth took candles, lighted them, and started the tender at Harelip's feet. He kicked in vain at the wood. His body thrashed like a snake in the beaks of an eagle. The effort fanned the flames of the tinder-dry wooden slabs taken from Spanish houses. The fire blazed. Harelip wailed. His eyes blended entreaty with horror. Domingo moved closer. *He smells like any other meat roasting. I wonder what he'd taste like.* Rancid smoke from Harelip's clothes and scorched flesh drove the thought from Domingo's mind. He gagged on the stench. Harelip's hair and the fancy feather smoldered moments before erupting into flame.

Harelip's screams engraved themselves on Domingo's ears.

Hardly thinking, Domingo notched an arrow and sent it into Harelip's chest.

Many in the crowd failed to notice, but Tupatu edged close and said, "Who do you think you are to interfere in our judgement?" The words were an indictment, but Tupatu's eyes flashed empathy.

"You are a good man," Francesca whispered to Domingo. "And I love you for it."

THIRTY EIGHT

The day after Harelip's execution, Domingo, Tupatu and Francesca set off for San Ildefonso. Francesca set a fast pace. Domingo forgot Harelip and the revolution after he caught his second breath and settled into the run. Toward mid-day Tupatu dropped out of sight. When Francesca reached a stream bed, she stopped to drink. Domingo caught up, drank, took off his moccasins, and waded in. The cool water shot relief up his legs. He looked around. The trees had turned yellow, and bright shades wrapped him in their color to remind him that fall approached. He wondered what the season signaled for the revolution. *Will Mexico send troops? Now that the Spanish know there's no gold here, maybe they'll leave us alone. Or is our land and labor worth as much as gold?* His shoulders sagged as he guessed the answer.

"You lost your stamina or are you afraid to ask my father for my hand?" Francesca stood hands on hips looking at him.

"I'm thinking of Tupatu." Domingo parried. "He needs time to catch up."

"That's good of you," Tupatu said, splashing into the stream. He had kept up most of the morning. Now, he was breathing lightly but holding his side. Domingo noticed that he had aged since they first met. He wondered about himself.

"Domingo won't say if he still wants to marry me," Francesca said to Tupatu.

"You can always marry *me*," Tupatu said. "I'd like a young wife. You can see I have plenty of stamina."

"If Domingo doesn't want me, I'm your's."

Domingo only shook his head, refusing to join the banter.

"Let's go," Tupatu said. "I'll beg your parents for your hand."

Domingo jerked his moccasins on. "You'll have to get there before I do, then." He raced ahead. Francesca stayed beside Tupatu, addressing him as husband in her clowning.

When Domingo reached San Ildefonso, Tupatu and Francesca remained out of sight. He went to her mother's. Juan came out to greet him; his wife climbed down from the roof top where she was drying squash. Juan looked askance, and Domingo broke the news about Cristina's death.

"We heard of so many deaths, your news is not a shock," Juan said.

Domingo's cousin bit her lip but did not cry. "And our other daughter?" she said. "Any news of her? She went in search of Cristina."

"She is behind me with a friend. A lieutenant of Po-pe."

They both frowned. "It might be best if you did not mention such a friendship to other people," Juan said.

At that moment, Francesca and Tupatu reached the plaza at a trot. Francesca broke into a run. She greeted her parents with a broad smile. A tear trickled onto her mother's smile.

"He's told you about my sister?" Francesca asked.

Juan and his wife nodded. "The revolution has taken so many lives." Juan choked on his words.

"Has it been worth it?" his wife asked Tupatu.

"It has," he said emphatically. "We have yet to experience the freedom. The joy of the old ways. To worship as we please. The kachinas will return now. Whenever they please."

"Your Po-pe preaches a return to the old ways, but he's acting like the governor," Juan said.

"Certainly *he's* not living the old way," his wife added.

Since Tupatu did not ask what they knew, Domingo did.

Juan looked at his wife. She jerked her chin toward him.

"He orders feasts for himself," Juan said. "To be served at a Spaniard's long table."

Domingo couldn't help thinking of the long table Po-pe had claimed to be his desk.

Juan's wife talked excitedly. "It's even worse. He demands dinners to be laid out on Spanish dishes with their silverware."

"Where was this?" Tupatu asked.

"At Santa Clara," Juan answered. "A few days ago. Just before he left for San Juan."

"Maybe he was ridiculing the Spanish," Tupatu said. "He never was very good at making a joke."

"He wasn't joking," Juan shook his head. "When one of the young women serving the meal dropped a wine glass, he knocked her down."

Juan's wife stared at Tupatu. "Do you call that returning to the old ways?"

"It will take a long time to revive all our customs. To know how to use our freedom. It's been eighty years under the Spanish yoke. Some of us became like their cattle."

"But we've kept so many of our customs!" Domingo was disappointed with Tupatu's argument. "Kivas right under the noses of the Spanish. Dances they never saw. We don't have to revive the old ways. We can bring them out in the open."

"So the women can see them!" Francesca tried to sound sincere, but Domingo heard the sarcasm in her voice.

"You see what the gods meant for you to see," Juan said to his daughter. "The men's secret ceremonies are a small part of the dances and rituals that are for everyone."

Both Francesca and her mother hid wry grins.

"The real issue now is if Po-pe can be trusted to lead us or if power has gone to his head?" Domingo didn't try to hide his anxiety.

"I've known Po-pe for years. He wouldn't betray all we have worked for." Tupatu pretended assurance, but Domingo saw doubt in his eyes.

"We must go to San Juan to see for ourselves." Domingo spoke as if he intended to leave immediately.

Francesca glared at him.

Domingo recovered quickly. "I want to ask my father to send a go-between." He looked at his cousin and Juan. Juan appeared perplexed, but his wife was smiling.

Domingo found himself stammering. "In times of revolution, things move swiftly. I...," Francesca glared again, "*We* want to do things right. But swiftly, in keeping with the revolution."

He stalled, baffled by Juan's looks. Obviously, Juan had no idea what he was talking about while his wife's smile widened. Francesca was shaking her head.

Tupatu broke up everyone. "I want you to make the arrangements for me to marry your daughter. That is, if my young friend cannot find his tongue."

"Will you arrange our marriage?" Domingo took Francesca's hand while he looked from Juan to his wife.

"We'd be happy to." Juan's wife answered. Juan finally beamed.

"I know the go-between should ask you." Words now gushed from Domingo's lips. "He will. That is as soon as I ask my father. It will be his brother. Well, if his brother is at home. Otherwise, he'll send someone else. I could come myself," he said looking at Francesca. "But I guess that wouldn't be right." Domingo felt so elated that he had no idea what he was saying. He didn't care if he sounded like a fool. He didn't care about anything at that moment, except Francesca. She couldn't contain her chortle.

"Things go too fast in a revolution. Spinning like a whirlwind." Juan gestured with his hand.

"It's all right, my father. We know what we're doing," Francesca said.

"But no one's asked if you're a hard worker." He looked at Domingo. "She is, you know. A real hard worker. Not a bad cook, either. Best of hunters! Well, you may not want her to hunt any more." He looked at the ground in his confusion.

"I'm sure she'll be a wonderful wife," Domingo said. "And even if we're rushing the marriage, we want everything else to be traditional. All our family here. The wise men's blessings. Everything."

Juan's wife interrupted. "It's getting dark, and I haven't even lit the cook fire. Dinner will be late. Daughter?" she looked at Francesca. The two went inside. In no time, Domingo smelled a rich stew. He wondered if the meaty smell could be venison. Or horse? His mouth watered at the thought of tortillas.

Hardly a word was spoken while they ate. Domingo kept glancing at Francesca. She licked her lips at him. Tupatu seemed far away. Once everyone finished the meal, Domingo talked of going to San

Juan. Francesca said she wanted to accompany him. Her mother begged them to stay a few more days.

"We should learn what others have heard." Domingo looked at Juan. "Have you talked with Little Pot?"

"Not recently," Juan said. "We meet tonight in the kiva. You can talk with him then."

The three men got to their feet. Francesca and her mother gathered up the pots and dishes.

At the kiva no one thought to ask Tupatu who had invited him. They had heard of his role in the revolution. A few, who had fought at Santa Fe had met him. Everyone greeted him and Domingo with warmth. For Tupatu's sake, they lavished praise on Domingo, recalling his part in their battle with the Apache. Domingo regretted that he could not tell of Francesca's role in the victory because he feared it would cause her problems, even delay their wedding.

After their accolades Little Pot and the War Chiefs motioned Tupatu and Domingo to a corner of the kiva to ask when they last saw Po-pe.

"Not since he left Santa Fe," Tupatu said. "More than twenty days ago."

"We heard disturbing rumors from Santa Clara," Little Pot said. "If they're true, you'd think Po-pe has forgotten he's Indian."

"Because he was feasting in the style of the governor?" Tupatu said.

"Not that so much. That didn't hurt anyone. But he and two other men—big men—broke into people's houses in search of gold and silver. They say one of the men was an Apache. That's not right! Breaking into other people's homes. And not even from the same pueblo." Little Pot's face flushed. The War Chiefs stomped their feet in agreement.

One of the senior War Chiefs spoke. "We might ask an outsider for advice, even to judge a matter, but never to find out if one of our own people has done something wrong. That's for us to determine." All the chiefs muttered their consensus.

Little Pot's news of Po-pe's behavior made Domingo want to leave for San Juan at once. He'd beg his cousin to allow her daughter to accompany him and Tupatu, but before he could say anything, Little Pot was praising the War Chief's wisdom. "We beg you to listen to our problem." He and the War Chief looked at Tupatu.

What now? We came here to discuss my problem. Now they've twisted things so we're included in their problem. An Indian way we'll probably never give up. Domingo gritted his teeth.

"We have the silver chalice from the church," Little Pot said. "Some wanted to throw it in the river. Others said it belonged to us. All the labor we gave to the church more than paid for it."

"Think of all the blankets we wove that the priest sent off to Mexico," a War Chief broke in.

"And so much time working the priest's fields that we didn't have time for our own," another said, his fists clenched. "We have earned the silver."

"But it's of no value now," Tupatu said.

"The Apaches will take it in trade. They're so dumb they'll never figure out it's worthless." The War Chiefs all laughed.

"We should be on our way to San Juan. I need to see my father," Domingo pleaded.

"It's all right for you to go," Little Pot said. "We want Tupatu to judge for us. The issue has divided us so badly we need an outsider's decision." He dipped his head to Tupatu, forgetting the stylized bow was out of fashion. "Everyone will respect your opinion."

Tupatu glanced at Domingo. Domingo realized he had no choice. "Francesca and I can make the trip alone. We'll be back and married by the time you've heard everyone's arguments."

Tupatu smiled. "I suspect you're right. Regardless, I'll stay here so I can witness your marriage. I wouldn't miss the feasting for anything in the world."

THIRTY NINE

Francesca and Domingo spent the night on the rooftop under a rabbit fur blanket. Both were too anxious for sex, but they savored the comfort of each other's arms. In the morning, Domingo was reluctant to leave Francesca's embrace, even after he smelled the morning cook fire with its message of tortillas. Francesca stretched, the two rolled onto their backs, and they watched eastern clouds turn from shades of pink to a gentle red.

Francesca rolled over and kissed Domingo on the cheek. "I could stay here with you forever."

"One of the best ideas you've ever had," Domingo said.

"Aren't you curious to see what Po-pe is doing in San Juan?"

"Yes. But more to the point, we invite my father to our wedding."

"Remind me," Francesca said. "When was it you asked me to marry you?"

"I've asked a hundred times. I've even pleaded. Begged you. How can you forget?"

"Did I say yes each time?"

"Once was enough." He pulled her to him and gave her a long kiss. They would have made love, but Juan called to them to tell them that mush was boiling and tortillas were stacked.

As the four of them ate, each recalled what they had heard of Po-pe's behavior. Domingo's stomach muscles tightened despite the warmth of the mush. He recalled Harelip's claim that Po-pe was beheading people and wondered if it could be true. No one at San Ildefonso had heard of such an act so Domingo had convinced himself that Harelip lied or at least exaggerated. *But what if he was telling the truth? Should I take Francesca with me? But what have I to fear. I've served Po-pe well. Too bad Tupatu won't be with us. But he'll come soon.* Domingo shrugged off his concern and took the tortilla that Francesca handed him. He scooped out the last of the mush hiding at the bottom of the pot.

After that the four joked about the bounty of food they would enjoy now that the Spanish could no longer demand a levy from them. Juan and his wife talked of having more than enough food for four people, even a fifth or sixth. Domingo knew he would be as welcome at San Ildefonso as he was in San Juan.

When the banter ended, Domingo and Francesca prepared to leave. He put his bow in a room rafter, but fastened his knife to his side. They started toward the San Juan path on the opposite side of the plaza. Half way across it, a man came running toward him. Domingo recognized him as a distant uncle. The man called out to announce his presence, then raced toward Domingo. He and Domingo no sooner exchanged greetings than Little Pot and two of the War Chiefs joined them. "I have news of Po-pe," the man said.

"From him or about him?" Little Pot asked.

"About him. News that you should know. He'll be heading here or to Santa Clara tomorrow."

"I suppose he expects a feast," one of the War Chiefs said.

"No. Much worse. He's looking for evidence about anyone who might be suspected of having betrayed him."

"Has he become some sort of god that he can read men's minds?" Little Pot said.

The man shrugged. "He's looking for anyone who didn't support the revolution. At San Juan he was judging people by what they said about him for killing his son-in-law."

"Can't the cacique stop him?" Domingo blurted out. A War Chief gave him a look to remind him it was his elders who asked the questions.

"That's just it. Two people claimed the cacique had urged people to wait until they saw how the revolt was going. They admitted San Juan had sent its warriors to Santa Fe, but the two informers claimed the force was a day late to start."

"Were the warriors late?" a War Chief asked.

"Who knows? Anyway, they say it's a way of letting Po-pe decide who will be the cacique. Or it may be, they say, that people with grudges against the cacique will testify that he sent his force late. Po-pe is questioning everyone about all sorts of things, even religious beliefs. He's behaving as if he's a judge in the Inquisition."

Domingo bit at his lip. He should be by his father's side. He turned to nod at Francesca. She had slipped on new moccasins and filled a flask with water.

Domingo's misgivings drove his legs. This time his pace made it impossible for Francesca to tease him. The two times they stopped, she had tugged at his arm and signaled she needed water. It was his turn to sip from the flask while she gulped.

San Juan would be over the next rise as they stopped a final time for water. The sun had passed its half way point. The day was at its hottest, the sky its deepest blue. Everything seemed to be accented. He smelled his sweat, even Francesca's as she handed him the leather flask. He emptied its contents.

"So you *can* run like an Indian," Francesca's eyes danced. "Maybe the revolution has changed you, too."

"The revolution has changed everything." Domingo was in no mood to return his lover's joking. "Not all for the best."

"You are worried, aren't you?" She put a hand on his arm.

"I have too many relatives in the pueblo. If Po-pe harms anyone, I'm likely related to them. What's worse, they could be his relatives, too. What kind of Indian would do that?"

"It's probably a good reason why he isn't harming anyone. That he's related to everyone." She dropped her hand to his and squeezed it. "So, don't worry."

"Are you forgetting he killed his own son-in-law?" Domingo whispered son-in-law. "The revolution has taken so many lives! Surely the death must stop now that the Spanish are gone."

"Especially if we're to return to the old Indian ways." She dropped his hand. "Speaking of which, I hope you're not forgetting we've come to invite your father and your other relatives to our wedding."

"How could I forget that?" He clasped the back of her neck and pulled her to him for a kiss. "First thing we do, we talk to my father and my relatives. Then we see what Po-pe is up to."

They jogged the down hill slope to the pueblo. On the outskirts they encountered four tall posts with some kind of decoration at their tops.

As they neared the posts, Francesca stopped.

Domingo turned to her. Her eyes, fixed on the poles, were frozen in horror. Domingo looked to the top of the poles. The decorations were heads. He gagged. The head closest to him was that of the cacique. *It can't be!* The next head belonged to his father. Drained of blood it looked livid, as if his father were ill. The eyes stared ahead. Domingo stepped closer. Splinters of wood propped his father's eyelids to the top of the sockets. Domingo bent at the waist heaving dry vomit. Francesca ran to his side and placed a hand on his back. He shook it off.

Oh my God. Blessed Virgin. His body shuddered. He fought to regain control. *Oh Mother Kachina! I swear to you that I'll kill whoever did this.*

"Do we go on?" Francesca asked.

"We must." Domingo broke into a run. The downhill slope leveled off, then slanted upward. The rise did nothing to slow his pace. Once past a row of houses, he saw the plaza. His grandfather was tied to the whipping post. His tunic had been torn from him and covered the ground near his feet. His back bled. A tall slim man raised a leather whip and cracked it above his head. His grandfather winced at the sound. The man flipped the whip behind him, ready for another stroke.

Po-pe chanted at the top of his voice how important it is to obey. Two large men stood beside Po-pe, echoing his words. The whipper waited for him to finish, a fiendish grin on his face.

Domingo drew his knife while he dashed for Po-pe. He felt Francesca by his side. They ran as they never had before. Po-pe stopped his chant. The two guards turned to look at their attackers.

Domingo could think of nothing but plunging his knife into Po-pe's heart. He had almost reached him when the two guards grabbed him by his arms and lifted him from the ground. He swiped at one with his knife, but he could only swing from his elbow. The man laughed and swore at him in gibberish that Domingo realized must be Apache. The other man had a Spanish dagger. He jabbed it into Domingo's side. The weapon broke on a rib.

Out of the corner of his eye, Domingo saw Francesca leap onto the back of the tall man with the whip. She slashed at his throat with a small stone knife. Domingo was conscious of blood spurting, a hideous red engulfing the whipper's chest. But half a dozen men leapt at Francesca, knives flailing. He called a soundless farewell to her.

The last thing Domingo felt was a jagged point reaching his heart.